Praise for the Mi

"Written with Ross's signature Southern charm and wit, th
Miss Julia will delight longtime fans of the series and will entice new readers to get to know her."

—*Booklist*

"As fast, feisty, and full of personality as its heroine."

—*Kirkus Reviews*

"Ross has a gift for elevating such everyday matters as marital strife and the hazards of middle age to high comedy, while painting her beautifully drawn characters with wit and sympathy."

—*Publishers Weekly*

"Ann B. Ross develops characters so expertly, through quirks, names, and mannerisms, that they easily feel familiar as the reader is gently immersed into the world Miss Ross has created. . . . A delightful read."

—*Winston-Salem Journal*

"Miss Julia is one of the most delightful characters to come along in years. Ann B. Ross has created what is sure to become a classic Southern comic novel. Hooray for Miss Julia, I could not have liked it more."

—Fannie Flagg, author of *The All-Girl Filling Station's Last Reunion*

"Yes, Miss Julia is back, and I, for one, am one happy camper."

—J. A. Jance, author of *Cold Betrayal*

PENGUIN BOOKS

MISS JULIA HAPPILY EVER AFTER

Ann B. Ross is the author of twenty-two novels featuring the popular Southern heroine Miss Julia, as well as *Etta Mae's Worst Bad-Luck Day*, a novel about one of Abbotsville's other most outspoken residents: Etta Mae Wiggins. Ross holds a doctorate in English from the University of North Carolina at Chapel Hill, and has taught literature at the University of North Carolina at Asheville. She lives in Hendersonville, North Carolina.

Also by Ann B. Ross

Miss Julia Knows a Thing or Two

Miss Julia Takes the Wheel

Miss Julia Raises the Roof

Miss Julia Weathers the Storm

Miss Julia Inherits a Mess

Miss Julia Lays Down the Law

Etta Mae's Worst Bad-Luck Day

Miss Julia's Marvelous Makeover

Miss Julia Stirs Up Trouble

Miss Julia to the Rescue

Miss Julia Rocks the Cradle

Miss Julia Renews Her Vows

Miss Julia Delivers the Goods

Miss Julia Paints the Town

Miss Julia Strikes Back

Miss Julia Stands Her Ground

Miss Julia's School of Beauty

Miss Julia Meets Her Match

Miss Julia Hits the Road

Miss Julia Throws a Wedding

Miss Julia Takes Over

Miss Julia Speaks Her Mind

Miss Julia Happily Ever After

ANN B. ROSS

PENGUIN BOOKS

PENGUIN BOOKS
An imprint of Penguin Random House LLC
penguinrandomhouse.com

First published in the United States of America by Viking,
an imprint of Penguin Random House LLC, 2021
Published in Penguin Books 2022

ISBN 9780593296486 (paperback)

THE LIBRARY OF CONGRESS HAS CATALOGED THE
HARDCOVER EDITION AS FOLLOWS:
Names: Ross, Ann B., author.
Title: Miss Julia happily ever after / Ann B. Ross.
Description: First edition. | New York: Viking, [2021]
Identifiers: LCCN 2020045756 (print) | LCCN 2020045757 (ebook) |
ISBN 9780593296462 (hardcover) | ISBN 9780593296479 (ebook)
Subjects: GSAFD: Mystery fiction.
Classification: LCC PS3568.O84198 M562 2021 (print) |
LCC PS3568.O84198 (ebook) | DDC 813/.54—dc23
LC record available at https://lccn.loc.gov/2020045756
LC ebook record available at https://lccn.loc.gov/20200457

Printed in the United States of America
1st Printing

Set in Fairfield LT Std
Designed by Cassandra Garruzzo

This book is for all the dedicated booksellers who make the final connection between book and reader. Thank you for introducing Miss Julia to so many for so many years.

Miss Julia Happily Ever After

Chapter 1

All things considered, you'd think we'd have taken it in stride, but no. I mean, people get married all the time, don't they? But just let someone mention the words *wedding*, *bridesmaid*, *engagement ring*, or the like and everybody gets all atwitter with excitement even though the happy couple may be the most unlikely pairing anyone could imagine.

As word of the currently forthcoming nuptials began to trickle out, I admit to a tingle of excitement myself, although my fingers were crossed behind my back whenever I passed the news along. Of course I wished them well and all that, but I couldn't help but wonder why they'd want to rock the boat. Their present arrangement seemed the best possible one under the circumstances, and they'd already lived down the rampant speculation and gossip that had stirred the town when she'd moved in, so why in the world would they want to start it all up again?

I didn't know, but one thing I did know and that was that Helen Stroud never did anything she had not thoroughly thought through and determined the benefit, or lack of same, to her. And if that makes her sound coldhearted and self-absorbed, I don't mean it to. What I mean is that Helen was clear-eyed and far-sighted. She knew what she was doing, even though nobody else could figure out why she was doing it. She already had Thurlow Jones under her thumb and his checkbook in her hand, so why in the world would she want to marry him?

Well, of course that was no more understandable than their original arrangement, which had stunned us all and become the subject of at least two sermons in a nondenominational church on the outskirts of town. No names were mentioned, as you can imagine, but when the preacher went off on a tangent about two people living openly in sin at an age and of a class that should've known better, they say everybody in the congregation sat up straight and nodded in agreement. I didn't hear the sermons myself, being a Presbyterian attending my own church where things are done decently and in order, yet our pastor touched briefly on being unequally yoked in marriage one Sunday when his topic was the wedding in Cana. He did a fine tap dance with that since Presbyterians aren't too liberal when it comes to drinking wine, either, but everybody knew who he was talking about.

And everybody knew that for many years of her life, Helen Stroud had been one of the most active women in our church. Why, she had been president of the Women of the Church at least twice, a Sunday school teacher for years, and a circle chairman several times. And when we finally got around to electing women to the Board of Deacons and to the Session, she showed her allegiance to Paul's admonition about women keeping silence in the church by refusing to run. We admired her for that.

Everything changed, though, when she moved in with Thurlow Jones. She hasn't darkened the door of any church since then, and as far as I know not one person from the visitation committee, much less the pastor himself, has gone to see her to urge her back into the fold. Let me tell you something, when a church drops you, you pretty much stay dropped.

I wonder, though, if that will change when a marriage certificate elevates her to legitimacy. But here's the thing: I'd have to be in worse straits than unwelcome in church to go to such an extreme as to legally bind myself to the likes of Thurlow Jones.

All I can say is that the stars must've been crazily aligned to have brought those two together. Helen was one of those neat, capable women, fastidious to a fault, who could've run a major industry if she hadn't first married a go-getter husband who overstepped himself into a ten-year sentence for fraud and embezzlement. But Helen was no Tammy Wynette. She divorced him as soon as the prison doors slammed shut behind him and went about arranging her life to accommodate the new reality of having to work for a living.

Thurlow, on the other hand, was the town buffoon, careless in dress, conversation, and attitude. Loaded by all accounts, he looked and lived like one of the bums who wandered the sidewalk on Main Street. He lived in his family's once-impressive mansion, which he had allowed to deteriorate on its overgrown city block not too far from my own house. He took inordinate delight in shocking the staid, upright ladies of the town, and he wasn't above sneaking a pinch of female flesh if you didn't keep your distance.

All of that changed when he climbed to the roof of his house to adjust a television antenna and fell three floors to the ground, breaking one hip, two legs, an arm, and several ribs. Laid up for an interminable length of time and having no wife or siblings, not even a cousin or two, to care for him, it was either go into a nursing home or come up with a suitable alternative.

That was where Helen came in. She needed a home and an income. He needed a nurse and a caretaker, and to all intents and purposes, Helen proved her negotiating skills. Not only did she move in, she agreed to oversee Thurlow's entire household as well as his medical needs with one caveat—he would provide the funds. She started by hiring a cook, a male nurse, and a house-cleaning crew. I don't know how Thurlow survived that because he was as tight as a tick with his money, which is why he had so much of it. But Helen demanded and was given unlimited access to Thurlow's bank account and permission to refurbish his one-hundred-and-twenty-year-old house, proving thereby that she was also an interior designer of great talent. So, in one fell swoop Thurlow got everything a wife would ordinarily have provided without getting any of the intimate privileges of having one—as far as we knew.

Of course there was talk, as well as whispers and gasps and images of impossible couplings, what with Thurlow encased in casts and strung up in traction. But Helen, the chatelaine, sailed untouched above it all, projecting by her serene competence that their connection was a commercial and not a romantic one.

But now they were going to marry? *Why?* I ask you.

Chapter 2

Drawn to the kitchen to have somebody to talk to, I found Lillian sitting at the table in front of a half cup of coffee. As I headed toward the coffeepot on the counter, she began to get to her feet.

"Don't get up," I said, waving her back. "I'll join you unless you're thinking on some deep, dark subject and don't want company."

"Well, I am," she said, "but I need some comp'ny 'cause I don't want to be thinkin' what I'm thinkin'."

"And what's that?" I drew out a chair and sat opposite her at the table. "I've been telling myself that with this beautiful spring we're having I should be feeling blessed and happy. But I'm feeling so low I hardly know what to do."

"Law, Miss Julia, me, too." Lillian leaned her head on her hand and gave me a forlorn look. "Guess who's gone an' got herself pregnant."

My head jerked up and I almost spilled my coffee. *"Not Helen Stroud?"*

"Who?"

"Oh," I said, wiping my hand across my face. "What am I thinking? Of course it's not Helen. She may look fifty, but she's well into her sixties. Sorry, Lillian, I've just had her on my mind wondering why she's marrying that crazy Thurlow Jones."

"Ev'rybody's wonderin' that, but it's not hard to figure out. Miss Helen, she sees what it's like to get old without enough to live on. Can't nobody blame her for that. No'm," Lillian went on sadly, "it's not her that's carryin' a baby. It's Janelle, an' I'm jus' sick to my soul about it."

"Oh, no," I said, leaning back in my chair and closing my eyes. Janelle was Lillian's bright young neighbor who had often helped out at my house. She was quick to learn and efficient in her work, never having to be told twice. I'd long been impressed with her and knew that she was graduating from high school in June with plans for college already made. "Oh, Lillian, I do hate to hear that. She's so young and has so much to look forward to. Why in the world would she ruin it all?"

"I don't know, Miss Julia. Her mama, she say she be glad to have another baby to raise, but what else can she say?"

"That sounds," I said carefully, "like Janelle's not planning to get married."

"No'm, from what I hear, he already left town. I declare," Lillian said with a sigh, "look like these young girls would learn not to believe half what they're told. But at least Janelle gonna have that baby 'stead of gettin' rid of it like a lot of 'em do."

"Yes, there is that, and I'm glad to hear it. But, listen, will she be able to graduate? Girls in trouble used to have to quit school, but everything's so different now. To have a baby out of wedlock used to stigmatize you for life, but now . . . Well, now it seems more a badge of honor than anything else."

"I don't know 'bout that," Lillian said. "All I know is she's lucky Miss Pearl wants to help her out, but then, what else is new? Grandmamas been raising babies forever."

I smiled and put my hand on her arm. "I know, and they have a special place in heaven, too." Lillian, herself, had raised a great-grandbaby after the mother left town and never came back. "Latisha is a blessing to you and to everybody who knows her."

"Yes'm, but she's gettin' to that age when some boy could turn her head and start it all over again."

"I know, and I worry about it, too. But pray about it, Lillian, and talk to her. Hold up all the possibilities that are open to her. Why, with her intelligence and her personality, Latisha can do anything she wants to do. If she doesn't let herself get waylaid along the way."

"I jus' feel so bad about Janelle," Lillian said, mopping her eyes with a napkin, "an' I'm mad at her, too. She knowed better, 'specially since she's not the first one that boy got ahold of, but at least Janelle's gonna finish high school, which they'll let her do from home. But she say she won't walk on the stage to get her diploma 'cause by June she'll be too big to get up the steps. She won't be goin' to no college, either, which I guess is just as well 'cause she's not likely to get any of the honors and scholarships she was in line for. No need givin' 'em to somebody who'll be stayin' home with a baby." She smoothed out the napkin, then mopped her eyes again. "Miss Julia, did you know Janelle is third in her class? An' she jus' throwed it all away. I could jus' cry 'cause anybody that smart ought not to get in such a mess. An' it makes me worry about Latisha that much more 'cause bein' smart don't always mean you act smart."

"That is certainly the truth," I agreed, thinking of a few questionable decisions I had made in the past. I considered myself on the bright end of the intelligence scale, yet on occasion I had made some poor choices—nothing irretrievable, I hasten to add, yet nothing to be proud of, either. "So what will Janelle do? Do you know?"

"Last I heard she's gonna find a job soon as the baby comes

’cause somebody gotta support it an’ the daddy’s nowhere to be found.” Lillian grimaced at the thought. “An’ her mama say Janelle gonna try to take a class ev’ry term out at the technical college.”

“Oh, good for her,” I said, then on further thought, added, “except at the rate of one class every term, it’ll take her about twenty years to graduate. Still, it’s better than nothing, and she might find a field that doesn’t take as long as a degree program, like cosmetology or childcare or nursing—something that she can make a living at.” I sighed, thinking that there would be a lot of intelligence and ability going to waste if Janelle contented herself with the technical, rather than the academic, route. Yet even uneducated people often made good if they had a strong work ethic. And there was such a thing as being self-educated. I mean, anybody can read, can’t they? Lillian had told me that Janelle’s mama had often complained about Janelle having her nose in a book. That seemed to me to be a hopeful sign.

The news about Janelle did nothing to lift my spirits, so I put on a sweater and wandered around outside for a while wishing that I had planted some spring bulbs back in the fall. Things had been awfully busy then, and I’d not even thought of jonquils or tulips or anything else. I missed them now, so it was a relief when Lillian called me in to the telephone.

“Julia,” LuAnne Conover said when I answered, “sorry to interrupt whatever you were doing, but I need to ask you something.”

“You didn’t interrupt anything, LuAnne. I was just surveying the yard to have something to do. How are you? It’s good to hear from you.”

LuAnne was a longtime friend who had suffered a recent

divorce from Leonard Conover, who'd been unwilling to give up a certain lady friend, also of long standing. Unhappily, Leonard had never been a provident provider, so dividing a little into two made for not much for either of them to live on. LuAnne, for the first time in her life, had been forced to find a job, and she'd lucked into the receptionist's position at the Good Shepherd Funeral Home.

"Well, listen, Julia," LuAnne said, "I think we ought to do something, and I'd love for the two of us to go in on it together. Your house has all the room in the world, while my condo wouldn't do at all. But we're her friends, at least I guess we are, but who knows now? So what do you think?"

"About what? I'm lost here, LuAnne. What are we talking about?" That was the problem with LuAnne—her mind skipped from one topic to another and very few of us were swift enough to keep up.

"Why, Helen, of course. I mean, it's not often we have a wedding to celebrate at our age, which may mean there's hope for me. But you know she'll expect her friends to do something for her. I'm thinking that a bridal shower probably won't do—you know how picky Helen is—but maybe a tea or something along those lines where we'd only invite women. I'm just not up to entertaining Thurlow even if he could get out of bed."

"Well, I'm in agreement with that. I'm not sure he's able to attend anything, anyway. I'm not even sure he'll be able to stand for the wedding. Have you heard anything? I mean, like, will it be in the church or will they go to the courthouse or what?"

"Your guess is as good as mine," LuAnne said. "Helen hasn't confided in me."

"Me, either. Do you suppose she's planning just a small, private affair? She may not want any kind of celebratory activities."

"I thought of that," LuAnne said, and then, revealing a seldom-noted sensitivity, she went on. "But you know Helen. She'd never *ask* for anything, but I know she'd appreciate our offering to do something. Marrying Thurlow is a huge step she's taking, so she has to be having some second thoughts. She needs to know she has friends who are happy for her."

"Well, I'm not sure I am," I said, "but don't tell her I said that. But you're right, LuAnne, we should offer to do something. And I agree that a shower wouldn't be appropriate, so let's invite her to lunch and just ask her. If she'd like a tea, we can do it here, or maybe we could offer to do the wedding reception."

"Oh, that would be nice."

"On the other hand, if they're just going to go down to the courthouse, they may not want a big to-do."

"That's true," LuAnne said, "and you know what? With Thurlow in the state he's in, they may be planning to just slip away and get it done with a small announcement in the paper afterward. A lot of families do that when they have an out-of-town funeral service, just to let everybody here know that they've buried somebody."

"Well, yes, I guess," I said, not exactly following her line of thinking. "So let's invite Helen for lunch and find out what she'd like. When can you be free?"

"Thursday, because I have to work the weekend. And, Julia, if you don't mind, let's go to the country club. I'll reimburse you for my share, but I never get to go there anymore since I had to resign my membership. I can't afford the dues. But I'll tell you what's a fact, I miss the club more than anything I lost in the divorce, and that includes Leonard."

Chapter 3

"Helen?" I said when the maid called her to the phone. While I had waited, I'd thought again of how smoothly Thurlow's house was now run in contrast to the unseemly way he'd lived there on his own. "It's Julia," I said when Helen responded. "LuAnne and I have been talking, and we would very much like to do something for you and Thurlow, either before or after the wedding. We're open to anything from an intimate dinner to the reception after the service—whatever you'd like."

There was a moment's pause, then Helen said, "How very thoughtful of you, Julia, but I haven't given much thought to anything like that. My days stay so busy with all I have to do here, you know."

"I can imagine, but we'd really like to honor the occasion with some kind of celebration. Could you have lunch with us at the club this Thursday? We could discuss the possibilities and see what would fit in with the plans of others who may want to do something as well."

"Oh," Helen said with a slight acerbic tinge, "I doubt there'll be a line forming to recognize this particular wedding. But it's very kind of you and LuAnne, so, yes, let's meet for lunch and discuss it. I'll be thinking what might be appropriate under the circumstances."

"Good," I said, noting but not commenting on her reference to the particular circumstances. It wasn't up to me to pass judgment on who marries whom, and I'd given teas, showers, dinners, and you-name-it to celebrate mismatched weddings before. A woman in my position in the town does the right thing regardless of her personal opinion of what she's celebrating. "Then we'll see you at noon on Thursday at the club."

"I can't wait to hear all about it," LuAnne said as the waiter scooted a chair under her at the table in the Azalea Room of the country club. LuAnne had ridden with me to the club and she had talked the entire time, chattering away about where the wedding would be, whether or not they would have a honeymoon, and how in the world Helen could bear being Thurlow's wife.

"Can you imagine?" she'd asked, shuddering, as I'd parked in the club lot. "I get nauseated at the thought of crawling into bed with the likes of Thurlow Jones."

Well, so did I, but that was Helen's problem, not mine. I had to assume that she'd counted the cost of becoming Mrs. Thurlow Jones and figured the gain to be worth what she'd have to put up with.

I had asked for a quiet table, so after meeting Helen in the foyer, we'd been led through the crowded main dining area to one of the more private rooms. Helen had attracted several stares as we'd progressed, but she'd held her head high, turning to neither the right nor the left, giving no one a chance to speak to her. Helen's icy control, however, did not stop LuAnne.

"So tell us how he proposed," she said eagerly, even before a napkin was in her lap. "I just can't imagine Thurlow being romantic, but when true love hits there's no telling how a man will change."

I couldn't help it, but my eyes rolled so far back in my head that they were in danger of lodging there. I sometimes wondered if LuAnne had a lick of sense, because anybody who talked as much as she did is bound to say too much sooner or later or, in her case, the wrong thing.

Helen stiffened, gave LuAnne a cool look, and shook out her napkin. "We came to that conclusion at the same time," she said in a tone meant to also conclude the topic of conversation.

"What?" LuAnne, who at times could be fairly dense, asked. "The conclusion of what?"

"The conclusion of what was best to do," Helen said in such a way that would have told me to change the subject.

"Let's look at the menu," I said, opening mine. "What would you like, Helen? The Caesar salad is always good. Or you might prefer a sandwich."

We busied ourselves with ordering lunch as the waitress jotted down our decisions, giving LuAnne something else to think about for a few minutes. As usual, she had several changes to make—no onions, for instance, in her Cobb salad, and a specific dressing "on the side," every drop of which she would later pour over her salad.

As soon as we were served, LuAnne took up her fork and her questions. "Is Thurlow going to give you an engagement ring? I don't see you wearing one, but I guess he's not able to go shopping, is he?"

"No, and I don't need an engagement ring," Helen said. Then, as a concession to the next question, she said, "I will wear his mother's wedding ring, which is in a safety-deposit box at the bank."

"Then it's likely to be in an old-fashioned setting," LuAnne said. "You should have it reset, Helen, to modernize it into something you'll be proud to wear. But tell us about the wedding. When is it? What will you wear? Who will be in the wedding party?" LuAnne's eyes glittered with excitement and, I thought, the expectation of being in that party.

"We've not yet decided when or where the actual wedding will be," Helen said, "although I will say that Thurlow does not wish to have it at the church. We all know how he feels about that."

Yes, we did. Thurlow Jones had an animus toward the church, any church, no matter the denomination, because, we had heard, some long-dead preacher had offended Thurlow's father in some way that no one remembered and Thurlow had used it as an excuse for non-membership ever since.

"So what will you *do*?" LuAnne asked with an insistence that made Helen put down her fork and take a deep breath.

"We've decided that it should be entirely private," Helen said, then went on, thinking, I assumed, that if she answered all the questions at once, maybe LuAnne would be satisfied. "It's quite painful for Thurlow to be moved, so I'll make arrangements for the magistrate to come to the house. We'll ask Mike, the day nurse, and Hannah, the cook, to be the witnesses. It can be done in fifteen minutes or less with no fanfare or inappropriate celebration. Going somewhere else or having a lot of people in would do nothing but agitate Thurlow and tire him out. So, as much as I appreciate what the two of you are offering, I've given it a lot of thought since you called, Julia, and I am going to say thank you, but no thanks."

"Oh, but you can't do that!" LuAnne said, truly shocked at the thought of a wedding without a celebration.

"We can, and we will," Helen said, firmly enough to put an end to the conversation with anyone but LuAnne.

"Well, I could just cry," LuAnne said, a lettuce leaf dropping from her fork to her lap. "It's not right to get married without friends around rejoicing in your happiness."

"Rejoice all you want," Helen said drily. "Just do it where it won't be a pretense. Listen, LuAnne, this is a marriage of convenience, and all the parties and receptions and rice-throwing in the world will not change that and there's no use pretending that they would. I am trying my best not to make it more of a travesty than it already is, so let's just drop the subject. Unless," she said, turning to me, "there's something you want to add, Julia."

"No," I said quickly, "I think that, under the circumstances, you're handling it just right. Why pretend it's something that it's not? If it suits you and Thurlow, that's all that matters. LuAnne and I just did not want to let it pass without at least offering to do something, but we understand, don't we, LuAnne?"

"Well," LuAnne mumbled, "I guess, but I don't see . . ."

"We're pleased for you," I said, overriding her, "and who knows? This marriage may be stronger and more long-lasting than one that starts off with stars in the eyes of two half-grown people who've seen too many Hollywood movies. We wish you well, Helen."

As I awaited the tab to sign for our lunches, Helen thanked us and excused herself, pleading her need to be at home to oversee Thurlow's physical therapy. LuAnne, having been silenced during the rest of our lunch, waited with me.

"I think it's a shame," LuAnne said, as soon as Helen had left us. "It's not right to have such a sham of a wedding. A magistrate, of all things, and in Thurlow's bedroom! With two people they hardly know as witnesses! Why, Julia, I'm not even sure that would be legitimate in the first place." She leaned across the table toward me. "What if it's not? What if they go through that charade and end up not even being married at all? Because nobody will know about it! What will happen if Thurlow kicks the bucket and she expects to inherit, and some distant cousin pops up to say they'd never been properly married? In fact, the church used to publish banns to let everybody know of an upcoming marriage, in case, you know, anybody knew a reason the couple shouldn't marry. Like if they were kin to each other or something."

"I seriously doubt that Helen and Thurlow are kin," I said, nodding my thanks to the club hostess as we left. "And it is the bride's prerogative to have the wedding of her choice. Helen knows what she's doing, LuAnne, and I think it's smart to have it as low-key as possible."

"Well," LuAnne said, "if I was in her place, I'd have a wedding to end all weddings so that everybody knew the knot had been tied good and tight, especially with his estate on the line."

"Oh," I said, opening the car door, "I expect she'll have a license and a certificate as proof. I don't think we need to worry about that."

"Well," LuAnne said as she slid into the front seat of my car, "you have to admit that it's a strange way of doing things."

I did, indeed, but even stranger things began to happen, so I had little time to worry about the status of that particular marriage.

Chapter 4

But LuAnne couldn't let it go that easily. She called me later that afternoon, saying immediately, "You know what that means, don't you?"

"I'm not following you, LuAnne. What does what mean?"

"It means that we won't be invited to the wedding. Which I think is about the tackiest thing in the world. We've been her friends through thick and thin for years, and she's not inviting us to her wedding? I think my feelings are hurt."

"I expect nobody is being invited. So it's not as if we're being personally excluded. Listen, LuAnne, you have to just accept it and let it go. It's an unusual situation to begin with and not covered by Amy Vanderbilt. And," I went on brightly, "just think. We don't have to bother with a wedding gift."

"Well," LuAnne said, "there is that, I guess. But we'd better read the paper carefully, Julia, or we won't even know when she's suddenly Helen Jones instead of Helen Stroud. *If*," she went on darkly, "she even announces it in the first place. But I'll tell you this, if I ever get married again, which is highly unlikely but you never know, I want it *all*. I want parties and showers and a walk-down-the-aisle wedding and all my friends celebrating with me. Because all I had with Leonard was one of those magistrate weddings at the courthouse, and it was as cut and dried as getting a driver's license and about as much fun."

Then she began laughing at herself, which was LuAnne's saving grace when she remembered to do it. "Well, just listen to me," she said. "What do I care what Helen does? Sorry, Julia, I got carried away."

"I know. You're concerned for her, and I am, too. But all we can do is stand by and be there for her if she needs us." I declare, I sometimes think that if we didn't have platitudes to fall back on, we'd have nothing at all to say.

I didn't sleep well that night, having had Helen on my mind in spite of what I'd said to LuAnne. I'd told Sam about our luncheon and about LuAnne's inability to turn it loose, yet I'd been unable to get Helen off my mind, either.

So I was slow with my morning toilette even though Sam was up and gone long before I'd crawled out of bed. He was having breakfast downtown at the Bluebird café with a group of men who were all retired and had too little to do but who were still interested in the town and what people were doing.

As I put a quick spray on my hair, I heard Lillian come in downstairs, then, surprisingly, walk through the kitchen and out into the hall.

"Miss Julia," she called up the stairs.

I went to the railing and looked over. "Morning, Lillian. You need me?"

"Jus' makin' sure you're up," she said. "I got something to tell you, an' I'm puttin' on the eggs."

"I'm on my way," I said, hoping that she didn't have more bad news about Janelle.

Sitting at the kitchen table, I yawned, still trying to wake up. I reached for the coffee cup as soon as Lillian put it before me.

"Thanks, I need this," I said. "What did you have to tell me?"

Lillian stood by the table, looking down at me. "Didn't you say Mr. Sam gonna be goin' outta town for a few days?"

"Yes, he's going with Mr. Pickens and Lloyd on their annual trip to south Alabama. It'll be during Lloyd's spring break, and they're going deep sea fishing, of all things." J. D. Pickens, Hazel Marie's swashbuckling husband, was a private investigator who had swept her off her feet and made her one of his multiple wives—all of whom, I quickly add, he had divorced or been divorced by. And Lloyd was Hazel Marie's son by her infamous attachment to my first husband, Wesley Lloyd Springer, now deceased. And if all those entanglements confuse and shock you, suffice it to say that we have worked them out to our mutual benefit and satisfaction.

"So," Lillian said, "you gonna be in this house all by your lonesome, is that right?"

"Well, yes, but I'll be fine. I'm not afraid to be alone."

"Well," she said, putting her hands on her hips and glaring at me, "maybe you oughta be. You know ole Miss Vinnie Worsham? Live over there on Wilson Street, hardly four blocks from here?"

"Yes, I know her. Why? She's a little . . . off, isn't she?"

"She jus' ole. Nothin' wrong with her mind, an' she know what she saw. So I'm tellin' you, you gotta be careful. Won't be nothin' in the paper about it till tomorrow 'cause it happened 'bout four o'clock this mornin'."

"What?" I asked. "Is she all right? What happened to her?"

"Lemme get these eggs done," Lillian said, pouring beaten eggs into a skillet. "Won't take but a minute." She scrambled them in the pan, then spooned them onto a plate with toast and a serving of grits, which she set before me. "Well, here's how it was, an' I heard it from Miss Onie Taylor who lives three doors from me, an' she heard it from Mr. Wilbur when he was gettin' in his car to go to work. And somebody right next door to Miss Vinnie had called Mr. Wilbur to tell him that the police had come out before sunup to see about her. So I call that pretty close to firsthand information."

"Well, tell me," I said. "What was it? What happened to her?"

"Well," Lillian said, pulling out a chair and sitting down, "seems Miss Vinnie don't sleep too good, an' she say she was up trying to get something on TV, but she don't have cable, so it was mostly static an' something about that Miracle Spring Water an' she'd about decided to order some 'cause her Social Security don't hardly cover anything, an' . . ."

"Lillian, for heaven's sake."

"Yes'm, I'm gettin' to it. Anyway, Miss Vinnie say she heard something on the back porch, something kinda clatterin' around, an' she thought it might be a possum or something like that tryin' to get in the garbage can. So she went tippy-toein' through the kitchen an' turned on the porch light right by the door while she was watchin' through the window, an' when that porch light come on, you won't believe what she saw."

"What?"

"A nekkid man, right there on her back porch!"

"Naked? *Really*?"

"Yes'm, stark nekkid, she said, with a golf club in his hand. An' she say she so shocked she couldn't do nothin' but stare at him while he stand there starin' back at her. Then he took a big jump off the porch an' hightailed it across the yard, an' that's the last she seen of him. But you know what?"

"No," I said, fascinated at the tale, "what?"

"When the police come, 'cause Miss Vinnie, she called 'em right away, an' they went lookin' 'round the yard, they found out that the crazy man had lopped the heads off ev'ry one of her jonquils an' her tulips—even the ones she'd planted in coffee cans on the porch. Just whacked 'em all off, an' they was lyin' all over the porch an' the yard, 'cause she planted dozens of 'em last fall."

"My word," I said, leaning back in my chair, "I've never heard of such a thing. You think he just doesn't like spring flowers?"

"No'm, it has to be more'n that 'cause why he take off his clothes jus' to mess up somebody's yard? That's what I can't figure out."

"What a shock that must've been to Miss Vinnie. Did she recognize him?"

"She say she wadn't lookin' at his face."

"I imagine not with everything else on display." I laughed. I couldn't help it, for the idea of a naked man wandering around somebody's yard—and it not even summertime—chopping off flowers struck me as funny.

"Well," Lillian said, "you can laugh about it now, but I'm tellin' you if you hear some noise at night while Mr. Sam's gone, don't be gettin' up to look outside. You might see more'n you wanta see."

"Oh," I said, "I don't think I need to worry. I didn't plant any spring bulbs last fall."

Chapter 5

"Sam?" I said, later that evening as we sat in the library after supper. "Did you hear about that naked man?"

"Uh-huh," he said, glancing up from the newspaper, "but don't look at me. I was home in bed."

I laughed. "Well, what did the breakfast club make of it? Any guesses as to who it was? Or why he was wandering around with no clothes on in April—and a fairly chilly April at that?"

"The best guess was that Miss Vinnie had had a nip or two and saw what she wanted to see."

"*No,*" I said, sitting up straight. "Does she drink? Really?"

"I don't have any idea, but apparently the deputies know the way to her house. At least, that's the word from the Bluebird." Sam snapped the paper open, then looked over the top at me. "I'd take her sighting with a grain of salt and not worry too much about it."

"Well, I'd like to know why he was whacking the heads off all her bulbs with a golf club. To me, that's just as strange as running around as naked as a jaybird."

"Um," Sam murmured, his interest centered on what he was reading.

"But see," I went on, "that brings up a problem that no one seems to have addressed. Just where did he leave his clothes? I mean, did he take them off in her yard when he got there? In which case they may still be there, which would be a clue to his identity. Or did he leave them at home, wherever home is? And does he live close enough to walk unclothed to her house or did he have to get into a car and drive there?"

"Could've been either way, I guess."

"If we knew that," I said, "we'd know where to look for him. You know, if he walked, that would mean he lives nearby, but if he drove, he could be anywhere in the county."

"I'm sure the deputies take that into consideration. But since I'm not looking for him . . ."

"But if he took his clothes off at home, then drove to Miss Vinnie's, I'll bet you he doesn't have leather seats. That's a good clue right there because it was in the forties last night, and you wouldn't catch me sliding in on a leather seat without a stitch on underneath."

"Julia, for goodness' sake," Sam said, laughing as he tossed the paper aside. "We're not ever going to understand why crazy people do crazy things."

"Well, I know, but it's good to keep the mind working on various problems, and this is an interesting one."

"Uh-huh, and here's another one for you. Guess who joined us for breakfast this morning?"

"No telling. Who?"

"Bob Hargrove," Sam said. "I expect it was the first Friday morning in thirty years that he wasn't in his office seeing patients. He's definitely cutting back, just as we'd heard, but only because he brought in that new fellow."

"Well, I hope that new fellow is better than the locum tenens he hired when he went to Europe. I couldn't stand another so-called doctor like him."

"Nobody could, but Bob checked this one out to a fare-thee-well and stayed in the office with him for weeks. In fact, this morning may have been the first time he's left him alone. Anyway," Sam said, stifling a yawn, "he now has something else to occupy his time and his mind."

"I hope it's a nice hobby," I said, "although doctors aren't known to do much more than practice medicine their entire lives. What has he taken up?"

"Have you talked with Sue lately?"

"Actually, no. Why? Are they doing something together? That would be so nice because doctors' wives are as married to a practice as their husbands are. I would think that Sue needs an interesting hobby as badly as he does."

"Not a hobby, honey. It seems that Christy's getting married."

"Oh, my goodness," I said, thrilled at the thought of the Hargroves' only child planning a wedding. "Oh, my, what a spring and summer we'll have. When is it? Everybody will want to do something for her. We'll be so social we won't be able to stand it. Start thinking of what we should do, Sam. I just love that Christy. She was always the sweetest child, and still is. And smart—my word, she sailed through high school and graduated magna cum laude from Duke, remember? And now she's in medical school, following in her daddy's footsteps. Can you imagine how proud the Hargroves must be? And she's just beautiful, too, like her mother. Oh, Sue must be thrilled. I'll call her first thing in the morning."

"I'd tread softly with that, honey," Sam said. "I got a real feeling that Bob's not all that happy about it. In fact, he didn't announce it at the table to everybody, just mentioned to me that Christy is home planning a wedding as we walked out to the sidewalk."

I stared at him as a few things, like Janelle's uneasy situation, began to come unbidden to the surface. "It's April," I said, rubbing my forehead, "the middle of a semester, and here Christy is, at home. Oh, my, Sam, that means that it might not be such a joyous occasion."

"Worse than that, maybe," Sam said. "Have you ever wondered why Bob never took in a partner even though he got busier and busier every year? He told me a long time ago that he was holding a place for Christy because she wanted to practice medicine with her daddy. He was so proud of that, yet now it may all be out the window. Because you're right, being home in April means she's dropped out of medical school. Or," he went on after a second or two, "medical school dropped her."

"No, I can't believe that. Christy is much too smart to fail at anything she does. Besides, they'd fail her at the end of a semester, not in the middle of it. Wouldn't they?"

We sat in silence a few minutes, both of us contemplating the disappointment that we assumed was being suffered by two of the most decent people we knew—Bob and Sue Hargrove. How often, I thought, did we pin our fondest hopes on our children and have them fail us in order to pursue their own? Which, I guess, is the way it should be in the long run, but I no longer felt that I had missed out by not having children of my own. After all, I had Lloyd who, so far, had never disappointed me or his mother.

"Well," I said to put an end to my doleful thoughts, "one thing is for sure—Christy must be doing what she wants to do." Whether or not, I thought, it's what her parents want her to do.

"So," I went on, "I guess this is the year of weddings. There's Janelle who needs one, and Helen and Thurlow who probably don't, and now Christy who seems bound and determined to have one. I mean, Sam, why didn't she at least finish the semester, get married this summer, and go back to school in the fall? I know for a fact that Bob and Sue have been saving tuition money for years. So it's not as if Christy needs to work, although . . ." I stopped to consider the possibilities. "Who is she marrying? Did Bob say?"

Sam shook his head. "Not a word, which is another reason I felt he wasn't so thrilled about it."

"I'll call LuAnne tomorrow. She'll know if anybody does, although since she hasn't called to tell me, she may not. But, Sam, I do have to call Sue because she'll know that Bob told you, and she'll wonder why I'm ignoring it if I don't. Besides, we may as well go all out to make it a happy occasion as weddings usually are, and there's all the more reason to do so since this one may not actually be."

I went to bed that night after two or three hours of being bombarded by various and sundry medical problems on television, none of which were fit to be mentioned in polite company. Yet there they were displayed in all their glory for the viewers' delectation. Maybe it had been concern over Christy's decision to forsake medical school that I had noticed so many advertisements for pills, potions, injections, and apparatuses guaranteed to ease pain or embarrassment or both. And most of the ailments could be self-diagnosed and self-treated, which was the reason they were being advertised. Maybe, I thought, Christy had seen the handwriting on the wall—what need would we have for physicians when all we had to do was turn on the television set?

Sooner or later some advertisement would address the particular ailment we happened to have, no matter how rare or tasteless it happened to be. I mean, have you ever heard of Peyronie's disease? Watch television for an hour or so and you'll learn about it, and it will change your attitude about shopping for vegetables at the grocery store. I concede that such matters would not normally be brought up as conversational topics at a formal tea, nor would bladder leakage or an over- or underactive bowel, but no one bats an eye when such matters are openly aired in every living room in the land.

But the worst, to my mind, are the ones that pretend to address one subject when they're really aimed toward another. Take the one with the hyped-up young man pedaling away but going nowhere as he yells to a bunch of constipated bicycle riders, "Come on, everybody, work it out!" which conjures up about the most graphic mental image I can imagine.

Chapter 6

A little uneasy about how best to broach the subject, I called Sue the next morning and soon realized that I had nothing to worry about. She immediately launched into news about the upcoming wedding, sounding for all the world as if she couldn't be happier about it, as if her only child hadn't abruptly given up what she'd dreamed of doing all of her life.

"She is so happy, Julia," Sue said, "so of course we are, too. Her young man is just outstanding—he's from an old Virginia family—and even though we'd hoped they would wait a few years, this is what they want. You know, I suppose," she went on, "that the medical year begins on the first of July, and since he has a prestigious surgical residency at Johns Hopkins, he has to be settled in Baltimore by the end of June. So there's a lot to be done in a short amount of time."

"What can we do to help?" I asked. "Sam and I want to do something, and of course I'm free to help you anytime you need an errand run or packages picked up or whatever."

"Thank you, Julia. I may call on you if you really don't mind. Right now I have a couple of carpenters working on a gift-display room. We've emptied one of the guest rooms and we're putting tables up around the room, all ready to set out gifts as they come in. I don't have enough tablecloths, so I'm using white sheets. They'll do, don't you think?"

"Oh, yes, everybody uses sheets. Just be sure you drape them to the floor so you can hide the boxes the gifts come in but still have them handy when you're ready to pack them up. You're always so organized, Sue, I'm sure everything will work out just fine."

"Well," she said, "I hope so, but a big church wedding really needs a year's worth of preparations, yet we're having to do it all in less than three months. Christy just got home last week, but she's selected her invitations and we have them on order. A rush order, I might add, because they have to be mailed six weeks ahead." Sue laughed, although it sounded slightly forced. "We'll be addressing them for several days *and* nights."

"What about her trousseau? Has she decided on a wedding dress?"

"She's wearing mine, and it only needs a few darts adjusted at the waist and the bust. But it's a real relief not to have to spend days trying on one dress after another. And," Sue said after taking a deep breath, "there's no need of a trousseau. Travis has to be at the hospital in July and Christy will start looking for a job. In Baltimore. So there won't be a honeymoon. They'll plan something special when he finishes his residency." After a pause, she added, "In four or five years."

I let that pass, and after offering again to help as well as to host whatever social occasion Christy wanted, I ended the conversation. I'd learned a lot, but not what I wanted to know. Which was, what was the hurry? Johns Hopkins in Baltimore wasn't that far from Duke in Durham. Christy and her young man could have easily continued their romance at such a short distance apart, allowing Christy to pursue her education even as he was pursuing his. I'd noticed, however, that Sue had not mentioned Christy's dropping out of school, which of course was obvious in light of all the wedding preparations. But it seemed likely to me that it hurt Sue too much to bring it up.

Of course it wasn't any of my business and no one had asked my opinion, but I couldn't help but wonder at the rush. For the truth of the matter was that I could come up with only one reason for a hurry-up wedding requiring Christy to give up her education, and that was the same reason that Janelle wasn't starting hers.

"Miss Julia?" Lillian said without looking up as she leaned over to empty the dishwasher. "You got time to talk?"

I stopped on my way to the coffeepot and stared at her back. "Why, of course, Lillian. When do I ever not have time to talk?"

"Well, I don't know," she said, turning her attention to the counter as she began wiping it dry. "I jus' got something on my mind an' I need to get it off."

"Then now's as good a time as any. I'm pouring the coffee, so put down that rag and sit down. We'll talk all you want."

Lillian took her time getting settled at the table, sugaring her coffee and stirring it a lot more than it needed. She sighed a couple of times as I sat across from her, waiting to hear what was on her mind.

Finally she said, "You know Mr. Chester P. Dobbs?"

"I know who he is, but I don't *know* him. He owns that pest-control business, doesn't he? I see his trucks all over town. Why're you asking about him?"

"Well," she said, looking intently at the coffee in her cup, "he's been comin' 'round lately."

I frowned. "What do you mean, coming around? Is he bothering you? Creating a problem of some kind?" I was immediately on the defensive for Lillian, feeling protective of her. Chester P. Dobbs was an elderly man who had long been a respected leader of the black community, keeping good relations between that community and the town fathers. Always neatly dressed and shaven, noted for his full head of white hair and the cane he carried jauntily, he commanded esteem from everyone who knew him or knew of him. Chester P. Dobbs, with his unfailing good manners and a sizable bank account, was a polite and gentlemanly force to be reckoned with.

"If that's the case, Lillian," I went on, "we can report him to Sergeant Bates as well as get Binkie to threaten a lawsuit or something."

"No'm, I don't think I wanta sue him, but he's about to wear me down."

"Wear you down? About what? What does he want?"

"He say he want me to think about marryin' him."

My mouth dropped open and I stared at her, almost too surprised to respond. "What? *Marry* him? Why, Lillian, the man is as old as the hills. Why in the world does he have marrying on his mind?" Then, abruptly realizing how I might have sounded, I quickly began to backtrack. "Of course, I can see how he or any man would want you—you're a prize. But why would you consider *him*? I mean, if you *are* considering him."

Lillian picked up a napkin and began to fold it into pleats. "He say," she said without looking at me, "he can make it worth my while."

"What does that mean?"

"He say he'll put me in his will."

"Well!" I said indignantly. "I should *say* he'll put you in his will.

As his wife, you'd get half of everything he owns whether he puts you in it or not." I leaned toward her and went on. "Don't you remember how Wesley Lloyd Springer tried to cut me out—*me*, his duly wedded wife of more than forty years? But the state laws wouldn't let him, so don't be fooled into thinking Mr. Dobbs is promising something special to you. The minute you both say 'I do,' you're in line for at least half of everything. And from what I hear, he has a gracious plenty of everything."

"Yes, ma'am, he sure do, least that's what ev'rybody say. An' he's got that big ole Cadillac he can't drive no more so he has to have a driver, an' he say I can drive him around. An' he say he hears I'm a good cook an' that ev'rybody say I got a good heart to look after people when they get ole. An' he say he got a big, roomy house—you know, it's that big blue one on the corner over there—so there's plenty of room for me."

"And for Latisha?"

"He don't say much 'bout Latisha so far, but he got to know that where I go, she goes, too."

"Not necessarily," I said and leaned my head against my hand. "Lillian, I declare, I've got to have time to process this because it sounds like you could be leaving me. And," I quickly added as I reached across the table to touch her arm, "I don't want to just be thinking of myself, but I'll tell you the truth. The thought of losing you makes the bottom drop out from under my feet. I know I'm being selfish, thinking only of myself, but I don't know what I'd do without you.

"On the other hand," I went on, "leaving Sam and me out of it for a minute, is it really a good thing for you? Because, frankly, so far it sounds as if he's looking for live-in nursing care."

"Yes'm, an' he wants me to fry him up some pork chops so he can see how good I do 'em."

"Lillian!" I cried, struck by the man's audacity. "He wants you to *audition* for the position? For all you know, he's got half a dozen other women frying up pork chops all over town, and he's planning to choose among them. On the basis of what? *Crispiness*?"

"That's what I been wonderin', too," Lillian said. "Still an' all, I been thinkin' it might be worth a few years of nursin' an' cookin' an' drivin' before he passes. 'Cept he's already eighty-nine years ole an' still on his feet. He could keep on goin' for lots more years, an' he's got lots of grown chil'ren who all work for him, so they drainin' whatever's been put away. I could wake up some mornin' when he don't and find out I'm poorer than I ever was."

"Oh, my goodness," I said, shocked yet laughing in spite of myself. "You are so wise! You've already thought of everything I was going to say. Of course, I don't want to lose you. You and Latisha are family, and I'd be lost without you. On the other hand, I don't want to stand in your way if you have a chance to better yourself financially and socially. I mean, I assume that being Mrs. Chester P. Dobbs would be a feather in your cap if you care about such things. It's just . . ." I stopped, wondering how far to go. "It's just that it may not be all it's cracked up to be. How're his children, who I assume all live close by, going to take to a new mother? You could have a lot of problems there." I stopped, took a breath, and looked her in the eye. "But, Lillian, here's the most important thing—how do *you* feel about it? What do *you* want to do?"

"Well," she said as she looked around the kitchen as if she'd find the answer there, "I figure I ought to think about it 'cause you don't get a proposal ev'ry day, least I don't. An' I figure I could handle the work, an' I wouldn't mind settin' in the front pew at church like he does, an' I figure Latisha's college might get paid easier than I could do it. But, Miss Julia, I tell you the truth, I jus' don't know if I could live with the smell."

"The smell? What're you talking about? What kind of smell?"

"The smell Mr. Dobbs got."

"You mean," I asked, leaning forward and lowering my voice, "he's not clean?"

"No'm, he's clean enough an' he oughta be 'cause he smell like a can of Raid. Ev'ry time he move around, I get a whiff of bug-killin' spray an' jus' about get sick to my stomach."

"Oh, Lillian," I said, "that's awful. But that's his business, so I guess his wife would have to get used to it."

But my heart soared to hear it, because I didn't want to lose Lillian by marriage or by any other means, although, of course, I didn't want to stand in her way. On the other hand, I'd stand in her way if I could.

Chapter 7

"Sam?" I said that evening when the house was quiet and we were waiting for the late news and tomorrow's weather forecast.

"Hm-m?" he said from behind the newspaper.

"Lillian is thinking of getting married."

The paper came down abruptly and he stared at me. "Married! Why?"

"Well, when you pare it down there're only two reasons a woman gets married. No, maybe three. The first is when she's so in love that she'll marry the worst possible person she knows, but because she has stars in her eyes she'll think he's wonderful . . . until, nine times out of ten, she's lived with him for a few months. The second reason is purely pragmatic—she wants a man with a good income and a regular job that will provide a home and all the necessities for a family. She might really care for him as well, but she wouldn't have looked at him if he'd been a ditch digger. And possibly a third reason is because all her friends are getting married."

"Julia," Sam said, "honey, that is the most cynical thing I've ever heard. You don't really believe that." He cocked an eyebrow at me. "Do you?"

"No, I guess I don't. I'm just making a general comment on the reasons behind some of the marriages I've observed. But you have to admit that there are very few that are as good and as fitting as ours."

"Well," Sam said, "I'm relieved that you think so. I've been sitting here wondering which reason you had for marrying me."

"Oh," I said with a knowing smile, "the first one, by far. I was so in love I couldn't see straight. But I lucked out by getting a man who's not only easy to live with but easy to keep on loving."

"I'm certainly glad to hear it."

"Oh, you," I said, laughing. "My point, though, is that most women—and men, too, I guess—don't know what they're getting when they marry. And it can be a shock when they find out what they have. But back to what started all this. How well do you know Mr. Chester P. Dobbs?"

"Fairly well, I guess. When I was a town commissioner, I pushed to give his business the pest-control contract for the civic buildings. He did a good job, and as far as I know he's still doing it. That's the closest contact I've had with him other than a chat or two on the street." Sam suddenly sat up straight. "Wait a minute! Are you saying it's Chester Dobbs that Lillian is thinking of marrying?"

"Well, yes, except apparently he's not yet out-and-out proposed. He seems to still be in the shopping phase. You know—seeing what's available and putting out a few feelers. Comparison shopping, I'd call it."

"Julia, for goodness' sake, is she seriously considering it?"

"Well, as I said, he's not actually asked her. He's just told her all the benefits of being his wife if he decides on her. As far as I can tell, she's not particularly thrilled by the idea—she falls into the second reason I gave for marrying. You know, so she won't have to worry about finances, having Latisha's college paid for, living in a big house, driving a big car, sitting in the front pew in church—that sort of thing. He assured her," I went on, "that he'd make it worth her while."

"Good Lord," Sam said, blowing out his breath as he leaned his head back against his chair. "What does that mean?"

"It means," I said, "that he told her he'll put her in his will, and I think she's really considering it as something too good to turn down. You know, like it's a job she might not want but that would pay better than any other and she'd be foolish not to take it."

"My goodness," Sam said softly. "Julia, remind her that Mr. Dobbs has three grown sons who now own the business. They may pay him a salary for advice or some such, but he no longer has anything to do with Dobbs Best Pest Control. Also—and I know this for a fact because he told me about it—all his rental property is tied up in life estates with the boys, which means that the minute he passes, they'll have full ownership. He may not have much to leave to anybody in his will, but of course," Sam went on, "I don't know the extent of his holdings. He's a good businessman, so he may have more assets, but he's already done a lot of estate planning in order to take care of his children."

"And grandchildren," I added.

Sam nodded. "Yes, and he has a houseful of them."

"That's right! And a bunch of them live in that big blue house that he held out as a temptation to Lillian."

"Yes, I think the youngest son lives there with his family, probably to keep Chester company and, I guess, to take care of him in his old age."

"Oh, Sam," I said with a moan, "I have to remind Lillian of that. I can't imagine she'd be welcome in another woman's kitchen, and two women in the same house is a recipe for a conflict of major proportions. You see my problem, though, don't you?

I'm trying my best to want the best for her, but what *I* want keeps getting in the way. And half the time I can't tell the difference between what I want and what would be best for her."

"Well, what about Lillian herself? How does she feel about *him*? If he didn't have two nickels to rub together, would she still be tempted?"

"No way in the world," I said. "She's already told me that the only things that make her even consider it are Latisha's college and her own old age being taken care of—sort of like having a guaranteed retirement plan, I guess. But what she'd have to go through to get to that point is what worries me, especially if he's already distributed most of his assets."

"Does she have any *feelings* for him? Companionship in old age is nothing to be sneezed at, you know."

"I do know, but not when your companion smells like a can of bug spray."

"Really?" Sam said, laughing. "Maybe he's more active in the pest control business than I thought. Come to think of it, though," he went on, "I've seen him coming and going from their warehouse several times. His boys just might welcome a new wife to keep him occupied and out of their hair."

"Well, tell me this, Sam. How in the world do I advise Lillian? Wait, though," I said, holding up my hand. "She hasn't exactly asked for my advice, but she's told me what's going on and been very open about her doubts as to what to do. So far, I've tried to be evenhanded, pointing out the pluses and minuses on both sides. But all I want to do is throw my arms around her and cry, 'Don't leave me, don't leave me!'"

"And," Sam said, "that makes you feel selfish and concerned about your own needs with no thought of hers."

"Exactly. I truly do want what's best for her, but when I think of her being tied to that old man for years and years, being treated like hired help, and getting nothing out of it because he's already given everything away, I could just cry."

"If she brings it up again," Sam said, "you might mention the retirement fund that you set up for her years ago. Just to remind her that she won't be totally dependent on Social Security, which you also pay for. And I know that you intend to help with tuition costs for Latisha. If I were you, I'd make sure she knows that she has a few things that might balance out Chester's offerings."

"She knows, Sam. I've not kept anything from her, but I haven't reminded her for fear of sounding like I'm trying to outbid Mr. Dobbs. I don't want her to think I'm trying to buy her."

"I doubt she'd think that. You've been planning for her and Latisha for years."

"That's true," I said, nodding. "But I haven't gone into detail about much of it. But an employee deserves to know exactly what she's making and what her employer thinks she's worth. Maybe I should give her some details so she can weigh what she has here against what Chester P. Dobbs is offering, and he may not come out smelling so good."

Sam grinned. "Right, and from what you said a minute ago, he already has an olfactory problem."

Chapter 8

"Julia?" Sue Hargrove said when I answered the phone the following morning. "If you're still interested in doing something for Christy, what would you think of having the bridesmaids' luncheon?"

"I would love it," I said, delighted to be offered the perfect entertainment option. It could be as elegant as I wanted to make it, yet there would be a manageable number of guests. "One question, though, Sue, and don't hesitate to say so if you don't like the idea. But I wonder if LuAnne could help? I know she'll want to do something for Christy, but, well, she's fairly limited in what she can do."

"Oh, of course," Sue said, fully aware of LuAnne's financial situation. "I'll call her today and ask if she'll go in with you to have the luncheon. The wedding will be on the third Saturday in June, so the luncheon should be the day before, if they don't change it. Christy's Travis is spending next week with us—how he has the time off, I don't know—but he's not shy about adding his two cents' worth to any plans we make." Sue then quickly added a penny's worth of her own. "You know I don't mean that, Julia. I'm just getting overwhelmed."

"Don't worry about it," I said, hastily jotting down dates and reminders on a pad beside the phone. "Having a wedding is always a hectic time. How many should I plan for?"

"She's having eight bridesmaids and two flower girls," Sue said as I heard the rustle of pages on another pad. "And, of course, Ellie Harris is the maid of honor—they've been friends since kindergarten. I talked Christy out of having a ring bearer, mainly because we don't know a little boy the right age. But I told her that this is not a royal wedding, so she doesn't have to have every position filled.

"Actually," Sue went on with a small laugh, "I now understand the benefits of an elopement. But of course I don't mean that. Christy is so in love that I want everything perfect for her."

"I know it will be, Sue, and I'm so pleased to be a part of it. Oh, one question. Should we include the flower girls' mothers?"

"They're already on the list since both are cousins and bridesmaids. The only extras are Travis's mother and his grandmother, if I haven't overlooked anybody. I'll email you a list with addresses, and you don't know what a relief it is to put this in your hands. I know it'll be done right."

"I'll certainly try, but one other thing. Will Christy want to hand out her bridesmaids' gifts at the luncheon? That will determine the kind of mementos LuAnne and I give."

"Yes, I'm sure she will," Sue said with a laugh, "if she and Travis ever agree on what to give them. Oh, if we only had a few more months. I hate to complain, but I'm so afraid of forgetting something—you know, like getting the invitations out, confirming the church, the photographer, the announcement in the paper, the caterer, the florist, and on and on. I get up every morning thinking of something else that has to be done."

"You'll manage, Sue," I said, wanting to encourage her but hearing a note of panic in her voice, "and I know it'll be perfect in every way."

Here, there, or where? Where should we have the luncheon? LuAnne answered that when she called not thirty minutes later.

"Why, at your house, of course," she said after she'd told me three times how excited she was that Sue had asked the two of us to have the bridesmaids' luncheon. "And let's just fill it with flowers, Julia. Maybe it won't be too late to have peonies, just great bunches of them, but we'll have to order them ahead of time. Do you know that I've not done any entertaining since leaving Leonard, not having the room to do anything, as you well know, so I want to go all out with this. Your table will seat ten, won't it?"

"Yes, with the leaf in, but that makes it the head table while the others will have to be seated at card tables in the living room. I'm thinking it would be better to move the sofas out of the library and set up card tables there so that we're all in the same room."

"Oh, yes, that would be better. That way, no one would feel slighted by not being at the head table."

"True. But think about this, LuAnne. Let's not overlook the possibility of having the luncheon at an unusual place. Of course I'd love to have it here, but let's at least consider somewhere else."

"Like where? Because I hope you're not thinking of some restaurant," LuAnne said. "I mean, what's available in this town? Smokey's Barbecue? The Bluebird café?"

"Oh, LuAnne, of course not. And I'm not thinking of the country club, either. The reception will probably be there, so we need to do something different, like that new inn at the top of the mountain, maybe. You and I could drive up and have lunch one day soon. I hear that the views are spectacular, and all we'd have to do is check out the food and the service, as well as how they're set up for a private party."

"Okay, we can do that. And check out the cost as well, because I'm sure they'll be more expensive than having it at home. Your home, I mean."

"Probably, but we'll see. I'm just trying to think of an unusual venue that would contribute to the joy and excitement of the occasion."

I had to leave it at that and hope that the newly opened inn would be the perfect place. It would certainly be more expensive than having Lillian prepare the food, so I'd have to be careful not to scare LuAnne off, and also not to present her with half of an inordinately high bill. Perhaps I could arrange something under the table, so to speak, with the inn.

It had suddenly occurred to me that we should plan to have the luncheon anywhere but at my house. It might well be that Lillian would be Mrs. Chester P. Dobbs by the third Saturday in June, and what would I do with a bevy of bridesmaids coming over with expectations of an elegant luncheon?

The fact of the matter was that every day that passed seemed to present something more to worry about where Lillian was concerned. And now she had become obviously preoccupied, but when I tried to draw her out, she seemed to draw into herself more.

That was unusual in itself, because if there was one thing Lillian was, it was being open and talkative. At one time or another she had told me about Latisha's mama, her own mother, her childhood, her neighbors, who she was going to vote for, and what her last visit to the doctor had uncovered. She and I had no secrets from each other, for she knew as much about me as I did about her.

This morning, though, she had closed herself off, not wanting to sit and sip coffee while discussing whatever was on our minds. And she had recently been forgetting minor things like making gravy but not the rice it went on, overcooking two layers of a layer cake, and going three times in one morning to the grocery store because she kept thinking of something else she needed.

Some ponderous problem was on her mind, and now I knew that it was Mr. Chester P. Dobbs and his tantalizing offer. I was so sure that she was seriously considering it that I was afraid to ask her straight out for fear of her answer. Not only that, I was sick at the thought that any day she was going to announce her intent to marry and her resignation at the same time. I had no doubt about that. Mr. Dobbs occupied a much too elevated position to want his wife working in somebody else's kitchen.

Not only would losing Lillian break my heart, it would leave me up a creek without a paddle if I'd planned a bridesmaids' luncheon and she was no longer with me. I didn't want to share that concern with LuAnne. Lillian had been my closest friend for so long that I could hardly conceive of life without her. Yet I knew that Mr. Dobbs would not approve of his wife continuing in an employed status, as well as being too much in need of her services his own self.

I could think of nothing to do other than wait for Lillian to make up her mind, although I made an effort to be available to talk. But she didn't seem to want to talk. She went about her work with a far-off look in her eyes, doing things by rote, and fully occupied by what was on her mind.

So there was a noticeable lack of back-and-forth between us, not as much laughter in the kitchen, and a lot fewer cups of coffee being poured. The house was quieter with both of us going about our business, locked in our own thoughts.

I tried to lighten things up by asking, "Lillian, have you heard any more about that naked man?"

"Which one?"

"Which one! You mean there's more than one? I'm talking about the one on Miss Vinnie's back porch."

"Oh," she said, turning back to the sink to scrub the egg skillet. "No'm, ev'rybody jus' keep their back porch light on, an' so far that's keepin' him away."

"Well, that's certainly an easy solution to the problem, but what did you mean by asking which one? Are there more naked men running around?"

"No'm, I don't guess so. I guess I jus' have that kind on my mind here lately."

She turned and looked at me, and our eyes met for a second. We stared at each other in surprise at the thought of just who another naked man might be, then we burst out laughing. And there, for a minute, we were of one mind again.

Chapter 9

"Hey, Miss Julia, how're you doin'?" It was a bright, cheerful voice that greeted me when I answered the phone later that morning. "It's Etta Mae Wiggins."

"Etta Mae! It's so good to hear from you. How are you?" Etta Mae Wiggins, my young—comparatively speaking—friend and ally in a number of adventures, had recently become the owner of the Handy Home Helpers, an in-home nursing service, for which she had worked as an employee for a number of years. Now, though, with a little help and a lot of encouragement from me, she was an independent businesswoman, a member of the Chamber of Commerce, and a weekly advertiser in *The Abbotsville Times*.

"Oh, I'm doing real good," she said. "I just thought I'd touch base with you and be sure you're getting my loan payments on time. And to see how you're doing, too."

"They're like clockwork, Etta Mae, and I hope that means that business is good and that all is well with you."

"Yes'm, everything's going so good that it sometimes worries me." She stopped and laughed. "You know me. If I don't have something to worry about, I'll worry about that."

"I'm delighted to hear it, Etta Mae. But I miss seeing you. Stop by sometime and visit for a while. I'd love to hear about the business and your love life as well. How's that handsome deputy you were with at Christmas?"

"Oh, he's still around and still driving me crazy. All I hear from him now is 'Let's get married, let's get married.' And I'm too busy to think of having one more thing on top of everything else I have to deal with."

Well, I thought, that's certainly a different tune from what I was expecting. Etta Mae had been in love with Bobby Lee somebody for years, but she'd never been able to pin him down. She'd tried the marital state with two or three other men, but none had lasted and, according to her, by now she'd been burned too many times. But I'd thought none of them had lasted because they'd all been substitutes for Bobby Lee. And here she was telling me that he was ready to marry but she wasn't?

"It sounds, then," I said, "as if you're putting first things first, and I'm happy for you."

"Oh, yes, ma'am, I am," she said with a lilt in her voice. Then after a second, she went on. "I just love being the owner, though I still can't hardly believe it. It's a whole different ball game to give the orders instead of getting them. But, well, uh, Miss Julia, one of the reasons I called is, well, I hate to ask you this 'cause you've already done so much for me, and I know it's still a long way off, but Bobby Lee wanted me to ask if you and Mr. Sam would consider voting for him for sheriff in November. He's real qualified, much better than anybody else who's running, and the old sheriff has endorsed him. He'd be real professional and get the whole department up-to-date with the best equipment and all. He'd be glad to stop by sometime if you'd like to check him out, and I hope you don't mind me asking you to vote for him."

"Why, Etta Mae, he already has my vote simply because you recommend him, and I'm sure Sam will feel the same way. I don't know why you'd hate to ask us."

"Wel-ll," she said with some hesitation, "Bobby Lee thinks maybe some people will think him and me ought to, you know, make it legal. So I didn't want to put you on the spot if you had a reason for not wanting to vote for him, like him being so footloose and all. I sometimes think that getting elected is the only reason he's so hot to get married, and I told him I'm not about to jump into another marriage just to get a few votes when it's not even me that's running.

"I don't know if you know this or not, Miss Julia," she went on as if delivering a suddenly realized fact, "but people treat you different when you own a business. For the first time in my life, I'm Miss Wiggins, sometimes Ms. Wiggins, and I want to enjoy that for a while before I take a step back and be Mrs. Bobby Lee Moser even if he does get elected."

"I'm proud of you, Etta Mae, and I don't blame you. What you're getting and what you most assuredly deserve is called respect. So enjoy it."

She giggled. "Oh, believe me, I am. And I'm enjoying Deputy Bobby Lee Moser not getting what he wants, too. Turnabout is fair play, I always say."

I was tempted to caution her about being too independent and losing what she'd wanted for so long. There was no reason she couldn't be a respected business owner as well as a happily married woman. But she knew that, so I refrained from giving unneeded advice and, after a little more back-and-forth, we hung up after promising to meet soon for lunch.

"Lord, goodness, Lillian," I said as I walked into the kitchen that Monday morning, determined to ignore what was beginning to feel like an extended chill between us. "It seems as if everybody and his brother is getting married. Or thinking about it or wanting to or something. I wonder if there's something in the air or maybe in the water that has so many people walking down the aisle."

I stopped then, for I'd put my foot in it without realizing what I was doing. Lillian and I had never before had to dance around any subject. We spoke our minds to each other, but now the one sore spot was whether or not she would marry. And what did I do? Just came right out with a complaint about people getting married—the one subject that had created the rift between us.

The evening before, Sam had about convinced me that I was reading too much into Lillian's silence.

"She's trying to decide what to do," he'd said when I had poured out my concern to him. "She's weighing Mr. Dobbs's offer against what she has here, because it's fairly obvious that she can't have both."

"Well," I'd said with a huff, "I would think that we'd continue being friends even if she does marry him. Does she—or he—think I'd just drop her if she stops working here? What kind of a friend would that be?"

"It could be awkward, honey," Sam had pointed out. "Not least because Mr. Dobbs might not want her to continue a close friendship. In other words, she'd be dropping *you*, not the other way around. He has a certain position in town to uphold, one that he's deservedly proud of, and his wife would be expected to share that position, not hobnob around with a former employer."

"What you're saying, then, is that he wouldn't want to be reminded that Lillian had been a maid? I think that qualifies as one of those 'isms' that everybody is accusing everybody else of. Although I don't know which one it would be.

"And," I'd gone on, becoming more defensive, "I hope to goodness that being friends with me would not be taken as of a lesser status than being his wife." I was just before being highly offended.

"No, honey," Sam had said, "it's not you personally, it could be the job that he'd object to."

"And why is that?" I had demanded. "Cleaning house and preparing meals—that's honorable work. And she makes more here than she'd make in any factory or store in the county." I'd gotten to my feet and walked around the room to calm myself. "I don't know where he gets off thinking that working for us is something to be ashamed of. Just where does he think she learned how to fry crispy pork chops, anyway?"

But later that morning when I walked into the kitchen and started in with a complaint about all the marriages that were being planned, Lillian kindly overlooked it.

"Miss Julia," she said as she turned toward me with something else on her mind, "that nekkid man been on the move again. You heard anything about that?"

"No, what's he done now?"

"Well," she said, drying her hands with a paper towel. "Somebody say they seen him on the golf course over at that country club last night. I don't know as I believe it 'cause what was the woman who seen him doin' on the golf course in the middle of the night her own self?"

"Good question," I agreed. "Who was it? The one who saw him, I mean."

"Somebody said she lives in one of the houses on the edge of the golf course, but there wasn't a full moon last night, an' it was cloudin' up when I went to bed, so she might not've got a good look."

"True," I said, "and there's nothing blooming on or around the golf course, so he couldn't have been there to deadhead anything." Then I had a sudden thought. "The golf club, Lillian! That has to be a clue to who he is. What's he doing, carrying a golf club around? Does he play golf? Or he could work at the golf course. Or just be a member there. I mean, not everybody happens to have a bag of golf clubs sitting around."

"No'm, I don't."

"On the other hand," I went on, "I expect whoever said she saw something just saw a cloud drift across the moon. Or maybe some teenagers who've been known to park around there."

"I hope that's all it was," Lillian said. "Something like a crazy man runnin' around with no clothes on don't make livin' by yourself real easy. I keep thinkin' what if Latisha happen to look outside and see that sight? Or what if he see her out in the yard by herself?"

"Oh, Lillian, I didn't even think of that. But of course it's a concern, and I hope the sheriff is aware of it. But surely he is. Maybe we all ought to call and demand he do something. Which reminds me, Etta Mae's friend, Deputy Moser, is running for sheriff this fall. If he gets elected, it'll be reassuring to have someone in office who knows us personally."

"I guess," Lillian said, "but I don't want to wait till the fall to put some clothes on that man. It's gettin' to where I hate to go to bed, wonderin' if he's out in the yard with that golf club of his." She turned back to the sink and said, half under her breath, "Make me think it'd be better to live with somebody more than just Latisha."

Oh, my word, I thought. If she's afraid to live alone, that could be just the thing to push her over the edge into Mr. Dobbs's arms. Living with a houseful of stepchildren and stepgrandchildren wouldn't be as off-putting as I had thought.

"Lillian," I said, "why don't you and Latisha come stay here until that man is caught? The more I think of being alone while Sam is gone, the less I like it. They're leaving for Alabama this weekend, and I'm feeling more and more unsettled about it."

"I tole you, you ought not be stayin' by yourself."

"I know, and you were right. But now that I know that you, too, feel uneasy, we would both be better off staying together. Please say you will."

"Well, maybe." And arching an eyebrow, she turned and said, "If that nekkid man knows what's good for him, he won't wanta take on both of us."

Chapter 10

The following day, LuAnne and I drove up the mountain to have lunch at the Inn on Jump-Off, a refurbished small hotel on the edge of a sheer cliff that overlooked a vast vista of the Blue Ridge Mountains. Long closed and abandoned, the inn had at one time catered to wealthy summer visitors, more of whom the new owners were obviously hoping to attract.

The grounds, as I turned into the drive, were beautifully landscaped and well kept. There was also a valet waiting to park the car, which was highly impressive to LuAnne but hardly necessary since there were only a few cars in the lot. But the inn hadn't been open very long, and I hoped it only meant that word hadn't yet gotten around and was not an indication of the quality of its offerings.

I admit, though, to a gasp of amazement when we walked into the lobby. The entire back wall opened through windows to a stone patio that gave onto a view of breathtaking expanses. Even LuAnne was silenced by the grandeur of rolling mountains covered in green new growth with the occasional church spire poking up above the treetops.

We introduced ourselves to the hostess, who had been expecting us due to the reservation I had made. She led us to a paneled room off the lobby and explained that it was for private parties. Its outside wall was also entirely made of windows and gave onto the same view as that of the lobby.

So far, I was quite pleased with its possibility as a venue for our bridesmaids' luncheon. We discussed seating possibilities and decided that one U-shaped table would be more conducive to conversation than individual tables.

"Let's have the table large enough," I suggested, "so that no one is seated inside the U. If we're all on the outside, everyone will be able to see the view."

LuAnne pointed out the lovely Federal side tables flanking the door, both with mirrors hanging above, and announced that they'd be perfect for large bouquets of pink peonies. On the back wall of the room, there was a large framed painting of a group of red-coated fox hunters galloping on horseback across an English countryside. That decided it for me. Even before we'd sampled the food, I knew there was nothing in Abbotsville classier than an English hunt scene hanging on a paneled wall.

The food was adequate, not outstanding, but what more can be done to chicken à la king on pastry shells? It was either that or chicken salad, because one can't serve shrimp or lobster, as there will always be one or two who'll claim to have an allergy. And beef isn't a luncheon choice—too hearty and filling as well as offering too many choices—rare, well done, medium, or barely pink—which creates havoc for the server.

The only sour note of our trial luncheon was the hostess, who kept suggesting various items on the menu, invariably phrasing them as being "beautifully plated." I declare, I get so tired of hearing nouns turned into verbs, not by adding suffixes but by simply using them as verbs. What's wrong with serving food instead of *plating* it? And why do we now *gift* someone instead of simply giving it? So if you feel the urge to *task* someone, please just give him a job to do.

But along with changing the usage of certain words, there are now words that can no longer be used at all. The problem with that is that I can't keep up with which ones have been banished and what, in turn, will happen to highly acclaimed books like *The Adventures of Huckleberry Finn*, as well as to hip-hop so-called music.

LuAnne and I decided that the inn would be a uniquely lovely place for the luncheon, so we reserved the private room for the third Friday in June, planned the menu, and told the hostess that we would be responsible for the centerpiece and other arrangements around the room. There would also be, we told her, other instructions as we thought of them.

"Julia," LuAnne said as we slid into the front seat of my car for our return trip, "what do you think about serving a little something beforehand? Like an aperitif or something?"

"I was thinking the same thing," I admitted. "I know that Sue wouldn't mind a small serving of, say, a sparkling drink of some kind, but I don't know about the groom's mother. And of course Christy and her friends are all adults and may well expect something. My only concern is the drive back down the mountain. I certainly don't want to be responsible for somebody running off the road and ending up in the hospital or worse."

"But if we serve something that's very lightly laced with just enough for the girls to get a taste, we'll get the effect without the problem. I mean, they're all going to be giddy with excitement anyway, so all we have to do is suggest, and they'll take it from there."

"I agree," I said. "At least I'm pretty sure I do. I declare, LuAnne, I sometimes think that I'm getting more liberal every day I live. A few years ago I would've been shocked at the thought of serving alcohol at a party. It wouldn't even have occurred to me to consider it. Now, though, it seems perfectly appropriate. And I don't even wonder what the preacher would think."

"Me, either."

"I hate to admit it," I went on, "but maybe we're just getting older and we've learned that there're more important battles to fight. Who cares if somebody has a little nip now and then? I'm sure I don't."

LuAnne cocked her head at me. "Does that mean that you do?"

"Do what?"

"Have a little nip now and then."

"Absolutely not," I said, tapping the brakes as the car entered a long downhill S-curve. "What do you think I am, anyway? I was speaking in general terms. No, I'm against alcohol in general, but I see nothing wrong with raising a small glass of punch in celebration of a happy occasion."

"That hostess was really pushing it, wasn't she? Something before we eat and something with lunch and a sweet something with dessert. I'd be thoroughly looped if I drank that much." LuAnne paused, then said, "Not that I drink at all. I mean, unless it's for something special."

"Well, me, too. But I think restaurants make their money on alcohol—wine and mixed drinks—so I guess she had to try." I smiled. "She just didn't know who she was dealing with—two dyed-in-the-wool Presbyterians with just a toe in the water."

We continued to talk, or at least LuAnne did, as I drove across town and pulled to a stop in front of her condominium.

"Come in for a while," LuAnne said, her hand on the door handle. "We haven't had a long talk in ages."

"I'd love to, but I need to get home. Sam's in the process of packing for his fishing trip and invariably he forgets something.

Last year he forgot his razor, although I doubt he would've used it if he'd had it. I don't think any of them shaved until the day they came home." I laughed at the memory, then abruptly stopped. "I declare, LuAnne, time is really passing. Little Christy is getting married, and even Lloyd is shaving now, not often apparently, but he has all the paraphernalia and it's another symbol of his growing up." I sighed. "I don't much like it."

"I know what you mean," LuAnne said. "I have a real sense of time passing and what's left is getting shorter and shorter. And what am I doing? Spending my time answering a telephone in a mortuary all day and rattling around in a lonely condo half the night. I tell you, Julia, I get so lonesome sometimes I don't know what to do."

"Oh, LuAnne, I thought you were enjoying your condo—having your privacy and doing as you please."

"Living alone is not all it's cracked up to be," she said with a sharp edge to her voice. "I've come to realize that I *liked* being a wife. Yes, I know how Leonard was, so don't remind me and good riddance to him. It's just that I think I was cut out to be a wife, like it's my calling. I need somebody to talk to and to do for, and somebody to worry about me if I don't come home even if it's only to cook supper." She wiped her hand across her face. "I want to be married to somebody, Julia. I want to be somebody's wife."

"Well, my land, LuAnne," I said, dismayed by her admission. "You sure had me fooled. I really thought that you had adjusted to the divorce beautifully. You found a good job and you're filling your time with volunteer work just as you've always done. And for the first time in your life, you can do as you please and not be at the beck and call of someone else. You do remember, don't you, how it felt to live with Leonard while he was living with both you *and* his girlfriend?"

"I remember, all right, and I'm not saying I wish I was still married to *him*. I'm just saying I want to be *married*, period. Although the number of available men in our age group is a big, fat zero. You know," LuAnne went on in a dreamy sort of way, "I used to dream that a knight in shining armor would come along, but now I'd settle for a little male company, even in pleated pants.

"Anyway," she said, opening the car door, "don't worry about me. I'm in no danger of remarrying anytime soon. Thanks for the ride and the lunch. Just leave the luncheon flowers to me, and I'll address the invitations, too. But let's be thinking of what we can do about some kind of mementos for the bridesmaids." She stepped out of the car, leaned in to thank me again, then walked away.

I watched as she went to her door, then, feeling sad and undone, I turned the car toward home. Here I'd been thinking that my friend was enjoying her freedom from a miserable marriage, and all the while she'd been longing for another one.

Not another miserable one, of course, but as I'd pointed out to Sam, you never know what you'll get until you're already in it. And to tell the truth, LuAnne's admission had stirred up real fears for her. As impulsive as she could be, it wouldn't surprise me to suddenly learn that she was about to join the ever-lengthening list of soon-to-be brides.

Chapter 11

Well, Lord, I said to myself and to Him, what do you do about that? LuAnne's admission had both stunned and saddened me, and it rolled about in my mind all the way home. You would think that after what Leonard had put her through, she'd be the last one to want to jump into another marriage. I mean, think of the shame and embarrassment she'd suffered on learning that her placid and plodding husband had been carrying on for years with an overgrown hippie who couldn't touch LuAnne in looks, manners, class, or status in the town. And he absolutely would not give up his sideline, so LuAnne had been faced with the choice of divorcing or sharing him. Since he was no prize to begin with, LuAnne bravely chose to reject joint ownership.

Yet now here she was longing to leap back into a marriage just for the sake of being married. The scary thing about that was the possibility that she'd end up in a situation so miserable that the one she'd had with Leonard would look good.

I knew she had financial limitations that could make anyone rethink just about everything. But being strapped financially was nothing new to her, although she and Leonard seemed to have lived as well as any of us. If it hadn't been for the occasional cutting remark from LuAnne about people who had maids and cooks and yardmen and you-name-it, it would never have occurred to me that the Conovers had less than anyone else I knew.

But compare LuAnne's situation with that of Helen Stroud, for goodness' sake. Helen had been the one left high and dry after an abrupt fall from what had appeared to have been real wealth down to pennilessness in a matter of weeks. After repaying what had been mishandled as well as the fines and penalties her husband had incurred, Helen was left with absolutely nothing. LuAnne was not in such dire straits, yet she'd sat right beside me and moaned about wanting to marry again, not because she couldn't make ends meet but because she wanted someone to talk to.

I should've pointed out the benefits of owning a dog. Just think, she'd be eagerly welcomed home each day and she'd have somebody to take care of and somebody to keep her feet warm in the winter.

Suffice it to say that I was not inclined to be sympathetic with LuAnne's tearful desire to remarry. As far as I was concerned, she was well out of an untenable situation and should've been at least somewhat gun-shy about the possibility of getting into another one.

But that hadn't been the way she'd sounded. There had been nothing said about falling in love, nothing about wanting a soul mate, nothing about needing financial help, nothing about wanting to share a life. She simply wanted to be a wife. *Any*body's wife. LuAnne did not often stop and think, but somebody could pop up at any minute. As far as I knew, there was no one currently on the horizon, thank goodness, and she'd have to go some to find a husband worse than Leonard had been, but it could be done.

That's what worried me, and I wanted to go inside and discuss it with Lillian that afternoon and with Sam that evening. Between those two, I would get a better understanding of my friend's needs as well as suggestions for the kindest way of talking her out of marrying the first man who happened to present himself. I thought then of the number of widowers who walked through the doors of the Good Shepherd Funeral Home, and a cold chill ran down my back.

Parking in my usual place in the drive at home, I quickly got out of the car and hurried in, eager to tell Lillian of my concerns and hear her sensible responses. Instead, I met her on her way out.

"I'm glad you came home," she said, tucking her huge pocketbook under her arm. "I left you a note, an' supper's ready to be heated up, but I got to go."

"Okay, but is everything all right?"

"Yes'm, an' I shoulda tole you this mornin', but I didn't know anything about it till a little while ago when Mr. Dobbs, he called an' say we eatin' with some of his chil'ren tonight. His driver's gonna pick me up."

"Oh," I said, immediately perturbed by Mr. Dobbs's apparently last-minute invitation and his assumption that she would obey his summons, as indeed she appeared to be doing. "It's all a little sudden, isn't it?"

"He 'pologized for that 'cause he wanted me to come special on Saturday night and Janelle's mama was s'posed to come tonight. But she has a bad cold an' he don't wanta get infected an' his daughter-in-law already workin' on a big supper, so he invited me."

"Well," I said, hardly knowing what to say, "what about Latisha? Will she come here after school?"

"No'm, Mr. Dobbs, he got one of his granddaughters to look after her."

Hm-m, I thought, he's thought of everything, and all Lillian has to do is fall in line. I so wanted to point this out to her, but I refrained. But there went our long talk together, as well as her good common sense that would have eased my concerns about LuAnne. Instead, I clearly had more than one friend in the throes of who, why, and whether to marry.

"Well, I must say," I said with a tinge of outrage, "he's thought of just about everything, hasn't he? Except for how you feel about having everything planned for you."

"Oh," she said, "I don't mind about that 'less it gets to be a habit. He thinks he's tryin' me out, but the fact of the matter is that it's me who's tryin' *him* out. An' so far he's not doin' too good."

"I am glad to hear it, Lillian," I said with some relief, "because I don't want him and all he has to offer to turn your head. It can appear very appealing, I know, at least from the outside. Dealing with it from the inside can be a different matter, but of course you have to do what is best for you. And for Latisha.

"Anyway," I went on, "I hope he hasn't planned anything for you tomorrow. I really need to talk to you about getting married and . . ."

"Law, Miss Julia, I'm not gettin' married. Not anytime soon, anyway."

"No, no, not you. I mean, I know you're *considering* it. No, it's LuAnne Conover who sounds like she'd marry anybody in pants who'd hold still long enough."

"Oh, bless her heart. Let's us talk about it tomorrow, 'cause right now I gotta get home an' put on something decent 'fore that driver come to get me." And Lillian edged around me on her way to the door, and there was nothing to do but let her go.

"Have a good time," I said, then mumbled, "but not too good."

I plopped down in a chair at the table, done in by Lillian's just up and leaving when Mr. Dobbs snapped his fingers. I didn't mind her leaving so much as I minded the reason for her leaving. That old man was *courting* her. And introducing her to his children meant that he was parading her as a possibility. How many others, like Janelle's mother, had he invited to dinner? Did his children grade each one? And how much credence did he give to their opinions?

Well, I reminded myself, Lillian hadn't seemed all that thrilled about being invited to dinner—maybe because it had sounded more like a summons than an invitation. I knew she had a good head on her shoulders and it was not easily turned, but to be wined and dined had long been part of a courtship. And she had been anxious enough to get home and prepare herself to make a good impression.

It was a fact that many women liked the masterful type or thought they did until they got tired of taking orders. My heart sank at the thought that Lillian might actually see Mr. Dobbs as her knight in shining armor, and the fact of the matter was that she deserved one to come riding up if anyone did. My problem, though, was that Mr. Dobbs seemed more of a Don Quixote—or maybe a Sancho Panza—than a Sir Lancelot.

I knew I had to be very careful. If I pointed out too many problems or asked too many questions, she could become defensive of him. On the other hand, he had been quite open in what he was looking for—essentially a nursemaid who could both drive and cook—so he wasn't flying false colors. And then it struck me. Both Chester P. Dobbs and Thurlow Jones were in need of the same thing and both were willing to pay for it.

Well, maybe not willing, exactly, but *able,* at least, to pay for it. And if that's not a pitiful comment on the marital state, I don't know what is.

Chapter 12

"Sam," I said later that evening, after we'd cleared the table and were seated in the library, "what should I do about LuAnne?" I had filled him in on the conversation in the car as we ate the supper that Lillian had left.

"Nothing you can do, honey," he said from behind the newspaper.

"Well, I'm thinking that if we, or maybe *you*, knew someone nice and single, we could introduce them and give her somebody decent to think about. That would keep her from latching on to someone totally unsuitable."

"Uh-uh," he said. "I'm not in the matchmaking business." He lowered the paper. "And you shouldn't be, either."

"I know, that's why I thought you could do it. But I'll tell you the truth, I don't understand her at all. After I found out what Wesley Lloyd had been up to, the last thing I wanted was to get back into a marriage that might turn into another three-way situation."

"That was before you considered me," Sam said somewhat drily. "Right?"

"Oh, right. You'd always been around—Wesley Lloyd's friend and attorney who was just a part of our lives. But it wasn't just you. I wasn't considering *any*body. I figured I was well out of it since Wesley Lloyd's heart attack had so conveniently taken him out of the picture. I certainly wasn't looking for anybody else."

Sam folded the newspaper and laid it aside. "That was before you realized what a catch I was, wasn't it?"

"Oh, you," I said, smiling. "Yes, it took me a while because once burned, twice shy, but I finally saw that I couldn't let you get away. But see, Sam, that's exactly what worries me about LuAnne, and about Lillian as well. LuAnne sounds as if she'd marry anybody who presented himself, while Lillian is fully aware of the drawbacks in her situation but seems willing to accept them. I don't know which is worse."

"It's a good thing, then," Sam said with a smile, "that you don't have to make the decisions."

"I know," I said, then sighed. "I know it's not any of my business except that they talk to me about it. At least LuAnne does. Lillian is another matter. I'm not sure what she's thinking. She just seems to do whatever Mr. Dobbs tells her to do—fry pork chops for him, go to dinner with him whenever he wants, sit in a lineup for his children, and who knows what else. I don't think she particularly likes being told what to do, but she does it, thinking, I guess, that it'll pay off in the long run. But what if it doesn't?"

Before Sam could answer, I went on. "And it just tears me up to think of that old man taking advantage of her. I mean, from the looks of him he could live to be a hundred and ten, and be written up in the newspaper for longevity as if he himself had anything to do with it. And Lillian would be standing in the background with a bedpan, a washcloth, and baby food ready to spoon into his mouth. I mean, he could outlive her, and she'd never get the payoff he's tempting her with. Sam," I said, tapping my mouth with my fingers as I thought of something else, "could you maybe find out just how well off he is—financially, I mean? You've said that he's done some estate planning, so how much does he have that he hasn't already given away or earmarked?"

I sat up straight with a sudden thought, and before Sam could open his mouth, I said, "You know what it could be? What if he's not looking to *hire* somebody to take care of him because he can't afford to pay anybody? What if the only way he can get the help he needs is to get himself a wife? Oh, Sam, you should look into this. We can't let Lillian be lured into becoming that old man's unpaid nursemaid."

"No, honey," Sam said. "There's no way I can find out what he's worth. Where would I look? Who would I ask?"

"Well, you could bring it up at the Bluebird, couldn't you? Your buddies there might have some idea of what he has or what he's done with what he once had. Anything would help."

"Um, well, I'll think about it. Most of it would be gossip or hearsay, anyway."

"You'd be surprised," I said, "at how often hearsay is right on the money—especially in this town. And if the word is out that Mr. Dobbs is as poor as a church mouse, I want to know about it. And Lillian *needs* to know about it. I mean, she's not exactly enamored by him, so it wouldn't break her heart. What he's proposing is more of a business deal than a courtship, anyway. And in any business deal you need to know if the one you're dealing with has the wherewithal to finance whatever deal he's proposing."

I left Sam in bed the next morning and was up, dressed, and sitting at the kitchen table when Lillian came in.

She stopped in surprise just inside the door and demanded, "What you doin' up this time of a mornin'?"

"Oh, no reason, just woke up early for a change. Coffee's ready, so have a seat and I'll pour us some."

She gave me a sideways look as she put her jacket and purse in the pantry, then with a heavy sigh she took a chair at the table. I put a cup of steaming coffee in front of her, pushed the sugar bowl nearer, and sat back down.

"Well," I said, "how did it go?"

Lillian raised her cup and looked at me over the top of it. "How did what go?"

"You know what I'm talking about—your date. How did your date go?"

"I wouldn't 'zactly call it a date, 'specially since that big supper his daughter-in-law was supposed to cook turned out to be take-out pizza. An' after I got all dressed up to go eat it."

"No! *Pizza?*"

Lillian set her cup down, then said, "Yes'm, an' I tell you, Miss Julia, that's a house in need of a strong hand. There was toys an' coats an' odds an' ends all over the furniture, an' two or three cats that kept curlin' 'round my feet, an' four littl'uns running 'round like wild Indians, screamin' an' cryin' an' yellin' an' spillin' things. I couldn't hardly hear myself think, an' nobody said a thing to 'em, like 'Set down an' be quiet,' or 'Mind your manners,' or even 'Kiss my foot.'"

"*Really?* Not even Mr. Dobbs?"

"No'm, Mr. Dobbs, he don't seem to mind. He jus' eat that pizza like it's the best in the world, an' all that racket didn't even make a dent. That's when I find out he's 'bout as deaf as a post when he turns off his hearin' aid. I tell you, I was wishing I had something to turn off, an' that girl didn't even say she sorry she didn't get anything cooked for comp'ny. It beat all I ever seen."

I tried not to smile, just shook my head in commiseration. "My goodness," I said, "I wonder what she'll serve Janelle's mother on Saturday night—the night you were supposed to be there. It sounds as if the poor woman has too much to do, what with all those children and then being expected to cook a big supper for a guest. Bless her heart, she needs help, and it's thoughtful of Mr. Dobbs to recognize it and try to do something about it."

Lillian stared at me with a look of dawning realization, then she said, "He's lookin' at the wrong woman if he thinks I'd take on that crew. But I think he knowed that 'cause he had his driver drive us around a while instead of takin' me straight home so we could talk in the back seat. An' I tell you, Miss Julia, that's real nice ridin' to have somebody else do the drivin', though I didn't much like havin' somebody else listenin' in on us."

"Is he a sweet man, Lillian? I mean, when you're alone or almost alone?"

"Huh, sweet got nothin' to do with it. All he said was he was thinkin' of moving out to a smaller place where he wouldn't step on a cat every time he picked up his feet." Lillian paused and got a thoughtful look on her face. "I take that to mean that he might not've heard all the racket but he figured I had, and it was his way of sayin' I wouldn't have to put up with it."

"I'd get that in writing," I said, "*if*, I mean, you're seriously considering moving in with him."

"I don't know if I am or if I'm not. I'm just waitin' to see how many others he's stringin' along. 'Cept now," she said as she leaned her head on her hand, "he say he can come to supper at my house Sunday night an' he sure do like pork chops."

"Why, Lillian," I said as my eyebrows went up, "he just invited himself? And told you what he wanted to be served? That's pretty presumptuous of him, don't you think?"

"Well, turnabout, I guess. Maybe when he see how Latisha an' me eat, he'll know I'm not used to eatin' in a three-ring circus." Lillian sighed. "I don't know, Miss Julia. I sure do like that big blue house—if it could ever get emptied out an' cleaned up. I guess I'll just wait an' see what he does an' who all else's in the runnin' to be Mrs. Chester P. Dobbs."

"You think there might be more than Janelle's mama? What's her name, anyway?"

"Pearl. Miss Pearl, we call her, and, yes'm, I'm pretty sure Mr. Dobbs is lookin' at some others. Maybe ev'rybody who don't already have somebody. Look like he's givin' ev'rybody a fair chance."

A fair chance! As if he were a prize for whom every single woman in town was panting! Who, I wanted to ask, would want him?

Chapter 13

Just in case Lillian decided that she couldn't resist becoming the queen of the local AME Zion church and ended up leaving me, I decided that if I was going to do something for Helen, I'd better do it soon. Delaying any longer could leave me high and dry with no help at all, pretty much putting an end to meeting my social obligations.

In addition, even taking into account Helen's saying that she wanted no celebration of her marriage at all, one did not marry every day and still fewer married twice, so I felt that some acknowledgment was called for. A small luncheon within the next week or so would be both appropriate and doable, even if Lillian gave notice.

That thought saddened me so much that I almost took to my bed. But I soldiered on, knowing that Lillian herself was still up in the air and might, when all was said and done, be content to stay where she was.

It occurred to me that it would be helpful to give her a raise, then I thought better of it since it could appear to be a bribe. But what was wrong with a bribe? And wasn't that what a raise was, anyway? It was an indication that an employer was pleased with the employee and wanted to keep said employee on. So I gave her a raise as if it had been my plan all along. And, indeed, she was accustomed to raises now and then, so if she wondered about the impetus behind this one, she didn't mention it.

But I did take the opportunity to mention that her retirement fund was doing quite well and that I'd made a recent addition to it. I refrained from saying that I hoped she wouldn't need it anytime soon.

So I called Helen and announced my intention to have a luncheon in her honor. "I know," I said before she could respond, "that you don't want anything special done, so think of this as just an opportunity for a few old friends to get together. I'm thinking of asking LuAnne, Emma Sue, Mildred, and Hazel Marie. With you and me, that's just six of us, so it barely rises to a celebratory occasion. Still, I would like to do it for you, Helen, so just think of it as a nice, friendly break in your daily routine."

"Well," Helen said, and I could tell from the warmth in her voice that she was pleased. "That sounds perfect, if you really mean it. No shower, no gifts, no cute games, just lunch and a chance to talk and visit with old friends."

"That's exactly what I was thinking." And we went on, after Helen considered and rejected one or two days, to set a date the following week on Thursday, from which I quickly assumed the probable date of her wedding.

"Lillian," I said when I found her in the kitchen, "I'm having a small luncheon next Thursday in honor of Helen Stroud. There'll be only six of us. You'll be here, won't you?"

She turned to stare at me. "Where else would I be?"

"Well, I don't know. I hope you'll be here not only then but forever. But I keep thinking that one of these days you're going to walk in and give notice."

"Huh," she said, turning back to the sink. "That may be what you think an' what Mr. Dobbs think, but I'm not studyin' givin' no notice."

"That is certainly a relief to me," I said, feeling a lightness in my soul. "Does that mean you've told Mr. Dobbs that you're out of the running?"

"No'm, all it means is he's not come up with anything that'll make me change my mind. I wanta know who all's in the runnin', an' I wanta know where he's plannin' to live, an' I wanta know what kinda man he is when nobody else is watchin' what he's doin'."

"Oh, Lillian, you are so wise."

"No'm, jus' usin' the little bit of sense the Lord give me. I wanta know what I'm gettin' into before I get in it an' can't get out. I don't b'lieve in gettin' divorced, so once in it I'm in it for good, an' no tellin' how long that would be."

"Then I'll say it again: You are the wisest woman I know."

She laughed, and it occurred to me that perhaps I didn't know that many wise women although I'd meant it as the highest of compliments.

"What you want me to serve them ladies?"

"Hm-m, I'm thinking that very good quiche you make would be perfect, and you might be able to find some tiny asparagus spears. And let's have blueberry muffins and for dessert your chocolate mousse. What do you think of that?"

"I'll put some fruit on the plate to fill it up and that oughta do it."

"Perfect," I said and turned away, feeling gratitude for how well we worked together and fear of losing one of the pillars of my life.

"LuAnne?" I asked, having dared to call her at the Good Shepherd Funeral Home. "It's Julia. Can you talk?"

"Oh, hey, Julia. Yes, it's slow right now, although you wouldn't believe the number of bodies that came in during the night. Around here, when it rains it pours, but it's the strangest thing, Julia. It seems that when one person passes, it's as if a door opens because a whole bunch will soon follow. Then we'll go for a day or two with no calls at all until all of a sudden we have a bunch of them again."

"Interesting," I said, although the subject wasn't one that I particularly cared about. "Well, listen, I'm calling to invite you to lunch next Thursday, and I hope you can arrange to be off. I would've checked with you first, but it's the best day for Helen and—"

"You're doing it for Helen?"

"Well, yes. Just a few of us, nothing elaborate at all. She doesn't want anything like a celebration, no gifts or anything like that—just old friends getting together for lunch."

There was silence on the line and I prepared to defend myself for not asking LuAnne to host it with me.

"Well," LuAnne said, "I thought that you and I were going to do something together."

"We were," I assured her, "but that was when we were planning something big. This is just six for lunch with no gifts or mementos or anything but good conversation. That's all Helen wants."

"I see. And that means that you get credit for doing something for her and the rest of us get nothing."

"Oh, LuAnne, don't be that way. I'm not looking for credit, and this is going to be so small and insignificant that it hardly counts. I couldn't imagine that you'd want to be involved when there's really nothing for either of us to do."

It took a while to soothe her hurt feelings, and I wasn't sure that I had entirely succeeded. Still, unless she wanted to go to the grocery store for Lillian, everything was already taken care of.

Afterward, I made calls to Mildred Allen, Emma Sue Ledbetter, and Hazel Marie Pickens, everyone except Mildred immediately accepting.

"Since it's spring break, Penelope and I were planning to visit Horace for a few days," Mildred said, and before I could express my disappointment, she went on. "But we can wait to leave till after lunch—he won't know the difference—if you could do it Wednesday instead of Thursday."

Well, why not? So after first getting Lillian's approval of the change, I called everybody again to see if Wednesday suited instead of Thursday. And it did, although each one wanted to talk about Helen or something going on in their own lives so that it took all afternoon before I had my invitations issued.

Mildred, bless her heart, had brought me up-to-date on the condition of her husband, Horace, who was now locked in a facility in Southern Pines with no hope of ever getting out except on a gurney. Mildred said that the only thing he remembers of his life with her was the little red Porsche still parked in her garage. Then she spent another fifteen minutes telling me how well her granddaughter was doing in school and what a blessing the child was to her.

Emma Sue, on the other hand, didn't have a word to say about her husband, Pastor Ledbetter, the former minister of the First Presbyterian Church of Abbotsville. She did tell me, though, that they now attend the Delmont Presbyterian Church although she misses all of us. I knew that it was common practice for a retired minister to refrain from attending services in his former church. Perhaps it was thought that his presence would be off-putting to a new pastor. Emma Sue, however, would be an addition to any congregation, for she felt that her calling was to volunteer for anything that needed volunteers, as well as for some that didn't. From the sound of her list of activities, Larry Ledbetter may have retired, but she hadn't.

And Hazel Marie, as sweet as she always was, brought me up-to-date with the twins, although it had been only three days since I'd last gotten a report. It seems that they were acing preschool, and J. D. Pickens, their father, was taking most of the credit.

"You should see him," Hazel Marie said. "Both little girls crawl into his lap and he reads 'Goldilocks and the Three Bears,' and they're just fascinated because he does all the voices. It's just the sweetest thing."

It might well have been the sweetest thing, but it was hard to imagine. I was still amazed that the man was proving to be such an admirable father, not only to his own little girls but to the light of my life, Lloyd, Hazel Marie's son by a previous liaison unauthorized by clergy.

As soon as I'd sat down to rest from my labors on the telephone, it rang again.

"Julia?" LuAnne said. "You didn't mention Sue Hargrove. Was that an oversight or aren't you inviting her?"

I blew out my breath because of course leaving out Sue was not an oversight. I'd gone back and forth about inviting her and had reluctantly decided against it. Now LuAnne was calling me on it and I had to explain.

"I'm not inviting Sue because for one thing it's only been a few years that she's been such a close friend to all of us and I'm still not sure how close she is to Helen. But the main reason I didn't invite her is because I would then have had to invite Christy. And since she, too, is a soon-to-be bride, I thought there would be too much of a contrast between her and Helen. And you know that with two brides at the table, we'd soon be talking about weddings and I have the feeling that that's the last thing Helen wants to discuss."

"Well," LuAnne said, "I hope you know what you're doing because I'm sure Sue's feelings will be hurt."

"I doubt that," I returned a bit sharply. "She's overwhelmed with preparing for Christy's wedding and will probably thank me for not adding another thing to do." I took a deep breath to refrain from further remarks, then said, "I have to go, LuAnne. Somebody's at the door."

There wasn't, but at least I was able to get off the phone with our friendship still reasonably, though shakily, intact.

Chapter 14

I spent Saturday afternoon helping Sam get ready to leave the next morning on his fishing trip. That help consisted of my putting a few things in his suitcase and him taking them back out.

"Honey," he said, watching me pack, "I don't need a dress shirt and I don't need a tie, much less two of each. We'll be eating at fish camps and we won't be going to church."

"Maybe not, but it seems to me you'd want to be prepared in case you change your mind."

"Well, I'll tell you what," Sam said. "If Pickens decides he wants to go to church, I'll gladly purchase a new shirt and tie. It would be money well spent, but for now the less I pack, the better. Besides, we'll be on the road all day tomorrow and next Sunday as well. And in between we'll be out on the boat every day with no time for anything but supper and bed when we come in."

"I hate to think of you out on the bounding main all day long in the blistering sun. You'll watch out for Lloyd, won't you, Sam? Make sure he doesn't fall off the boat and that he uses sunblock and wears a hat and a shirt. And you, too, of course."

"You know I will. I'll watch out for Lloyd and me, and we'll just let Pickens manage on his own."

"I didn't mean it quite like that," I said a little defensively. "But I do worry about all of you when you're gone."

"It's just a week, honey, and we'll be back before you know it. And speaking of worrying, I'm glad Lillian and Latisha are staying with you this week. I feel better knowing you won't be by yourself."

"Why?" I asked, wondering if he knew something that I didn't. "Have you heard anything more about that naked man?"

"No, not really. We were talking about it at the Bluebird the other day and Ed Hollins said he'd heard of a sighting out near Edneyville a couple of nights ago. The deputies didn't find anything, though."

"No lopped-off tulip blooms?"

"Not a one."

"It wasn't him, then," I said, "apparently. But don't worry about me. I'll be so busy while you're gone that I wouldn't notice if I met that man face-to-face or whatever-to-whatever. I have the luncheon for Helen on Wednesday, and Sam, I'm just sure that if she's not already Mrs. Thurlow Jones, she will be soon. In fact, I may call on them in a day or so, maybe take some fruit and magazines to Thurlow. And LuAnne and I have so much to do to get ready for Christy's bridesmaids' luncheon, and LuAnne's about half mad at me, and Lillian is still keeping too much to herself, and, well, the days will be full, but not so full that I won't miss you. I'll be glad when you get back home."

"Me, too," Sam said. "The best thing about going away is coming home again."

I saw them off fairly early that Sunday morning with the trunk of Sam's car packed with suitcases, fishing gear, and empty coolers they hoped to bring home filled with ice and whatever they happened to catch. Sam and Mr. Pickens had had their usual back-and-forth about which car they should take. Since Mr. Pickens's car was much too small for three people on a long trip, he had wanted to rent a large SUV. Sam, on the other hand, had pushed for his roomy four-door sedan, which was equipped with all the comforts of home and then some. With Mr. Pickens at the wheel of Sam's car, it was obvious who had drawn the short straw.

I walked out to the curb and leaned over to speak to Mr. Pickens and Lloyd, both of them grinning with anticipation.

"You'll be careful, won't you?" I said, noting the winter pallor of them both. "Watch out for each other and don't stay out in the sun too long."

"Don't worry about us," Mr. Pickens said as if nothing would dare to bother him. "We're gonna bring home more fish than you can eat."

Lloyd leaned forward from the back seat. "I'll be helping with the driving, Miss Julia. Now that I have my license, we're taking turns so nobody gets too tired."

That announcement only gave me one more thing to worry about. "How long will it take you?" I asked.

"Oh, eight or nine hours, depending," Mr. Pickens said. "We'll stop for lunch and probably a few more times as well. But we'll be there by dark. Check in on Hazel Marie now and then, if you will."

"Oh, yes, of course I will," I said as Sam came up behind me with a bag of snacks. He gave me a kiss, then got inside as Mr. Pickens put the car in gear. "Bye!" I called, stepping back. "Be careful!"

As Sam's car disappeared around the corner onto South Oak, I turned and went inside, locking the door behind me. The house had a quiet and empty feel to it as I thought of how infrequently

I was ever in it by myself. Lillian would not be coming in for she would be preparing dinner for Mr. Dobbs that evening, although she rarely worked on Sundays anyway. So the day stretched out before me with little to do but go to church, which I did, only to come back to the same emptiness.

After a small lunch, I wandered through the house, mentally listing what needed to be reupholstered and what could last another year or so. Tiring of that, I finally succumbed to the silence of the house and took a nap.

When I woke, I found that Sam had texted me when they'd stopped in Montgomery for lunch. I quickly responded to him so that he'd know I was all right. By that time, though, I realized that my nap had turned into a full-blown slumber for it was nearly five o'clock. I'd slept the day away, yet time still hung heavy on my hands. At least, I reminded myself, *Masterpiece* would be on at nine, so there was something to look forward to.

As I ate a few leftovers for supper, my mind wandered to Lillian and how she was getting along with her guest. Mr. Dobbs would be at her table by then, as would Latisha, whose opinion I was sure would have great influence with Lillian. How Mr. Dobbs would react to her was another matter, as indeed would her reaction to him. I spent a great deal of time that evening imagining what was going on in Lillian's house and becoming more and more eager for her and Latisha to come over for the night. Yet *Masterpiece* came and went as did the late news with no word from Lillian.

Was Mr. Dobbs lingering on and on? Wasn't a guest supposed to know when his time was up? The next morning was ordinarily a school day and children needed to be in bed at a reasonable time. Did that mean that he was intentionally waiting for Latisha to go to bed to afford him time alone with Lillian?

Finally at a quarter to twelve, the telephone rang.

"Miss Julia?" Lillian said. "I hope I didn't wake you up, but Latisha an' me, we won't be comin' over tonight. She's already sound asleep an' I still got dishes to wash, an' we'll just wait till tomorrow if that's all right with you."

"Why, Lillian," I said, "do you mean that Mr. Dobbs has just left?"

"Yes'm, he surely did just leave. That man stayed an' stayed with his feet up on my ottoman an' talked and talked. Wouldn't even hear of me puttin' up the leftovers much less clearin' off the table, an' you know how I hate to leave a dirty kitchen."

"Yes, I do know. But what did the two of you talk about for so long?"

"Well, he did most of it an' I just listened an' dozed off an' on. I tell you, that man can talk an' he can eat pork chops. I think I got a good grade on them, but I don't know if I can put up with listenin' to him ramble on for hours an' hours. Anyway, I got to clean up the kitchen—that fryin' pan'll take an hour to get clean, an' gettin' Latisha up to come over there is more'n I can handle right now. So we'll spend the week with you like we planned, jus' startin' tomorrow instead of tonight."

"That's fine, Lillian. I'm glad you called. I was beginning to worry about you."

"Yes'm. Me, too."

Well, that left most of the night stretching out before me with no hope of sleeping through it. Wrapped in a heavy robe, I ended up on the sofa in the library trying to find something on television to pass the time. I learned more about antiaging creams than I ever wanted to know, as well as about the benefits of various kitchen gadgets, most of which could be obtained for a mere nineteen dollars and ninety-nine cents, with free shipping, and an extra gadget thrown in for an additional fee.

Hearing the rumble of thunder and seeing the television screen go blank for a second from a lightning flash, I went around the room making sure that the blinds were down and the curtains drawn. Not that either would keep out a lightning bolt, but doing something made me feel better.

I walked into the kitchen, meaning to check the back door again just as rain began drumming down in torrents. As my hand felt for the light switch, another flash of lightning lit up the entire room, as well as the backyard and, for all I knew, half the town. It had been so bright that the following darkness seemed deeper and blacker—except for the blurred image impressed on my mind's eye. Somebody or some*thing* had flown past the side window so fast that all I saw was a pale streak in the downpour of rain.

For a second, I couldn't move. I stood there in the dark, afraid to turn on the light and afraid to leave the room. Had I just seen the naked man? If so, what was he doing running around my house in a rainstorm? He was certainly out of luck if he'd been looking for a jonquil or a tulip in my yard.

Calming my racing heart, I took a deep breath and reassured myself of the unlikelihood of being the focus of any prowling man, naked or not. The pale flash zipping past the window could've been anything, a newspaper whipped by the wind and rain, a sheet ripped from a clothesline—if anybody hung clothes outside anymore. Very sensibly, I told myself that nobody in his right mind would be sneaking around during a thunderstorm and that the image in my head bore no resemblance to any man I'd ever seen.

Of course I immediately realized that anybody who wandered around with no clothes on wasn't in his right mind to begin with and that my knowledge of what naked men looked like was too limited to be used as a comparison.

Finally talking myself out of a paralysis of fear, I left the kitchen and returned to the library, where the television was back in its normal advertising mode. Knowing that I wouldn't be able to sleep if I went to bed, I wrapped up in an afghan on the sofa and prepared to stay up all night.

It occurred to me that perhaps I should call the sheriff and report what I'd seen, but then I decided that I wasn't sure of exactly what I'd seen. That being the case, I also decided that it would be best not to tell either Sam or Lillian. There was no use distressing them over something that was probably nothing more than a trick of the eye. Besides, I reminded myself, if it had been the naked man, he was long gone by now and, I devoutly hoped, thoroughly drenched for his efforts.

Chapter 15

After the disarrangement of my sleep patterns, Monday was all but a lost day for me. I felt logy and sleep deprived but resisted succumbing to another nap in the middle of the day. Lillian didn't help matters by being so closemouthed. She wasn't at all forthcoming about her dinner date with Mr. Dobbs even though I tried to draw her out with a few polite questions to indicate my interest.

All she would say was "Latisha, she need to learn herself some manners." And from that I assumed that Latisha had been less than welcoming. But since she was at the Boys and Girls Club for the day, I could get no information from her, either.

A phone call from LuAnne gave me something else to think about. "Julia," she said in a businesslike way when I answered, "we need to decide what kind of invitations we want. For the bridesmaids' luncheon, you know. I can run by the Print Shop on my lunch hour and see what they have." She paused, then went on. "Unless you want to pick them out."

"Oh, no, please go ahead if you don't mind doing it. You aren't thinking of having them printed, are you?"

"No, not really. I'm thinking of the fill-in-the-blank kind with something sweet and flowery on the outside."

"Just not too cutesy, LuAnne. But," I went on hurriedly, "you have very good taste, and whatever you choose will be fine with me. But don't you want me to help address them?"

"No, as soon as Sue gets the addresses to us, I can do them right here at my desk. We're going through a slow phase now, so I may be able to get them done before people start dying again. Oh, and one other thing," she said. "What do you think of us giving each bridesmaid a tiny charm of the initial of her first name? They all have charm bracelets, don't they? And if they don't, they can wear them on a chain around the neck. What do you think?"

"Well," I said, choosing my words carefully, "I'm not sure that anything from us is really called for. Christy will give out her gifts and that may be all that's needed."

"What's *needed* isn't the point, Julia," LuAnne said as if exerting great patience. "It's what we want to do to make the occasion memorable. And if you're worrying about the cost, don't, because I'm not thinking gold charms. I think sterling silver will be fine and quite fashionable these days. They're even showing gold and silver bracelets on the same arm in *Marie Claire* and *Elle*, so it's a very *in* look."

"That sounds fine," I said, deciding that tiny silver charms weren't worth upsetting LuAnne any more than she already was. "Thank you for thinking of it and for doing the invitations."

"Well," LuAnne said, "what I'm planning to do is to put each charm in a tiny box and wrap them with paper and ribbons. Then with name tags on them, they can serve as place cards. What do you think?"

"I think that would be lovely. I always like doing things with you, LuAnne. You have such good ideas, and you're so easy to work with."

Now, I thought, as we said our goodbyes and hung up, maybe she'll be over her huffiness at me by Wednesday when I entertain for Helen. I declare, it seemed that whichever way I turned, somebody had to be handled with kid gloves, and I'd about had enough of it.

So I marched myself out to the kitchen and said, "Lillian, you know, don't you, that you can talk to me about anything in the world and it won't go any further. People make themselves sick sometimes by keeping everything inside, so if you need to discuss something, I just wish you'd do it." I took in a deep breath, then went on. "I can't get anything done for worrying about you, not knowing what you're thinking or planning or anything else. I mean, I know you may not know what you're going to do yet, but I'd really like to know which way you're leaning."

"Well, Miss Julia," Lillian said, fitting a lid on a saucepan, "fact is, I don't know which way I'm leanin' my own self. One day I'm thinkin' that Mr. Dobbs might be the onliest chance I'll ever get to be somebody, an' the next day I wake up thinkin' I can't put up with a man that smells like he do an' that talks my ears off an' that 'spects to be waited on hand and foot. So I don't know what to talk to you about 'cause I don't know what I'm thinkin' I might do."

"That's completely understandable," I said, pleased that she'd opened up enough to at least state the problem. "You're in a quandary, that's for sure. But that's all the more reason to discuss it with someone who has your best interests at heart."

"I don't know about no quand'ry, but it sure is a predicament. Looks like whichever way I decide, I'm likely to regret it. On the other hand," she said, hanging a washrag on the faucet, "I don't know why I'm lettin' it bother me so much, 'cause far as I know, he's still lookin' around."

That was a pleasant surprise because it seemed to me that any man who was in the market for a wife would need to look no further than Lillian.

"An' see, Miss Julia," Lillian went on, "I don't know if I jus' want to come out on top an' beat all the others he's lookin' at or what. 'Cause I already pretty much know I'd prob'bly wring his neck if I had to put up with him for the rest of my life."

"Oh, Lillian," I said and started laughing. "That could be said for most of the men I've ever known."

She laughed, too. "Yes'm, an' that's why I've been single for so long." She adjusted the flame under the saucepan, then turned to me. "You want some coffee?"

As we sat sipping coffee, mostly in companionable silence, I suddenly had what I thought was a good idea. "Lillian, what do you think of asking Janelle to help with our luncheon?"

"Law, Miss Julia, I don't need no help with lunch for six people. What would she do?"

"Well, she could keep you company for one thing," I said with a laugh. "No, really, I was thinking that she might need the money, so anything you can think of for her to do—set the table or whatever—would be helpful. Just nothing too strenuous."

"Yes'm, we could do that, an' I know Miss Pearl would 'preciate it, an' Janelle would, too."

"Then let's do it, and you know what else?" I sat back, having realized there was much more that could be done. "It was just last year that Hazel Marie bought twin beds for the little girls, which means that she has two cribs to get rid of. I wonder what she did with them because Janelle could certainly use one of them, unless, of course, she's having twins, too." Worriedly, I asked, "She's not, is she?"

"No'm, thank the Lord, she's not. An' that's a good idea, Miss Julia, 'cause far as I know, Janelle don't have anything for that baby."

"Then I'll call Hazel Marie and ask her because I know she'll want to help. She thinks the world of Janelle. I just hope those cribs are folded up and stored in the garage, and not already given away."

Unhappily, that was not the case, for Hazel Marie had donated both cribs to the Goodwill resale store several months before.

"But let me call them," Hazel Marie said. "They may still have both of them, or at least one. Oh, I wish I'd known they'd be needed, but I guess you can't predict who'll be expecting and who won't. But I'm sorry to hear about Janelle. She's such a deserving girl, isn't she? Now," she went on, "I'll buy back a crib if they still have one, and while I'm out, I'll go by Toby's and get a mattress. I threw away both mattresses. I mean, who would want a previously used mattress for a new baby?"

"That's very good of you, Hazel Marie," I said. "I know Janelle will be thrilled. And her mother, too."

"Oh, I'll enjoy doing it. And, come to think of it, while I'm at Goodwill, I'll look for a good car seat for the baby. Or I'll just go ahead and get a new one, except those things aren't used long enough to get hardly any wear on them. And isn't it funny?" Hazel Marie said. "Here I've been thinking that I needed something worthwhile to do and now I have it."

I was happy for her, but the fact that I didn't have anything to do was brought into clear focus. I'd told Sam that I would be so busy during the week he was gone that I would hardly miss him. Yet, all of a sudden, other people were taking up the slack and leaving me with nothing to do. There was LuAnne writing, stamping, and mailing the invitations, then purchasing silver charms and wrapping them, as well as taking care of the floral arrangements for Christy's luncheon. And there was Lillian taking care of everything needed for the luncheon for Helen, and there was Hazel Marie essentially taking over the outfitting of Janelle's nursery. All any of it had required of me was a statement of need and others had jumped in to fill it, leaving me with a lot of empty time on my hands.

So what was left for me to do? I needed something to occupy my mind and my time while Sam was gone and while I was still seeing a pale streak dash past a window every time I closed my eyes.

I went to the phone and tapped in a number before I could come up with a dozen reasons for not doing what I proceeded to commit myself to doing.

"Helen?" I said, surprised that she, and not a maid or a social secretary, had answered. "I'm a little at loose ends this week, and I'm wondering if Thurlow would like a visitor this afternoon—to pass the time if nothing else. It must get awfully boring to lie in bed all day, and I thought—"

"Oh, Julia," Helen said, "that is so thoughtful of you. In fact, you're a lifesaver. Thurlow's nurse, Mike, broke a tooth this morning, so he's at the dentist's office, and I have several errands downtown that really should not be put off. And Thurlow gets increasingly bored and restless as the day goes by, so I don't like to leave him alone. Of course Hannah and Ellie will be in the house, but they're not very good company for him. I think Thurlow intimidates them, so it would be helpful if you could sit with him for about an hour and, you know, give him something new and different to think about."

To tell the truth, I'd really thought that Helen would be cool to the idea of a visit. She certainly had not previously encouraged friends to drop by, nor had she welcomed flowers or gifts to the bedridden. Deep down, I had thought that I'd get credit for offering, but I wouldn't have to follow through. Now, though, I was caught, so I proceeded to prepare myself for an hour in the company of the most uncouth and ill-humored man in Abbotsville.

Chapter 16

On my way to visit Thurlow, I stopped by the Fresh Market and purchased a small fruit basket, then on impulse a pound cake as well. Normally, I would've asked Lillian to bake something since anything she turned out was always welcome. But with her mind so taken up with the pros and cons of Mr. Dobbs's courtship, I decided not to burden her with a request for a last-minute pound cake.

A maid, who I assumed was Ellie, appeared when I rang the bell at the freshly painted door of Thurlow's refurbished house. She seemed to have been expecting me. She took my offerings and indicated the stairs to Thurlow's room. Helen had prepared her well for my visit.

When I entered the bedroom at the top of the stairs, the first things I noticed were the aroma of air freshener—meadows and rain, I thought—and the flickering of scented candles placed around the room. Below the aromatic layers, however, I detected the old, musty odor of dead skin accumulating inside Thurlow's several casts. He was lying in bed—one of the new automated king-size beds, I noted, which was slightly elevated. A sheet covered most of his body, but my first glimpse of his face told me that he was not a well man. The cot on the far side of the room confirmed that he needed someone with him both day and night. I wondered who that someone was—Mike or Helen?

Steeling myself, I breezed in and took a seat in the chair beside the bed. "Well, Thurlow," I said, "how are you? I've been keeping up with you through Helen, and she assures me that you are well on the way to complete recovery."

"Then she's lying," he snarled, which was no more than I expected from someone who looked as ghastly as he did. He'd lost weight and gained wrinkles, neither of which improved either his facial expression or his irritable personality.

"Oh, I doubt that," I said, reminding myself that sick people need to be encouraged. "I'm sure Helen is taking good care of you. Why, your house is in the best condition it's ever been, and you have all the help you need to get you back on your feet. What in the world would you have done without her?"

"I'd've had a lot more money," he said, his dark eyes glaring at me. "She's putting me in the poorhouse as fast as she can."

I didn't believe him for a minute. For one thing, if Thurlow was headed for the poorhouse, Helen certainly would not have been accompanying him.

"Oh, come now, Thurlow. What's money for if not to use it when you need it?" Then, thinking that I should get him off the subject of Helen's expenditures, I went on. "I understand that congratulations are in order, so I extend them to you. You know, of course, that the bride is never congratulated, but the groom is and should be. You've won an outstanding person, and I'm sure you'll both be very happy."

As I think I've said before, good manners require overlooking the truth in many cases.

Thurlow stirred under the sheet, shifting his heavy, cast-laden legs. "Yeah, and lightning'll probably strike me, too. I'll tell you, Madame Springer or Murdoch or whoever you are, don't get old or sick. You'll be at the mercy of every grasping, money-grubbing hag that comes along."

Well, that did it for me. I was willing to overlook Thurlow's complaints—they were nothing new from him. I was also willing to discount his referring to Helen as grasping and money-grubbing—sick people deserve some leniency—but calling her a hag? No, that was too much.

"Then why are you marrying her?" I snapped, forgetting my intent to comfort the sick. "Don't you understand that Helen is the only thing between you and a nursing home? Take your pick, Thurlow. It's either Helen or an impersonal, half-staffed, *inordinately* expensive nursing facility, which should teach you not to climb three stories to fix a television antenna. If you hadn't been too stingy to pay the bill, you would've called somebody who knew what he was doing. But that's beside the point now. What you ought to do is be thankful that Helen is willing to take care of you. She's worth every cent you have and then some."

Thurlow turned his head to the side and moaned. "You don't understand. She's got me over a barrel."

"It was you who got yourself over that barrel, and I'm telling you that you should be thankful for Helen. You need to be doing some positive thinking, Thurlow. Remember that book? I hope you read it because you are the most persistently negative person I've ever known."

"I am not," he said, pulling the sheet up to his chin.

"Well, you certainly are. Why don't you try showing a little gratitude? I can assure you that there's not another woman in town who would put up with you, I don't care how much money you have."

"You certainly know how to treat a sick man," Thurlow mumbled. "I don't know why you bothered to come."

"I came to cheer you up and to remind you how fortunate you are to have Helen. You should be counting your blessings, not wallowing in self-pity and calling her ugly names."

I do believe that he gnashed his teeth, although I've never been sure of exactly what *teeth gnashing* sounds like. All I knew at the moment was a sense of impending disaster if the proposed marriage came to fruition. What was Helen getting herself into? Was she aware of the depth of resentment that Thurlow seemed to have toward her? Would we wake up one morning to learn that some horrific crime had been committed?

Goodness knows, I am not one to interfere in the personal lives of my friends, and surely Helen would be safe as long as Thurlow was confined to bed. But what about later on when he had regained the use of his limbs and could take out after her?

The sound of voices floated up from the hall downstairs and soon I heard the tap of heels on the stairs. Thurlow turned his face toward the door to the hall where Helen appeared.

"There you are," he said. Then more pityingly, "Why were you gone so long?"

To my amazement, Thurlow's eyes filled with tears as Helen walked over to the bed and took his hand. "It's all right," she said. "I'm home now. Did you and Julia have a good visit? Hannah is cutting up some of Julia's oranges for you—won't that be good?" Helen straightened the sheet over Thurlow's body and plumped up the pillow on which his cast-laden arm rested.

"Julia," she said, turning to me, "thank you so much for visiting with Thurlow. I'm sure you've done him a world of good."

Taking my cue, I rose from my chair and, with effort, pretended that I was not shaken by Thurlow's tears and Helen's tenderness toward him. "I'm happy to help anytime," I said, edging toward the door. "Thurlow, take care now and get well soon. Helen, if you need me again, just let me know."

Before stepping into the hall, I turned to look back and saw Helen sitting on the side of the bed as Thurlow took her hand with his one good one. "Don't go off again," he said.

"Only when I have to," she said, leaning over to brush back his hair. "But I'll always come back."

I walked slowly down the stairs, mumbled my thanks to Ellie, and left the house as that last scene replayed in my mind. After regaining my car, which was parked in Thurlow's front drive, I could do nothing but sit and ponder what I'd seen. I had gone from postulating a horrific crime scene some dark and stormy night to witnessing a most improbably tender and touching moment between two antagonists.

Where was the truth of the matter? Well, of course it wasn't up to me to decide, but what I had seen and felt between those two before I left made me sit up and take notice. I had to recalibrate my thinking about the entire situation. Surely Thurlow's misogynistic rampages posed no threat to Helen, nor did her need for financial security mean that she was a cold-eyed gold digger who was after all she could get.

I felt somehow better about that marriage by the time I got home, although I still didn't know when or if it would take place.

I should've just asked him, I thought, or her, but I hadn't wanted to appear to be prying. Helen had said that the ceremony would be private, so for all I knew it had already taken place. Maybe she'll announce it to us at the luncheon, because surely she'll want her closest friends to know of her changed status. But who knew with Helen?

I parked in the drive at home and hurried inside, that last bedroom scene playing again in my mind.

"Lillian," I said, plopping my pocketbook on the table and myself on a chair, "it is certainly the truth that no one knows what goes on behind closed doors, but I've just had a glimpse."

Chapter 17

"So," I said, concluding a recap to Lillian of my visit to Thurlow, "I don't know what to think. Are both of them just out for what they can get? And resentful of the one they have to get it from? Or do they really care for each other?"

"Maybe a little of both," Lillian said.

"Maybe so, but I'll tell you, they are the most mismatched couple I've ever known. There's not a more fastidious and particular woman in town than Helen Stroud, and Thurlow? Well, we all know him and I'd be surprised if he bathes more than once a week. If that often. No," I said, shaking my head, "I just don't see it. Helen needs security and Thurlow needs hands-on care. It's a business deal, and if it works, then good for them. But mark my words, Lillian, when Thurlow gets out of his casts and is on his feet again, the fur is going to fly."

"You thinkin' he might get rid of Miss Helen when he gets well? Divorce her or something?"

"I wouldn't put it past him, and I don't doubt that Helen has thought of that and planned for it—which is probably why she's willing to marry him. A wife is harder to get rid of than an employee."

"I don't know, Miss Julia," Lillian said, shaking her head. "Lots of strange people fall in love an' change their ways. Mr. Thurlow, he pro'bly never knowed a fine lady like Miss Helen, up close, I mean. But he got to know how lucky he is to have her. He might want to hold on to her whether he stays sick or gets well."

"Well, I hope you're right, but I keep thinking how I'd feel if I were in Helen's place." I shuddered at the thought. "And had to crawl in bed with the likes of Thurlow Jones. And not only that. Think how you'd feel if you had to live day in and day out with somebody who turns your stomach."

"Miss Julia," she said, heaving a great sigh, "that's about all I think about these days."

I stared at her for a second, realizing that she'd just revealed her state of mind about being in the same situation as Helen—being offered financial security in return for services. I wondered if she recognized the parallel, but I could not bring myself to point it out.

Instead I said, "That reminds me of something you said this morning that's been on my mind ever since. You said that Mr. Dobbs might be the only chance you'll ever have to be somebody, but, Lillian, don't you know that you're already somebody? And a very important somebody, too."

"Hah!" she said with a laugh. "You jus' don't know, Miss Julia. Nobody's somebody like Mr. Dobbs is. An' Miz Chester P. Dobbs will be right up there with him at least on the outside. But what goes on on the inside could be a whole lot diff'rent, an' I'm not sure I wanta fetch an' carry an' tote an' pick up after any man, much less one that thinks he's so high-and-mighty he can have his pick of all the ladies in town."

"Well, be careful, Lillian. If he really thinks he can pick and choose any woman he wants, he'll want the very one who doesn't want him. You know how playing hard to get works, don't you?"

"Yes'm, an' I been thinkin' about that. So I'm real sweet an' nice to him. But to tell the truth, I think pretty soon I'm gonna have to mess up a batch of pork chops."

"Oh?" I said, a feeling of dread running down my back. "You think he might be getting ready to propose?"

"Well, he sure did make hisself at home in my house Sunday night. An' I don't wanta brag, but he tole me Miss Pearl's the last one on his courtin' list an' for me to jus' hold on a little longer. He as good as tole me he's about ready to make his choice."

"Then," I said, "invite him to supper again and let me fry the pork chops. That'll get you off his list in a hurry."

We both had a good laugh over that, but it didn't last long for me. A cloud of worry engulfed me the rest of the day, and not even Latisha's joining us for supper lifted it. I kept thinking that any day could be Lillian's last one in my employ.

But the day wasn't through with me because Sam called just as I was about to crawl into bed that night. My first thought when I heard his voice was that something awful had happened.

"No, we're fine," Sam said. "I'm just calling in case you happen to see Pickens in Abbotsville. He's on his way back."

"*Tonight?* Is Hazel Marie all right? What's wrong?"

"No, nothing like that. Everybody's fine. He had a call from one of the insurance companies that has him on retainer. They need him for something, so he rented a car and is on his way to Atlanta. He'll fly to St. Louis from there, but Lloyd and I decided to stay the week, so we'll be back Sunday just as we'd planned."

I had to think about that for a few seconds, acknowledging that as much as Mr. Pickens irritated me on occasion, his presence with Sam and Lloyd also gave me great comfort. How would they fare on a boat in high seas, wrestling with a large fish or being alone in a strange town without him?

I cleared my throat and said, "Will he come back down later in the week?"

"Probably not. He said it'll take two or three days to do whatever it is, so he'll fly home afterward. We'll plan another trip later on."

"I kind of wish," I said wistfully, "that you and Lloyd had come back with him."

"And disappoint Lloyd? No, honey," Sam said with a laugh, "we just got here last night, and we're still aiming to bring home a load of fish. But don't worry about us. We'll be going out with the same captain we always have, so we're in good hands."

I didn't like it, but what could I do? I would've liked it even less if Sam and Lloyd were driving through the night, and even more so if they were flying. Of course that's exactly what Mr. Pickens was doing, so I added his safety to my list of things to worry about and pray for.

The next morning after breakfast and after sending a response to a text from Sam, I called Hazel Marie to make sure that she still had a husband.

"Oh, yes," she said, "he'll be in St. Louis in an hour or so. This is what happens when you're on retainer, but he'll be home in a day or so. I'm almost used to it by now, but I'm sorry he's missing the week with Sam and Lloyd. He'd really been looking forward to it."

So, since the sudden change of plans hadn't distressed her, I turned my attention to my own business. Lillian and I started by removing a leaf from the dining room table. With only six for lunch, I wanted to make our gathering as warm and intimate as I could. I figured that, with Thurlow's inclination to find fault with everything and everybody, Helen would get gracious little warmth or intimacy in her marriage.

When the doorbell rang at midmorning, I was surprised to open the door to Sue Hargrove. She was not one to drop by without calling, but I was delighted to see her.

"Sue! Come in, come in. It's so good to see you. Let me ask Lillian to put on a fresh pot of coffee."

"No, please don't do that. I can't stay, and I apologize for not calling, but I wanted to give you a list of the bridesmaids and their addresses. And since I had to be in town anyway, I . . ." Tears filled her eyes, and before I knew it, they were running down her face.

"Oh, Sue, what is it? What's wrong? Here," I said, taking her arm and leading her to the sofa, "sit down."

"I'm sorry," Sue said as she pulled out a handful of Kleenex from her purse. "So sorry. Just overlook me. I'll be all right." She blew her nose. "Just give me a minute."

"Take all the time you want, Sue, but something has to be wrong. This isn't like you. What's happened to upset you so badly?"

"Ohh," she said, leaning her head back against the sofa as if to give up. "Julia, I am so undone, so worried, so angry. It's just one thing after another and Christy won't stand up for herself, and I can see it all falling apart."

"What? You mean the wedding?"

"I *wish*!" she said vehemently. Then waving her hand, she said, "No, no, I don't mean that, not really, but Travis is on his last rotation at Duke, which apparently doesn't give him enough to do. He's in and out of here all the time, suggesting and directing everything, and Christy falls in with whatever he says. Every time I turn around, here he is again." Sue suddenly sat straight up and demanded, "And of course Christy drops everything else when he's around, and now her feelings are hurt because I put Travis out in the guesthouse. But, Julia, I may be behind the times, but I'll have no cohabitating in my house before they're married."

"Why, of course not," I said, shocked that the engaged couple expected anything different, although what this last-minute, hurry-up wedding had put in my mind earlier came rushing back. Janelle may not have been the only gravid young woman in town.

"It was well after Christy was born," Sue said, wiping her eyes, "before I felt comfortable sleeping with Bob in my parents' home, yet now it's as if there're no rules, no consideration, and no shame. And on top of that," she went on, "do you know what Travis wants to do now?"

"No," I said, shaking my head.

"He wants to have a *destination* wedding! In *New Orleans*! Can you believe that?"

"Oh, my word, no. It's a little late for that, isn't it?"

"It's a little late for everything," Sue said. "Including a wedding anywhere!" Then she started crying in earnest. "Oh, Julia, I'm sorry, I don't mean that. Not really, I don't think. But he's just taken over Christy's *life*! Got her to drop out of medical school because two doctors in one family are too much, *he says*. And *he says* that she'd probably give up her practice when children come, anyway, so it'd be better for her to drop out now. And she *agreed*! And," she went on bitterly, "of course it was never even suggested that he give up *his* plans. And now he wants to have a destination wedding because he wants to show Christy around New Orleans! And because *he* wants it, we're expected to put up the entire wedding party in a hotel, plus pay their travel expenses, and who knows what else. And we've already ordered invitations saying that the wedding will be here in our church. What're we supposed to do with them? Throw them out and order more? And how many of our friends would fly to New Orleans for a thirty-minute wedding?"

"Not many," I murmured, because it was a rhetorical question. Besides, I wouldn't fly to New Orleans for anything.

"And," Sue continued, "I don't know why I've brought you the bridesmaids' addresses. If he has his way, we won't have a luncheon at all because the girls will be flying in all that day. And Christy thinks he's just so sweet and thoughtful!"

"My word," I said. "Why doesn't he just take her to New Orleans for their honeymoon? That's the groom's responsibility, anyway."

"They're not having a honeymoon, remember? He has to be on the surgical floor July first and his new wife has to find a job. It's just starting off so wrong, and Christy's head is so far off in the clouds that she doesn't see . . . Well, anyway," Sue said, a sob in her throat, "what can we do?"

"You can put your foot down and say no," I said. "Or Bob can. That's what I would do. It's up to the bride's family to do the wedding—the planning, the arranging, the size—everything, including paying for it. So," I added, carefully, "Christy should remind him that Amy Vanderbilt says it's your prerogative to make those decisions."

"But that's the thing!" Sue exclaimed. "That's what upsets me so much. She just agrees with everything he comes up with. She never questions anything or disagrees with him, or even thinks that she might want something different. She doesn't realize that it's setting a pattern for the rest of their lives together, and Julia, I am just sick with worry about it."

"Yes," I murmured, "I would be, too." In fact, I already was.

Sue said, "I just don't know what to do."

"Well," I went on, "one thing you could do is just give them a check for what you'd planned to spend on the wedding and tell them to do it their way. That might wake them up."

"Yes, that's what Bob said," Sue said, nodding her head. "He's just furious about the whole thing, but mostly because Christy dropped out of med school without talking to us. But, Julia," she went on, "I don't know what to tell you or anybody else. We may have a wedding and we may not, and I've already reserved the church and the pastor and the country club for the rehearsal party and the reception, and you're preparing the bridesmaids' luncheon, and I don't know what to tell any of you. You and LuAnne may want to throw up your hands and forget it."

"No, don't worry about us. We can either do it or not, however it works out for you and Bob. And for Christy, of course."

After listening to a few more words of encouragement from me, Sue prepared to leave. She thanked me for listening and for offering a shoulder to cry on, but what are friends for?

As I closed the door behind her, I recalled giving Sam my flippant list of the different kinds of marriages and realized that Christy's upcoming one certainly fit one of them. But, I reminded myself, Christy was not of the generation that made their beds, then felt obligated to lie in them for the rest of their lives. She was a bright young woman, and sooner or later her head would come down out of the clouds and she'd realize, to her sorrow, what she'd married. I knew she would, for I'd done the same thing my first time around. By that time, though, if children were involved, it wouldn't be so easy to start over.

Chapter 18

Sue, I realized, had left me in a quandary. Should I warn LuAnne that Christy's wedding might be in New Orleans and not in the Presbyterian church across the street? Should I cancel the luncheon reservation in the private room at the inn up on the mountain? And what about the invitations and silver charms that LuAnne was buying, to say nothing of the dozens of peonies that she was placing on order?

On the other hand, it wasn't up to me to pass the word along. For all I knew, the wedding would proceed as planned regardless of the groom's high-flown aspirations. Sue had left me with no idea of what she and Bob would do, but surely she was aware that decisions had to be made and that friends and family had to be forewarned one way or the other.

So I said nothing to LuAnne, knowing that if I had it would've been all over town by nightfall. But I did speak to Lillian about it.

"I don't know how Christy can be so thoughtless," I said, fuming as I recalled the hurt in Sue's voice. "It's not like her to think a wedding can be turned on its head in a matter of weeks, and that fiancé of hers certainly isn't starting off on the right foot with his in-laws. I've never heard of any groom planning a wedding, knowing full well that somebody else has to pay for it."

"He prob'bly don't know no better," Lillian said, " 'cause somebody else always pay his bills."

"Yes, you're probably right about him. But Christy has always been so levelheaded. It's just amazing to me to think that she's letting him call the shots. I mean, it's *her* wedding. He's just the groom. All he's supposed to do is show up. Anyway," I went on, "I just went online and—"

"By yourself? I thought you always got Lloyd to do that for you."

"Well, how can I? He's off fishing somewhere. Besides, I can do a little of it, but, Lillian, I declare I don't know where we got the idea that computers helped anything. They don't cut down on paper or time or anything else. For instance, have you ever tried to find someone's phone number? They don't put out phone books anymore, you know, so if you try to look up a number online, it'll cost you ninety-five cents to do it, and I'm not about to pay for a phone number. Except," I mused, "I think it'll also tell you if the person has ever been arrested, which could be worth ninety-five cents to know.

"Anyway," I said again, "I found Christy's bridal registries and now I don't know what to do about a wedding gift. I know Sue has been adding to her silverware at Christmas and birthdays for years, so I thought of filling out her place settings if she doesn't have twelve. Or maybe some serving pieces if she needs them. She has Strasburg by Gorham, you know, which is an old and beautiful pattern, but it's not listed anywhere."

"Maybe Miss Sue already give her all she needs," Lillian said, "but she might need some trays for when she has a tea or something."

"Right. That was my next thought. Everybody needs a few silver trays except, apparently, Christy. She has a note on her registries that she doesn't want silver. Can you believe that? Doesn't that girl know that if she doesn't get silver for her wedding, she'll probably never get it?"

"Miss Julia," Lillian said, as if stating a firm fact. "Young girls today more likely to serve on paper plates with plastic cups and plastic forks than they are to use fine silver."

"Well, maybe so, but I doubt they'd appreciate a dozen paper plates as a wedding gift. I'll just have to come up with something else."

"Well, I know what they all want."

"Then tell me."

"Money. Just write a check, and they'll be happy. Fact is, they'll have a special bowl or basket settin' out on a presents table at the reception to put your checks in. I heard that the Givens girl had a Fund Our Honeymoon jar at her reception."

"That is just so tacky," I said, sniffing just a little as I refrained from saying what I thought of the Givens family. "I mean, there's nothing wrong with close family members giving checks since it can be done privately. But the idea of taking up an offering at the wedding itself is beyond the pale. It's like putting out a jar by a cash register to collect change for the SPCA.

"Actually," I continued, "it's tacky to wait till the wedding itself to get your gift to the bride. It should be sent or taken to the mother of the bride's house days, even weeks, before the wedding so it can be displayed for viewing. Friends, in fact, will come by just to see who's given what. And, of course, giving them in a timely manner helps the bride get all her thank-you notes written. I've always felt sorry for the brides whose friends and relatives bring gifts to the wedding. How in the world is she to enjoy her honeymoon with a dozen or more thank-you notes hanging over her head?"

"Well," Lillian said, "I guess I never looked at it that way. If I ever get married, I'll be happy to get anything any way anybody wants to give it."

"Oh, Lillian," I said—almost moaned—at the thought of her getting married.

"Well," I went on, shaking off the thought, "how is Janelle doing? Is she coming Wednesday to help with the luncheon?"

"Yes'm, she happy to come, an' she happy that Miss Hazel Marie brought her a crib an' a mattress an' some sheets to fit it. Miss Pearl, she cried when she seen it."

"I'm so glad to hear that. I should've called Hazel Marie to see if she'd found one of the cribs she'd given away."

"No'm, she didn't. Two somebodys already bought both of 'em, so Miss Pearl said it was a brand-new crib, an' she's real happy to have it for her grandbaby."

"That sounds just like Hazel Marie. When she decides to do something, she doesn't fiddle around. Anyway," I went on, "I still have to decide what to give Christy. She's listed several things that I've never heard of—kitchen appliances, they sound like. And I don't think Christy even cooks. I remember Sue saying that even as a little girl Christy would rather make rounds with Bob than help her make cookies.

"Anyway," I said again, "I just don't think I want to give a KitchenAid mixer that's so garishly colored it looks like it's been run through the paint shop of a Moroccan tile company. It'd do nothing but sit on a kitchen counter and never get used anyhow."

On that note, I started out of the kitchen, then stopped as I recalled why I'd gone there in the first place.

"Did I tell you that Christy's young man has come up with the idea of going to New Orleans to get married?"

Lillian turned to stare at me. "You mean he wants to run off an' not have a big wedding?"

"Oh, no. Apparently he wants a big wedding, but he wants everybody to go with them and have it in New Orleans. A destination wedding, they call it. Everybody flies or drives in the day before, and the whole wedding party stays in the same hotel, and the bridesmaids all get dressed and made up that morning. I just read an article on how it's done—the bride, or rather the bride's mother probably, arranges to have several beauticians come for the morning to do hair and makeup. Then they all pile into limousines to go to a strange church for the ceremony, then to a reception somewhere—all arranged and paid for by the bride's parents."

"My goodness," Lillian said, "how many people would go that far for a wedding?"

"Not many, I would think, including me. Yet a wedding should be a time when people who've watched you grow up come out to celebrate. Who would want to be married by a strange preacher in a strange place with only the wedding party in attendance? I told Sue that she and Bob should put their foot down. I mean *feet* down, both of them, especially since it wasn't even Christy's idea. Besides, invitations to the Presbyterian church have already been ordered."

"I 'spect, wherever it gets done, Miss Sue be glad when this one's over."

"Unhappily, that is the truth," I said. "And it is a shame. The Hargroves have only the one child and her wedding should be a happy time for them all. It's that groom who's causing all the trouble. Or no, maybe it's Christy who's letting him call the shots, which—if it keeps on—she will regret to her dying day. I learned that lesson the hard way."

"I know you did, Miss Julia," Lillian said, "I used to wonder if you'd ever get a backbone, but you fin'lly did."

"It took me long enough," I said with a laugh. "Actually, I didn't know that you'd noticed."

"Oh, yes, ma'am, an' I took a lesson from it, too. A wife can't ever turn everything over to her husband—he'll start thinkin' he can't ever be wrong an' get so big-headed can't nobody stand him, includin' the woman he married." Lillian stopped, stood stock-still for a second, then said, "Don't pay me no mind, Miss Julia. I don't need to be talkin' like that. But a good man like Mr. Sam is hard to find. I wouldn't mind havin' one of them, if he'd have me."

"Oh, Lillian," I said, feeling an urge to hug her but restraining myself, "any man would be fortunate to have you, but I hope my experience has pointed out that just having a husband, no matter how well off, isn't the be-all and end-all."

"Uh-huh," she said and leaned over to reach for a frying pan. "I guess I'll have to think about that 'cause sometimes it look like it is."

Which, I thought to myself, wasn't all that reassuring, but at least she was opening up and expressing her feelings a little more.

Chapter 19

That afternoon, after an early lunch, I took myself downtown to the Flower Basket just to get out of the house. I could've, of course, simply called and placed an order for a centerpiece and, in addition, had it delivered to my door. But I wanted something simple for the table, something that looked freshly picked from the yard and hand done by the hostess, rather than a professionally structured arrangement. For that, I wanted to select the flowers myself and watch them being put together.

My plan was to give the arrangement to Helen when the luncheon was over—a pleasant custom that acknowledges the guest of honor without going overboard with a gift.

As I walked back along the sidewalk to the car, I gingerly held the box in which the arrangement had been carefully packed. As I came abreast of the Main Street Drugstore, I glanced to the side and almost dropped the whole thing. Sitting at a window table of the drugstore, a coffee cup and a piece of pie in front of her, was LuAnne Conover with only a large pane of glass between her and me. But she wasn't looking my way. She had eyes only for the gentleman seated across from her.

Adjusting my grip on the box, I hurried past and on to the car, feeling a suspicious dampness on the bottom of the box. It was a wonder I hadn't tipped the arrangement onto the sidewalk, but who wouldn't have been surprised? Even shocked? LuAnne was supposed to be working. What was she doing having dessert with a perfect stranger at one o'clock in the afternoon, which probably meant that they'd had lunch together?

Who was he? I hadn't gotten a good look, just enough to know that I didn't know him. But I'd seen enough of LuAnne and had recognized the look on her face. I'd seen it before. I'd seen the smiling, teasing, eager-to-please expression that always came over her face in the presence of an unattached male. And this had occurred often enough when she herself had still been attached.

She couldn't help herself. LuAnne liked to please, and if that required a little flirting, well, she liked that, too. She didn't mean anything by it, but a stranger might not know that. And now that she no longer had Leonard as a backup—a husband in the background was often enough to deter an interested party—who knew what kind of trouble she could get into?

I slid into the car and sat for a few minutes to calm my nerves. I declare, I don't know why I was so concerned that LuAnne might've seen me. It should've been the other way around, yet there she'd been in full view of anyone on the sidewalk or in the drugstore.

Well, but why not? She was free to have lunch with anyone she wanted, which, unhappily, could've been anyone at all. I mean, she had as good as told me straight out that she was open to whoever was available.

I turned the ignition and guided the car out onto the street, telling myself that what LuAnne did was not my business. I would, however, have liked to have known who her table companion had been. Where had she met him? How long had she known him? Was he married? And if not, why not? There were very few unmarried men in our age group, so where had she found one if, indeed, she had?

Maybe, I told myself, she'd tell us about him tomorrow at the luncheon. LuAnne wasn't known for keeping much to herself, and I'd been the one to whom she'd told everything Leonard had done or said during the long, tedious process of their divorcing each other. I knew more about Leonard Conover's personal habits than I'd ever known about Wesley Lloyd Springer's and I'd been married to him.

So it stood to reason that sooner or later LuAnne would tell me about the man in the window.

"If it's not one thing," I told Lillian as I put the box on the kitchen counter, "it's two more. This is the centerpiece for the table if it's survived almost being dropped. I declare, Lillian, I can't keep up with what all is going on in this town."

"What all's goin' on now?" she asked.

"I wish I knew. I saw LuAnne Conover having lunch with a strange man, and how did she meet him, I'd like to know." I took off my jacket and began to remove the newspapers packed around the arrangement. Lifting it out, I said, "I wish I didn't worry about her so much, or rather, I wish she wouldn't give me reasons to worry about her. But sometimes I wonder if she has good sense." Setting the arrangement on the counter, I studied it from all angles. "Oh, of course I don't mean that. It's just that sometimes she gets a little close to the edge. What do you think of this, Lillian? It looks quite nice, don't you think?"

"Yes'm, an' it's just the right size for the table. But what's Miss LuAnne done to make you worry about her?"

"She was having lunch with a strange man in the Main Street Drugstore, sitting in the front window where everybody passing by could see her. Them, I mean."

"Well, what's wrong with that?"

"Why, Lillian, people talk. You know that, but it was as if she didn't care who saw her."

"Maybe she didn't. I mean, she's not married, and if he's not married, maybe neither one cares who sees them."

"Yes, but we don't know what or who he is, do we? No, don't roll your eyes. I just mean that sometimes LuAnne doesn't think ahead. It's as if she doesn't take into account how something might look, and yes, I know it's none of my business, so I'm through complaining about it."

Lillian laughed. "Well, good, 'cause you can't do nothin' about it anyway. Oh, an' by the way, Miss Hazel Marie called. She say she'll talk to you later 'cause she has to be out this afternoon, but she tell me that James thinks he saw that nekkid man run through their yard last night."

"What!" I stopped on my way to the dining room with the arrangement and stared at her. James lived in the garage apartment at the Pickenses' house and cooked for the family. He was also delegated by Mr. Pickens to look after the family during the many times that Mr. Pickens had to be away, as he apparently had been since leaving Alabama. "Oh, my goodness," I said, my heart rate accelerating, "was he sure?"

"No'm, she said he said it was jus' after dark an' he didn't have the yard lights on yet, an' by the time he got 'em on, whoever or whatever it was was gone. James said it was more like a flash of white streakin' 'cross the yard."

"Oh, my goodness," I said again, thinking of the streak of white I'd seen in the rain torrents a few nights ago. "I guess that means Mr. Pickens is still in St. Louis. Maybe we should ask Hazel Marie and the twins to come stay with us."

"I don't know, Miss Julia. We'd have to have James, too, an' I don't think I can stand having him underfoot."

"Oh, Lillian," I said, laughing, "you're right. James can be a problem. But I'll talk to Hazel Marie, and if she's afraid to be in the house alone, I'll see if she wants to come over. Nobody's going to bother James—he's safe enough over the garage."

"That's right," Lillian said, turning with a surprised look on her face. " 'Cause when you think about it, that nekkid man only showin' hisself to ladies by theirselves. Think about Miss Vinnie Worsham, an' Miss Hazel Marie, an' maybe that lady that lives over by the golf course."

I did think about it, and wondered whether I ought to add my name to the list of women who'd been alone at a sighting.

I said nothing to Lillian about it, mainly because she left to pick up Latisha at the Boys and Girls Club, where she had been spending her days during spring break. As much as Latisha seemed to enjoy her time there, I thought she was about tired of it. She was fussy and argumentative with Lillian, not at all her usual enjoyable self. So we had a quiet supper that Latisha only picked at before Lillian took her upstairs for an early bedtime.

I spoke with Hazel Marie on the phone during that time and got a firsthand account of what James had seen the night before.

"He's just sure," Hazel Marie said, "that it was a man without a stitch on that he saw running across the backyard. Although he does say that he hadn't yet turned on the yard lights, so I guess it could've been something else, although I don't know what. Surely if it had been a white dog or something, James would've recognized that even in the dark."

"But you didn't see anything?"

"No, but I wasn't looking. I had the twins in the bathtub, so anything could've happened in the backyard and I wouldn't have noticed."

"Well, if you're uneasy, you know you're welcome here. Lloyd's room is made up and ready for you. Either the girls can sleep with you or we can make them pallets on the floor. No man, naked or not, would dare come to a house with all of us in it."

Hazel Marie laughed. "You're right about that, but we'll be okay. I think James is planning to sit up late tonight just in case, and J.D. should be back sometime tomorrow. But, Miss Julia, I saw something else today that I want to ask you about. I had to go to the Fresh Market and passed by the Good Shepherd Funeral Home about five o'clock, and I saw LuAnne leaving with a gentleman I didn't know. Is she seeing someone now?"

"Well," I said, blowing out my breath. Then I proceeded to tell her what I'd seen in the window of the Main Street Drugstore. "I don't know who he is, Hazel Marie. I mean, I'm assuming we're talking about the same man. He may just be someone who works at the funeral home, but it had to be the same one. I can't imagine that she's all of a sudden seeing two different men. There're not that many available in this town. What did he look like?"

"I only got a quick glimpse as I passed, but I wasn't going very fast. My impression was that he was slim, not very tall but taller than LuAnne, and nicely dressed in a jacket and tie. He might've had a mustache, which I always notice because my husband has one. So distinguished, you know."

I left that alone, but my instinctive reaction was one of distrust of any man with facial hair, counting them either too lazy to keep themselves shorn or too taken up with trimming and combing and caring for fancy beards and mustaches. But that was my personal opinion, which I generally kept to myself.

"Well," I said to Hazel Marie, "I don't know what's going on, but maybe LuAnne will tell us tomorrow at the luncheon. If he works at the funeral home, they could've just happened to leave work at the same time."

"Um, I don't know," Hazel Marie said. "My feeling was that it was more than that. Maybe it was the way he held her elbow as they walked down the steps to the sidewalk. But again, I could've gotten the wrong impression."

"Then let's not mention it to her and just wait and see if she'll bring it up. If she's serious about him, she won't be able to keep it to herself. We'll hear all about it."

"I can't wait," Hazel Marie said, and giggled.

Chapter 20

I didn't have to wait for the luncheon. LuAnne called that very evening while Lillian was still upstairs getting Latisha ready for bed.

"Julia," LuAnne said, just breathless enough to let me know that she had something important to tell me. "You won't believe this, but I'm here to tell you that prayers are really and truly answered. So if there's something you really want, keep praying about it and don't give up hope."

"I already know that, LuAnne. Not many of Pastor Ledbetter's sermons made an impression on me, but the one he gave on prayer did. Prayers are always answered, he said, but not always the way we want. They're answered with 'yes,' and you get what you want, or by 'no,' and you don't, or by 'later,' when you have to wait a while. So you're not telling me anything I don't already know except what it was that you asked for."

"Well-l," she said, drawing out the word to lengthen the suspense, "I've been praying that the Lord would send me somebody, and He has. At least, I think He has. You know, Julia, that there's a dearth of available and *acceptable* men in this town, yet I am convinced that I am meant to be married. So it came to me that the Lord would not have made me this way without a way to remedy it.

So I decided to be on the lookout because nobody is going to walk up with a sign on him saying 'This is the one,' are they?"

"Uh, no."

"So, when Mr. Cochrane told me how nice I looked a few weeks ago, I sat up and took notice. I mean, big things start from little ones, don't they? And when he kept coming in to pay on his bill, I made sure to be helpful and to make a little conversation."

"Wait a minute," I said. "You mean that this 'answer' to your prayer owes money to the funeral home? Why? Is he paying for a funeral?"

"Well, yes, but so is every man who comes into the funeral home, unless it's a nephew or somebody too young to notice. They come in either to pay for a funeral for somebody else or to prepay on their own. Or, of course, some come in for a visitation, but they're usually in and out fairly quickly, and they sort of have their minds on mortality rates or something like that. Anyway, I made a special effort to explain the receipt when Eddie, I mean, Mr. Cochrane, came in to make a payment, and he was so appreciative. One morning he brought me a cappuccino, which was so nice, and one thing led to another, and we've had lunch together. He's very nice, Julia, and very particular about the way he eats and the way he dresses—something that, as you know, I'm not accustomed to with Leonard. But he's lonely. He and his wife had just moved here when she got sick, so he doesn't know a lot of people."

"So he's a widower?"

"Yes, of course. It's the way we met. I just told you—he's been coming in on a regular basis to pay on his bill. Or her bill, if you want to be specific."

"Are you saying," I said, aghast, "that he didn't have the money to bury his wife, so he put her on a *layaway* plan?"

"*Julia!* No! It's not like that at all. Layaways are for Christmas, not for . . . *forever.* And he has money. It's just that it's all invested, so he has to use his current income to pay his bills. He explained it all to me. I didn't even have to ask. If he took a lump sum out of his investments, he'd have to pay taxes on it. So he made arrangements with the funeral home to pay a little at a time."

"So he avoids taxes but pays interest on a loan," I said, because I knew how things worked.

"Well," LuAnne said defensively, "all I know is that Leonard wouldn't have known enough to make any arrangements whatsoever. I don't know how in the world I would've gotten buried with him in charge. The funeral home would've probably had to take him to small claims court."

"Not so small," I murmured, recalling the cost of Miss Mattie Freeman's last rites, of which I had been in charge. "Anyway, that's all behind you now. And I'm glad you've met someone nice. I look forward to meeting him."

"Well, not anytime soon, Julia. I'm keeping him to myself until I get to know him better. I'm not rushing into anything."

"That," I said, "is the most reassuring thing you've said. Good for you, LuAnne."

"Well, I do have to tell you, *he* is eager," LuAnne said with a tinkling little laugh. "He's lonely, you know."

Which, I thought but didn't say, was not at all reassuring.

"Miss Julia," Lillian said as she came into the library, "you want a fried apple pie? I still got some in the freezer I can heat up."

"That does sound good," I said, rising and following her out to the kitchen. "Is Latisha down for the night?"

"Law, I hope so. That chile's about to get too big for her britches.

She's gettin' sassy with all that back talk to anything I say. I don't know what I'm gonna do with her."

I pulled out a chair at the table as she turned on the oven, then went to the freezer.

"Well, Lillian, she's getting to that age, you know, when hormones start acting up. She's growing up right in front of our eyes, and that's not easy for her, much less for us."

"Yes'm, I know, but I think it's more'n that. 'Cause ev'ry time she get on her high horse, she have something to say about Mr. Dobbs."

I perked up at that. "Like what?"

"Oh, I don't know. Just some little thing like I'm too busy to do something she wants or I don't listen to her 'cause my mind's somewhere else or I go off ridin' around when she need me—that kinda thing. I guess I've spoiled her, but she's gettin' kinda hard to live with."

"She's worried about you and worried that her life will change if you marry Mr. Dobbs. And of course it will. She's used to having you to herself without having to share you with a houseful of other people." Carefully, but truthfully, I said, "It could get worse, you know."

"I do know," Lillian said, and sighed. She put the pies on a cookie sheet, which went into the oven, then sat beside me at the table. "We went by the house today to get her some clean clothes an' there was Mr. Dobbs settin' out in his big ole Cadillac, jus' waitin' on us. So I had to ask him in, an' he set down in my livin' room while Latisha got her things together, but she didn't like it. She went to th'owin' things around and stompin' up an' down, an' flingin' herself ev'ry whichaway." Lillian sighed again at the memory. "Then Mr. Dobbs, he chimed in to tell me what he said he was tellin' all the ladies on his list."

"My goodness," I said, surprised at the man's self-confidence, "he's certainly not shy about having a list of ladies. Wonder what he'd do if one of those ladies took her name off of it?"

"I don't think he ever thought of that. Fact of the matter, the only reason he was waitin' on me to come home was to tell me not to buy no white hats."

"What? What do white hats have to do with anything?"

"Maybe one of the ladies on his list is gettin' ahead of herself an' 'spectin' to be invited to join the White Hat Ladies' Club. Least that's what I thought at first, but then he tell me that he saved all his first wife's white hats an' don't nobody need to buy no more. Whoever he chooses can have all of hers."

"What's the White Hat Ladies' Club? I've never heard of it."

"The first Miz Dobbs—Miss Edna her name was—started it up years ago, an' only the finest ladies get asked to join. They have to be married or a widow lady, have a good name around town, do lots of good works, an' be about fifty years ole. They don't want no young, flighty members. An' the members get to wear big white hats to church an' when they have a meetin'. Ev'rybody wants to be a White Hat lady, but lots go to their graves still wantin' an' not ever gettin'."

"My word, Lillian, that's the most exclusive club I've ever heard of. Was Mr. Dobbs hinting that the second Mrs. Dobbs would automatically become a member?"

"No'm, he wadn't hintin'. That's what he was sayin', looked like to me." Lillian leaned her chin on her hand and smiled. "I sure would like to see that closet full of big white hats. Seemed like the first Miz Dobbs wore a new one jus' about ev'ry Sunday that rolled around."

"Well," I said, getting up to check on the fried apple pies, which were smelling up the kitchen and apparently forgotten by Lillian, "well, just remember that Sunday is only one day of the week. You'd still have six days every week to get through without a big white hat, but with Mr. Dobbs."

"I know it, but I can't help thinkin' how people would set up and take notice if I was to walk in church an' see all them big white hats scattered around, an' have one on myself. An' maybe a white dress an' white shoes, an' walk down the aisle an' take my place on the front pew."

"Why, Lillian," I said as I placed the pies on dessert plates, "I didn't know you were so socially inclined. But of course there is a certain dignity involved with being part of an exclusive group."

"Well," she said, accepting the plate I handed to her, "it's not just bein' dignified. It's livin' like ladies supposed to live, 'cause the young girls look up to the ones who wear the white hats an' want to be like them. We, I mean *they*, give scholarships to the girls who stay outta trouble an' go to school, which is one reason I get so tore up over Janelle. I don't doubt for a minute that she woulda got the White Hat Ladies' Club's scholarship this year, an' it woulda been in the newspaper, an' ev'rybody woulda been so proud of her."

"It is a shame, I know," I said, placing a fork beside her plate. "But we can still do something for Janelle and, who knows? She may still make us all proud of her, even though she may never be able to wear a white hat."

Chapter 21

I barely slept a wink that night, rolling and turning and going to the bathroom a half dozen times. As soon as I worried awhile about LuAnne and her eagerness for someone to marry, I'd flip over and start worrying about Lillian and her heretofore unknown longing for a white hat—with Janelle and her lost opportunities thrown in for good measure.

And then, toward daylight, Helen Stroud insinuated herself into my tortured thoughts. I can't say that I actually worried about her, because Helen was strong enough to get herself out of trouble if that's where she found herself. I just had a feeling that she and Thurlow had tied the knot within the past few days and were now settling down into a loveless relationship that nonetheless met their immediate needs. And thinking of them led my thoughts into philosophical directions.

Sam enjoyed reading history, not historical novels but real history, and more than once he'd told me of the marital customs of earlier eras. People married then primarily to have a family, to unite properties, or for dynastic reasons. They married for children, for the state, and for a warm body in bed. Some grew to care for each other, but the idea of meeting and marrying your one true love and living happily ever after was not part of the equation. He'd told me of one young heiress who'd been betrothed at four, married when she was seven to an elderly duke who soon died, and married again at fourteen, all for dynastic reasons. Bless her heart.

Hollywood, I suddenly realized, had been the source of the culture's current emphasis on romantic love that was written in the stars and that would prove to be endless. And this in spite of the shuffling of marital partners by the actors and actresses who played the parts.

Maybe I was judging too quickly—maybe Chester P. Dobbs was going about it in a sensible way. He had in mind the criteria he wanted in a second wife, and I vaguely wondered if his first one had met them. Maybe he learned from her what he didn't want rather than what he did. But I just could not get over his supreme self-confidence that any woman he chose would be thrilled to step into her shoes. Or wear her hats, as the case might be.

Dressing slowly and carefully that morning, I wondered why a bed looked so much more inviting when you had to get out of it than when you had to get into it. I put on a silk blouse, a nice skirt, and sensible but fashionable shoes. Make no mistake about it—shoes can make or break an outfit. Then I went downstairs to await our luncheon guests.

Turning aside on my way to the kitchen, I surveyed the dining room table. The centerpiece was still perkily fresh, and the six linen placemats were carefully set with silverware, service plates, and crystal stemware. Pleased with our preparations, I pushed through the door into the kitchen.

"Good morning," I said as cheerfully as I could manage, given my lack of sleep. Then, noticing the young woman who was carefully adding sugar and lemon juice to a pitcher of tea but not wanting to draw attention to the reason she was out of school and available to help, i.e., the protuberance in her midsection, I said, "Oh, Janelle, thank you so much for helping us out today. We're so happy to have you."

She smiled and looked down at the floor, mumbling a response as Lillian asked what I wanted for breakfast. "I got some fresh cinnamon rolls," she said.

I started to pull out a chair at the table, but Lillian stopped me. "Why don't you go set in the lib'ry while the coffee heats up? I'll bring it to you in a minute."

When Lillian used that particular tone of voice, I was always inclined to do as she said. So I went to the library and waited for her.

She came in with a breakfast tray, set it down on a table, and said, "Janelle, she 'shamed for you to see her 'cause she say when a baby start showin', everybody know what you been doin'."

"Well, that's pretty obvious, given how babies are conceived. But I'm sorry she thinks I'd say anything about her condition or embarrass her in any way. I would never do that." I reached for the coffee cup. "Are you sure she's not having twins?"

"Yes'm, she's sure. But she tell me her boyfriend come back to town an' say he'll help her out if she need him."

"*If she needs him?* I should think she does. Was that a marriage proposal or what?"

"Don't matter what it was," Lillian said. "He don't have a job an' don't want one, so Janelle, she say she have her hands full takin' care of a baby, so she can't take care of him, too. She give him his walkin' papers an' say for him to keep on goin'."

"Well, good for her. I always knew that Janelle was a bright young woman, and that just proves it."

"Yes'm, he cooked his goose good when he run out on her. I don't know why she got mixed up with him in the first place. That boy's been in an' out of trouble since he was twelve years old. But you know, Miss Julia, Janelle'll do all right on her own. She's smart an' a hard worker an' she got a good head on her shoulders. She'll do all right."

"I agree, and I'll let the ladies know that she's available for day jobs that aren't too heavy. Things will look brighter when she has a little money in the bank."

"You can say that again." Lillian turned to leave, then stopped and said, "I just feel so bad, though, 'cause she's ruint her chances to ever be in the White Hat Ladies' Club."

"Well, Lillian, things may've changed by the time she gets close to fifty. Why, things that were only whispered about yesterday are openly celebrated today, so you never know."

"Uh, uh, no, ma'am," Lillian said as she left the room. "Not for them ladies."

When the doorbell rang a few minutes past eleven, I knew it would be LuAnne. She always came early, so I hurried to open the door.

"Hey, Julia," she said, breezing into the hall, "I know I'm a little early, but you're always ready ahead of time. How are you?"

Before I could answer, LuAnne thrust a small, nicely wrapped gift toward me. "Where do you want this? Do you have a gift table?"

"Oh, LuAnne, Helen didn't want any gifts. She was quite firm about not having a shower."

"Well, I'm sorry," she said in a tone that was anything but regretful, "but I just could not ignore a traditional gift-giving occasion. It's nothing much, anyway, just some informals with her new initials."

"That was thoughtful of you. Everybody can use informals if they're not already addicted to email." I placed the gift on the hall console and hoped its presence wouldn't make the others feel bad for coming empty-handed.

LuAnne sat on the sofa, smoothed her skirt, and said, "Isn't that the truth. But, you know, I had the hardest time deciding how to have her initials printed. I finally decided on HSJ for Helen Stroud Jones because I didn't know her maiden name, except everybody knows her as Helen Stroud, anyway. But the printer reminded me that a lot of people put the last initial in the middle, so that would've been HJS with the J a little larger than the other two, and I almost chose that until he told me it cost more—used more ink, I guess." She opened her purse, looked through it, then snapped it closed. "Do you think she's actually going to marry him?"

"It certainly looks like it, but you know Helen. She doesn't explain or defend anything she does. She makes up her mind and does it."

LuAnne shuddered. "I don't know how she could. But then again," she went on, "there's that huge house and all the wealth he has—supposed to have, that is, so that kinda balances things out. And," she said after a pause, "he is a man, and I am more and more convinced that a woman is incomplete without a man. And vice versa, I guess. Two halves make a whole or something like that."

"Oh, LuAnne, you don't mean that. A lot of people get along

just fine by themselves, much better, in fact, than being married to the wrong half. As you should know, just as I do."

The doorbell rang again and I quickly got up to answer it, glad to put an end to that particular conversation.

I opened the door to Emma Sue Ledbetter, our former pastor's wife, and almost gasped. The woman looked tired and haggard, and all I could think of was that she must be working herself to the bone. Emma Sue did more for others than for herself even though she could've used help from somewhere.

Right behind her came Hazel Marie, who greeted me with her sweet smile, after which I accepted a hug and a kiss on the cheek from her.

"Come in, come in," I said, opening wide the door. "It's so good to see you. How's Pastor Ledbetter, Emma Sue?"

"Playing golf, would you believe?" she said indulgently. "But he needs the exercise."

So do you, I thought but didn't say. Looking past them as they came through the door, I saw Mildred Allen, my wealthy, overweight neighbor, coming up the walk.

"Did you walk over?" I asked as she gained the porch.

"I sure did," she said, panting. "I'm trying to walk a little every day, but I may have to call Ida Lee to drive over to get me back home. How are you, Julia?" Ida Lee was Mildred's right-hand woman. Professionally trained in New York, Ida Lee did for Mildred what most women do for themselves but not as well.

"I'm fine. Come in, everybody's here but Helen, and . . ." I stopped as a car pulled to the curb. "Here she is now. Go on in, Mildred. I'll wait for her."

I greeted Helen, who looked remarkably well put together as she always did, as she approached the door.

Lowering her voice, she asked, "Are they all here?"

I smiled and nodded.

She leaned close and whispered, "I'm only doing this for you, you know."

"I know, and I appreciate it." But she was wrong, for I was doing it for her to absorb from friends the first spate of questions that were in the minds of everybody who'd heard of the most improbable marriage since Beauty married the Beast. And come to think of it, Helen and Thurlow seemed to be doing a remake with the ending yet to be determined.

We sat in the living room talking and catching up with one another, as Lillian and Janelle moved silently around the dining room table. Then Lillian nodded at me, so I arose and led the ladies to the table.

Seating Helen at the head of the table in front of the bay window, I noticed how the lilac vine around the porch outside seemed to frame her. She was a lovely woman who deserved more than she was getting, I thought to myself. Knowing that Hazel Marie and Mildred were the least likely to ask unwanted questions, I seated them on either side of Helen.

I sat at the foot of the table nearest to the kitchen with Emma Sue on one side and LuAnne on the other, either of whom would be most likely to ask what everybody wanted to know but didn't have the nerve to ask. They did.

Lillian and Janelle swiftly served the plates that had been prepared in the kitchen, Emma Sue, as she expected to do, returned thanks, and then I lifted my fork as a signal to begin eating.

"Mildred," I said to forestall any personal questions aimed at Helen, "tell us how Penelope is doing. She came to visit last week, and that child has really come out of her shell."

"Oh, Julia, she is the love of my life. We have such a good time together. I don't know how I got along before she came. Well, I do know—not very well."

"You've done wonders with her," I said, "and just since Christmas, too." Penelope was the adopted daughter of Mildred's transgendered child, Tony, now Tonya, who had abandoned the child to her mother's care. Drawing on a bevy of Atlanta lawyers, Mildred had turned the tables on her by suing for custody of Penelope in a state that wasn't as woke as some, and winning.

"And," Helen said to Mildred, "tell us how Horace is doing." Mildred's husband, who was once a sedate fixture on the local society page, was now existing in a locked facility in Southern Pines, some hundred or so miles from Abbotsville.

Mildred sighed, then took another bite of Lillian's excellent quiche. "Who knows?" she said. "He's so polite when I visit that it's obvious he doesn't have a clue as to who I am. He asks how I am, how my children are doing, and if my husband is working. He talks to me as if we've just met and he's trying to put me at ease. Bless his heart, he's always had the loveliest manners." After a sip of tea, she said, "Penelope and I are leaving later today to visit with him for a few days. I'm trying to fortify myself."

"I am so sorry," Helen murmured as tears sprang up in Hazel Marie's eyes.

To lift the pall that had fallen over the table, LuAnne blurted out brightly, "Helen, why don't you tell us when the wedding will be?"

Without turning a hair, Helen said, "It was last week."

"*What!* You've already done it?" LuAnne's fork fell from her hand, clattered onto her plate, then dropped to her lap. Lillian appeared with a towel and another fork. I almost choked.

Mildred, in her laconic way, said, "Congratulations. I hope you'll be very happy."

Hazel Marie laid her hand on Helen's arm and said, "I'm sure you were a beautiful bride. I'm so happy for you."

Stunned and momentarily at a loss, I thought of and then discarded one subject after another to get the conversation onto a more even keel. Helen herself came to the rescue.

Chapter 22

Coolly ignoring LuAnne's shocked response to her announcement, Helen took a sip of tea and moved to another subject. "Has anyone heard any more about the crazy man who's running around town?"

Janelle came in from the kitchen and began removing the empty plates as Lillian entered behind her, placing a serving of chocolate mousse before each guest. Tea glasses were removed and replaced with cups and saucers, as Janelle followed, filling each cup from a silver coffeepot.

"You mean," Mildred asked, "the one who thinks he has something worth showing off?"

Everyone, seemingly relieved to take up a topic about which they were all in agreement, began talking at once.

Hazel Marie said, "He scares me to death."

"That kind won't hurt you," Mildred said as if she were well acquainted with that kind. "But he ought to be horsewhipped."

"Exposing oneself," Helen said, "is a sign of much deeper problems."

Emma Sue nodded in agreement. "The man needs to open his heart to the Lord. Oh, if somebody would only reach out to him."

"Well, Emma Sue," Mildred said, "I wouldn't recommend that you do it. No telling what you'd grab."

Everybody except Emma Sue laughed. She said, "*Some*body should. He's just pitiful."

"He's a freak," LuAnne said, "and that's all there is to it."

Seeing Lillian smile at Janelle as they went back to the kitchen, I looked forward to sitting with them after the guests were gone and hearing their comments. A kitchen debriefing after a social get-together was always the high point of any entertaining I did.

As we removed from the dining room, Helen sidled up to me. "Julia, thank you so much for this. I'm glad to have the wedding out in the open, and I must say that it was easier than I thought it would be."

"You handled it just right," I said. "But a small announcement in the paper might forestall any more questions. Most people will just accept it and move on."

"Yes, except for people like LuAnne." Helen smiled. "I expect she'll call for details. But if you'll forgive me, I must run on. Thurlow gets distressed if I stay away too long."

Helen said her goodbyes to the rest of the guests at the living room door, then turned to thank me again. "You're a good friend, Julia," she said, "and I thank you."

Closing the front door behind her, I wondered if she would prefer to keep on walking rather than return to the dreary routine to which she had now legally committed herself. As I went back to my remaining guests, I sighed, for no one truly knows the heart of another person.

"Well," LuAnne said, breaking into the murmured conversation as I appeared, "she didn't look any different, did she?"

Mildred said, "What in the world do you mean?"

"I mean," LuAnne said firmly, "that you would think that anyone who'd been to bed with Thurlow Jones would show some signs of it. Be changed in some way. I know *I* would."

"What kind of signs?" Hazel Marie asked, leaning forward as if wanting to know what gave away one's personal activities.

"Yeah," Mildred chimed in, "tell us what to look for, LuAnne. Because given the shape Thurlow is in, I'd bet money that nothing has happened. Nothing that you're thinking of, anyway. But we sure want to know what to look for when it does."

"Oh," LuAnne said, slightly addled at being called on to justify herself, "you know what I mean."

Hazel Marie came to her rescue by standing and saying, "If you don't mind, Miss Julia, I'd like to speak to Janelle before she leaves."

I nodded, took a seat, then turned as Hazel Marie stopped and said, "I won't be but a minute, but, Mildred, don't leave. I'll take you home unless you want to walk."

"I never want to walk," Mildred said with a laugh. "Take your time. I'll be ready whenever you are."

Emma Sue decided it was a good time to take her leave as well. "I have a meeting, so I'd better run along. Julia, this was just so nice. Thank you for having me. I miss seeing you all every Sunday, so if any of you would like to get together every week for a prayer session, just let me know."

"We will, Emma Sue," I said as I walked with her to the door. "We could all use more prayer time. Take care of yourself, and thank you for coming."

Returning to the living room, I smiled at the thought that I was left with the two most outspoken women I knew. And they soon proved it.

LuAnne was still stewing about Helen's secret, or rather her previously unannounced, wedding. "I just don't understand it," she said. "It doesn't matter *why* she married him, it's the fact that she actually did that's important. You don't just do it and then keep it a secret. Why do it at all if you're not going to tell anybody?"

"Oh, LuAnne," Mildred said, "you're just mad because you weren't invited. Get over it. Nobody was. Unless"—she turned to look at me—"you were, Julia."

"No, it was as much of a surprise to me as it was to you. I had no idea, although I had a feeling it would be soon."

"Well," LuAnne said, unable to drop the subject, "it just seems to me that any woman who'd spent even one night with Thurlow Jones would be changed in some way. I mean, you have to admit that he's not your normal bridegroom. You'd think that it would take a while to get used to somebody like him."

The cot that I'd seen in Thurlow's bedroom suddenly came to mind, and I wondered if perhaps Helen had long become accustomed to spending her nights with him.

Hazel Marie rejoined us, smiling as she took a chair. "Janelle is just the most remarkable young woman," she said. "I talked with her about doing some office work for J.D., and she's interested." Hazel Marie's handsome husband had a thriving business investigating theft, fraud, and other deceitful activities not, I assure you, in Abbotsville but in the surrounding states. He was, therefore, often away from home.

"That's a wonderful opportunity for her," I said, pleased that Janelle was being considered. "Did she tell you that the boyfriend is back in town?"

"You mean," Hazel Marie asked, "the one who got her in trouble?"

"The very one," I said tightly. "According to Lillian."

"Well," Hazel Marie said, shrugging. "I hope she doesn't get tangled up with him again, whoever he is."

"I don't think she will," I said, recalling Lillian's account of Janelle's reaction, which had come straight from Janelle's mother. "But for her to have a good, steady job will certainly help. Mr. Pickens was good to think of her. And office work is perfect for someone in her condition."

"Huh," LuAnne said, "she should've thought about the consequences before she got herself in that condition."

Mildred's eyes rolled back in her head, then, using the arm of the sofa to heft herself to her feet, she said, "Hazel Marie, if you're ready, I need to get home. Julia, this was lovely. Thank you so much."

LuAnne suddenly let out a little screech. "My present! Helen didn't get my present. Now I'll have to take it to her."

With all of them leaving at once, I tried to reassure LuAnne that she could drop off her gift at Thurlow's house on her way home. "A young maid, Ellie, I think is her name, will come to the door and you can give it to her. You won't even need to go in."

"Well, if I have to go at all," LuAnne said in a martyred tone, "I might as well go on in and visit."

"You just want to see what's going on," Mildred said with a touch of accusation.

"I do not," LuAnne shot back. "I got Helen a *personalized* gift, and I want her to have it."

"I'd just drop it off," I said before the two of them came to blows. "I think Thurlow has physical therapy about this time, anyway. Maybe call later and invite Helen to lunch. She probably needs to get out now and then."

"Well, you know what they say," LuAnne said as she picked up Helen's gift. "When you make your bed, et cetera, et cetera. Besides, my lunch hours are pretty well filled up now, but I'll see. Thanks, Julia, I'll talk to you later." And, leaving me with a whiff of worry about just how her lunch hours were filled, she left.

Chapter 23

"Lillian," I said, pushing through the swinging door into the kitchen. "Everything was perfect. Thank you and Janelle so . . ." I looked around. "She's already gone?"

"Yes'm, she looked tired, so I sent her on. But I give her your check an' she was real happy with it."

"Well, good. Did you hear that Mr. Pickens is thinking of hiring her for some office work? I don't know what that means, exactly. I didn't even know he had an office."

"James say he uses that downstairs bedroom of theirs. Got it full of papers an' boxes an' files an' first one thing and another. He prob'bly needs somebody to keep things straight for him."

"I wouldn't be surprised. Anyway, I hope it works out. It would be ideal for Janelle." I went to the sink for a glass of water. "Did you hear Helen say that she and Thurlow are already married?"

"No'm, but I heard y'all talkin' about it. How long they been married?"

"We didn't get that far. Helen changed the subject so quickly it was hardly noticeable. She brought up the naked man, and everybody started talking about him." I thought about that for a second. "Actually, it was a brilliant move. Thurlow is interesting because he's so outrageous, but a man running around without any clothes on goes way beyond that—as a matter of conversation, that is."

"Well, I jus' hope he don't come around here. That's one thing I could go the rest of my life without seein'."

"You and me both," I said.

With the house quiet and back in order, I went upstairs with a short nap in mind. Instead of falling asleep, though, snatches of the luncheon conversation kept passing through my mind until the truly worrisome one got there and stayed: LuAnne and her busy lunchtimes. Why couldn't she occasionally meet an old and valued friend who truly needed some companionship?

Since it was LuAnne, there was only one answer—she was lunching with a man. What was his name? Eddie something-or-other, unless she'd met someone else since I'd seen them at the Main Street Drugstore. I declare, the woman worried me to death. She seemed bound and determined to find someone to marry, and it didn't seem to much matter how congenial the two of them were, as long as he fit a certain predetermined pattern. And apparently this Eddie did—he dressed well, had good manners, seemed well-to-do—and he was available and, maybe most important, he was interested in her.

That was a powerful draw to someone who'd been discarded by a husband. I should know since it had also happened to me, although, I thought as I turned over again, I hadn't been actively seeking a replacement as LuAnne was. Far from it, in fact, and I smiled to myself as it occurred to me. I hadn't been in the mood to trust anyone as far as I could throw him.

Thank goodness Sam had been a patient man. But what kind

of a man was this Eddie what's-his-name? Well, for one thing he didn't let the grass grow under his feet. He was already looking for a substitute before he had his first wife fully put away. That should tell you something right there.

At least it told me something, and as I thought that, I sat straight up on the bed. Why not engage someone to look into this Eddie—his background, his résumé, his character in general? Wasn't that what private investigators did? LuAnne wouldn't have to know, unless, of course, something so unsavory was uncovered that she'd have to be told.

That, I decided, is exactly what I would do. At least then I'd be able to close my eyes and take a nap without being flooded with images of con men, scam artists, and others who prey on needy women. But, having decided what to do, I proceeded to do it by reaching for the phone.

"Hazel Marie?" I said when she answered. "Do you know when your husband will be home?"

"He's home now, Miss Julia. I can call him to the phone or give you his office number."

"Oh, well, since this is a business call, I'll take his office number."

And to my surprise, although it shouldn't have been since Mr. Pickens was known to be a fast worker, when I dialed the number, a soft female voice said, "Pickens Investigations, Janelle speaking. How may I help you?"

"Janelle? My goodness, you sound so professional. This is Julia Murdoch. I'd like to speak with Mr. Pickens, please."

"Just a moment, please," Janelle said. "I'll put you through to his office."

Smiling, I pictured her handing the receiver to Mr. Pickens, who was probably seated next to her in the one-room office that had once been a first-floor bedroom in the Pickens house.

"Pickens here," he said in his abrupt manner.

"It's Julia Murdoch, Mr. Pickens. I wonder if you're free to take on a small investigative matter for me?"

"I'm always free for you, Miss Julia. What do you have in mind?"

"Something entirely between you and me. It must never go beyond the two of us, and if you can't assure me of that, I will have to go elsewhere."

"Miss Julia," he said, "you have touched on the bedrock of Pickens Investigations. Put your mind at ease. We are the very epitome of secrecy. Why, sometimes not even I know what we're doing. Well, wait, I always know what I'm doing. I just don't always know why I'm doing it."

"That," I said, knowing, as usual, that he was patronizing me with his brand of humor, "is exactly what I want. I want you to do something without knowing why I want it done. I will pay your going rate, whatever it is. This is a business proposition."

"Then I'm your man. Would you like to come in and discuss the details in my office, or just give them to me now?"

Thinking of Janelle possibly overhearing anything said in his office, I said, "Over the phone will be fine, although you must be careful of what you say in front of your office help."

"Have no fear. My office help is required to wear ear muffs at all times."

"Well," I said, caught slightly off-balance since I never knew when to believe him, "if you need me to sign a contract or something, perhaps you could drop by here."

"Right. Now tell me what I can do for you."

I drew in a deep breath and said, "Mr. Pickens, I must again impress upon you the need for absolute secrecy. If it got out that I'm doing this, I could lose friends right and left, and no telling what else."

"I assure you, Miss Julia, no one will know from me. Or," he went on as if just having thought of it, "from anyone in my office. I have a special safe just like the ones used by the CIA where I keep my most secret case files. Feel free to tell me what you need."

There was a pause as I gathered the courage to interfere in a friend's life until Mr. Pickens suddenly lowered his voice and whispered, "This wouldn't be about Sam, would it?"

"Sam? No, why would you think that?"

"Because nine times out of ten when a wife calls, it's about her husband."

"Well, not this wife, and I resent the implication."

"Sorry," he said. "Shoulda known better. So who's the target? I need a name."

"Eddie."

"Eddie who?"

"Well, I'm not sure. I mean, I've heard his last name, but it just won't come to me right now. But whatever it is, he goes to lunch with LuAnne Conover, so whoever you see her with, that's him. I want to know who he is, where he came from, and what he's doing courting her while he still owes for his wife."

"He's behind on divorce payments?"

"I don't know what their marital status was. I only know that he's left with making monthly payments on a funeral that he probably wants to pay off with a lump sum, if he could find a lump sum. So let me tell you, Mr. Pickens, and this, too, must not go any further, but LuAnne has a way of implying that she is more well off than she actually is. In other words, she makes herself a perfect target for an unscrupulous man on the make."

"My goodness," Mr. Pickens said in his serious but questionable way. "I'd better be on my toes with this one. Don't worry, Miss Julia, I'll have a report for you in a few days. Then," he went on, "you can decide if you want me to take him out or what."

Never knowing when he meant what he said, I simply told him to do his job and nothing else. For the time being.

Chapter 24

Having put my problem into capable hands, I lay back down with a feeling of luxury that I still had time for a nap. I'd barely turned over when the phone rang.

"Julia?" the caller asked when I answered. "It's Sue. I hope I'm not interrupting anything."

"Not at all," I assured her. "I've been thinking of you. How are you?"

"Better. At least I think I am. I'm calling to let you know that the bridesmaids' luncheon is back on track and so is the wedding. It'll be in our church on the third Saturday in June, as planned, and Christy and I are addressing invitations now."

"I am happy to hear that," I said. "I'm sure it's a great relief for you."

"You just don't know," Sue said, blowing out her breath. "I feel as if we've been to you-know-where and back. But Christy finally realized what an imposition a destination wedding would be on the guests. We went through our list of more than two hundred people, most of whom live right here in Abbotsville, and I told her to estimate how many would fly or drive to New Orleans."

"That was a smart thing to do," I said. "How many did she come up with?"

Sue laughed. "About fifteen that we were sure of. When she thought about being married in an empty church, she began to change her tune."

"Well," I said, smiling, "it's a settled fact that there're not many jet-setters in this town. But I'm happy that it's worked out."

"Me, too, but I'm not sure just how well it's worked out. I'm trying not to worry about it, but apparently Travis isn't all that happy, but . . ." Sue said, then stopped. "I'm sorry. I shouldn't be talking so much. It's just that he is so typical of surgeon's syndrome . . ."

"Surgeon's what?"

"Syndrome. You know, docs with the attitude that they're the top of the heap, plus being aggressive, demanding, and never wrong about anything. That may be fine in an operating room, but not in a living room. Or a bedroom, either." Then, as if to counteract the bitterness with which she'd spoken, Sue said, "Well, of course, they're not all that way. Most, in fact, aren't. It's just that there're enough of them to keep the stereotype alive, and it looks as if Travis is one." She paused briefly, then with another touch of bitterness said, "He's apparently used to having all of his ideas approved and implemented. Forthwith."

"Oh, my," I said, thinking briefly of Wesley Lloyd Springer, my deceased first husband, who hadn't been a surgeon but had certainly fit the stereotype.

Sue went on. "I'm sorry for being so outspoken. I know I've got to put it all behind me. It's no way to start an in-law relationship. I just worry so about Christy. She's idolized her daddy for so long, yet now she's switched it all to Travis, and Bob is so hurt. But the worst thing is that it's no way to start a marriage—nobody needs to be idolized and obeyed." She managed a small laugh. "Bob certainly doesn't get anything like that from me."

"He gets it from his patients," I said. "And you from your

friends, Sue. But Christy is smart. I'm sure she'll learn soon enough to stand up for herself."

"Well, let us hope. Anyway, I wanted you to know that everything is working out just as we'd planned from the beginning, and Christy and I are looking forward to the bridesmaids' luncheon."

After exchanging a few more niceties, I hung up the phone and got up from the bed. Too late in the day for a nap, anyway. I'd heard Lillian leave to pick up Latisha at the Boys and Girls Club, smelled something delicious in the oven, and decided there were better things to do than lie in bed all afternoon.

After getting up, though, I couldn't think of even one better thing to do. Finally I sat down to compose and send a long text to Sam. I told him in the abbreviated shorthand used by experienced texters (which I was gradually learning) about the luncheon, Helen and Thurlow's marriage, Janelle's new job, Christy's renewed wedding plans, and how much I missed him. That took me about an hour, after which I decided that email was a better option for anything more involved than a grocery list.

Hearing doors opening and closing and footsteps in the kitchen, I glanced at my watch. Lillian was back with Latisha, but it had taken quite a long time to pick her up. They, however, were guests spending the week with me and free to come and go as they pleased. Still, I wondered what the holdup had been.

The silence was heavy when I joined them in the kitchen. Latisha's face was sullen, and Lillian was busily ignoring her.

"How are you, Latisha?" I asked, pretending that all was well. "Did you have a good day at the club?"

"No'm, I'm tired of that place. I'm ready for school to start back up an' things to get back to normal."

Lillian looked up from the roast she'd pulled from the oven and gave her a sharp look. "Well, that's a new one."

Latisha was fiddling with her bookbag on the little table in the corner. She turned to her great-granny and said, "You'd be tired of it, too, if all you had to do was play an' eat an' play an' eat. An' then go home an' set an' wait while somebody talks an' talks an' talks."

Lillian rolled her eyes, lifted the roast onto a platter, and said, "Go wash your hands. We 'bout ready to eat."

As Latisha left for the bathroom, I edged closer to Lillian and whispered, "What's that all about?"

"She just mad 'cause Mr. Dobbs was waitin' for us in his big ole car. I don't know how long he was settin' out there, but he wasn't in no hurry to leave. That man can surely talk, an' it took me the longest to find out why he was settin' out there waitin' on me."

"Oh, Lillian," I said, my heart sinking. "He's smitten with you. Why else is he coming around and waiting for you to show up? He knows you're staying here while that naked man is running around, so the only time he can catch you is when you go by the house with Latisha. So," I said with a shuddering breath, "please tell him he's welcome to visit you here anytime he wants. I wouldn't want to be a disruption in his courtship, and, in fact, I'd be happy to entertain Latisha if you and Mr. Dobbs would like an evening out." It took a lot for me to say that, but I could not stand in Lillian's way if she decided that her life would be better as Mr. Dobbs's wife.

"Law, Miss Julia," Lillian said with a laugh, "you don't wanta be babysittin' Latisha. That girl's gettin' to be a handful."

"We get along fine, Lillian. She's no problem for me. In fact, she's good company, so if you want to go out with Mr. Dobbs, go right ahead. The better the two of you know each other, the better your relationship will be."

Lillian busied herself with a potato masher, adding salt and pepper, butter, and cream to the cooked potatoes. She didn't respond to my offer until the potatoes were mashed to a fare-thee-well.

"I'm not interested in gettin' to know that man any better than I already do," she said, whacking the masher on the rim of the saucepan. "An' if anybody thinks I'm jus' mad 'cause he picked somebody else, they'd be wrong. I already decided that I was gonna turn him down if it was me. I already decided that I don't care how much money or hats he's got, an' I already decided I like settin' in the back of the church where I can get out fast an' easy." Lillian started to say something else but bit her lip, then said, "He thinks he's bein' a real gentleman, comin' to my house in person to ease my disappointment. He say he's sendin' ev'rybody else a notecard. But here he come to my house, smilin' like a possum. Didn't even give me time to turn him down before he tole me it wadn't me. That's what makes me so mad 'cause then he went right on tellin' me what a good woman I am, but that he had a higher callin' an' he had to listen to it. And he knew I would agree with him when he tole me who he'd picked out."

"Well?" I asked, my spirits soaring because Lillian had lost out, although I ached for her disappointment. "Who has he picked? Who in the world is a better choice than you?"

She turned, looked straight at me, and said, "You won't believe it. I can't hardly believe it myself, but he said her name come like a bolt outta the blue to him, an' even though my pork chops is better'n anybody else's, he has to put aside his personal feelin's."

"But who is it, Lillian? Tell me."

"Janelle. He picked Janelle, an' she don't even know it yet."

Chapter 25

"*Janelle!*" I shrieked. "How could he? She wasn't on his list!"

"Tell me about it," Lillian said, her eyes wide with outrage. "*No*body knowed she was in the runnin'. That ole man got his nerve, though, comin' 'round to tell me before he even tell Janelle."

"Wait, wait," I said. "You mean Janelle doesn't know he wants to marry her?"

"Not jus' wants, he say he intends to. She needs a husband an' he needs a wife—one that's young enough to keep up with him. That's what he say come to him outta the blue. Have you ever heard of such a thing?"

"No," I said, flopping down in a chair. "No, I haven't. What does Miss Pearl say? Or is she in the dark as well?"

"Oh, Miss Pearl, she'll say her prayers just got answered, but she don't know it yet, either. See, Miss Julia, he's so sure of his-self, he come to tell me about it before he even find out what Janelle thinks, much less her mama."

"Well," I said, trying to absorb all the ramifications of this stunning announcement. "Well, he may get his comeuppance when he does let her know. Janelle has a good job now, and she may not be as entranced with what he can offer as he thinks she'll be. And," I went on, "how does he think she can take care of him and a baby, too?"

"I don't think he thinks about that. All he say is she's young an' healthy an' could use a husband. He did say she too young to be a good cook, so he want me to show her how I fry pork chops."

"They Lord! The gall of the man is beyond words. Lillian," I said, leaning forward, "do you think she'd actually accept his proposal? I mean, it seems so . . . so inappropriate, don't you think? The age difference for one thing."

"Yes'm, Janelle, she's not eighteen yet an' he's eighty-nine. I'd say that's a pretty big difference."

"Of course," I went on, "she'd be financially set, and that could be very appealing to someone in her situation. And there're all those hats and the dignity of being Mrs. Chester P. Dobbs. He may really be an answer to prayer for her."

"Answer to prayer, my foot," Lillian said, whacking a spoonful of mashed potatoes into a bowl. "That's what he say to me, that he has to put aside his wants an' do his Christian duty, which he says is takin' care of a little lost lamb like Janelle."

"Does he really believe that or is he just a nasty old man hoping to take advantage of a young girl?"

"Miss Julia," Lillian said, picking up a carving knife and attacking the roast she'd just taken out of the oven, "I wisht I knowed. Ev'rybody look up to him, but, I declare, this is jus' more'n I can stomach." She suddenly whirled around, waving that knife, and said, "You know what it makes me think of?"

"No, what?"

"Well, I ought not to say," she said, lowering the knife. "But it puts me in mind of Mr. Thurlow an' Miss Helen. It's like ole, crookedety men buyin' what they want, an' the ladies bein' too far up a creek to help theirselves."

"I don't know why you shouldn't say it because you're absolutely right. The only difference is that Helen is old enough and knowledgeable enough to know what she's getting into and Janelle isn't."

I stopped, considering the two similar situations, which then sparked a memory of something that had happened some years back. "Lillian, do you remember old man Willard Pyles? Remember what happened to him?"

"I sure do, an' he didn't marry outside of his age, either. But that woman was somethin' else, wadn't she? He didn't make it through his weddin' night. She had to call the EMTs about seven-thirty that night."

"Oh, my goodness," I said, patting my chest. "I just remembered he wasn't the only one. Remember what happened to Etta Mae Wiggins?"

"Oh, Law, I sure do, but that wadn't her fault. Ole Mr. Conard's heart jus' couldn't stand the strain. Least that's what they say. He died on his weddin' night, too, didn't he?"

"Yes," I said, nodding, "and I'll tell you what Etta Mae told me. He didn't die from wedding night exertions, as most people think. Etta Mae said she was just crawling into bed when his heart failed him." I thought for a minute, then added, "But she still feels really bad because she said she'd taken her time in the bathroom and drawn it out as long as she could because she dreaded going to bed. She thinks it was the long wait that did him in, an' she should've just jumped into bed and gotten it over with, and he'd have been all right."

"Oh, bless her heart," Lillian said. "She ought not to take the blame for that. Ole Mr. Conard was in bad shape to start with."

"No worse than Mr. Dobbs, though, and younger, I think."

"Maybe so," Lillian said, looking off in the distance as she thought about it, "but if Janelle could count on Mr. Dobbs doin' like Mr. Conard did, then she could jus' marry him an' be done with it. She'd be the Widow Dobbs an', like I said before, be set for life."

"Lillian!" I said, slightly shocked, but thinking that she'd come up with the perfect outcome. Perfect outcomes, however, were few and far between, and Janelle was more likely to be waiting hand and foot on an invalid for years to come.

About that time and just in time, Latisha, with her face still tight and unhappy, pushed through the kitchen door. "What y'all talkin' about? I thought we was about to be eatin' supper."

"We are," Lillian said. "So set on down. We jus' talkin' about how Mr. Dobbs is about to get married."

Latisha went stiff as a poker, her eyes widening as she stared at her great-grandmother. "To *you*?"

"No, ma'am, not to me."

"Then bring on the food," Latisha said, plopping down at her usual place.

The meal was a quiet one, with Lillian and me absorbed in our thoughts and Latisha's appetite considerably restored. After thinking over Lillian's news, I found that I was sickened by Mr. Dobbs's choice of a barely nubile young woman who would be hard-pressed to pass up the opportunity he offered. But mainly I was filled with concern for Lillian. Obviously, I was much relieved that Mr. Dobbs had not chosen her as the winner of the Next Mrs. Dobbs Contest. On the other hand, I couldn't stand the thought that she was hurt by the loss. How much better it would have been if he had chosen her, thereby giving her the opportunity to turn him down. She would forever have been the woman who had refused to trade herself for a front seat in church and a closet full of white hats.

If, I thought, she actually would have turned him down.

Chapter 26

I declare, if I didn't soon get back into my normal sleep routine, I didn't know what I'd do. That night was another one of rolling and turning and pushing off the covers and pulling them back up, dozing and waking up again. And I'd not even gotten a nap during the day, although I'd tried hard enough.

My problem was missing Sam. The bed was too wide with no one beside me, and of course not just anyone would do, only him.

I pictured him and Lloyd, miles to the south, sleeping soundly after a day of reeling in fish. I smiled in the dark, hoping that they'd had a successful day and were enjoying their time together. And that led me to Mr. Pickens, who should've been with them but who was now engaged in uncovering any dark secrets in the life of a certain Eddie.

My eyes sprang open as I thought, And if he does, what do I do then? I shuddered at the thought of going to LuAnne and confessing that I'd hired a private investigator to look into the background of the man who was buying her lunch at the Main Street Drugstore. At least I assumed he was paying for it, but who knew? Who was paying for what was one of the things I hoped to know when Mr. Pickens got through investigating. But there was one thing I already knew: LuAnne would never forgive me, even if, or maybe especially if, Mr. Pickens actually uncovered something nefarious in Eddie's life.

But, I assured myself, if nothing questionable turned up, LuAnne would never have to know of my interference in her affairs. But it's a fact that if she'd ever shown the least amount of sense about men in general, I would never have interfered in the first place. So it wasn't my fault.

And poor little Janelle, I thought—fatherless, husbandless, and moneyless. What a decision she would have to make as soon as Mr. Dobbs announced his choice. And how would he do that? Would he propose on his knee in his old-fashioned, gentlemanly way? Surely he wouldn't attempt to kneel with his bones creaking and muscles trembling. He might never get up.

Perhaps, though, he would speak to her mother first as was properly done in the olden days. But why, I wondered, had he told Lillian before he'd spoken to either mother or daughter? Confidence, I answered, complete and unhampered confidence in his own desirability as a husband to a little, lost lamb. I shuddered at Janelle's vulnerability and thanked the Lord that Mr. Pickens had been moved to give her a job. Maybe, I thought, just maybe that would be enough to make Mr. Dobbs's proposal easy to reject.

And Helen? Was she even now in bed with her new husband? What did she think of in the dark hours of the night when she, too, lay sleepless beside him?

And Christy? Was she starting a life of giving in, holding her tongue, trying to see things from Travis's viewpoint? Like Sue, I realized the danger in such a marriage.

And Etta Mae? Sweet Etta Mae Wiggins, feeling now for the first time in her life the pleasure and comfort of being self-sufficient. Whenever I felt the pangs of having possibly interfered in someone's life, all I had to do was think of Etta Mae. Yes, at the time some might've called my help meddling, but she didn't and neither did I.

Now, though, I had to wonder how a marriage—even if it was the one she'd always wanted—would affect her newfound independence and self-esteem. A lot would depend on just what Deputy Bobby Lee what's-his-name wanted in a wife—an equal partner or an adjunct to himself.

Thank goodness, I thought as I turned over again, these matters weren't up to me to resolve. Deciding to leave them all in the hands of the Lord, where they already were to begin with, it suddenly came to me what to do about Christy's wedding gift.

That's the way the mind works sometimes. If you stop worrying something to death, you'll find the decision made for you. I would give Christy one of the garishly painted kitchen appliances on her registry—maybe the coffeepot, which she might occasionally use. And because weddings meant silver to me, I'd also give her a silver tray. Christy might not appreciate it, but her mother would.

With that decided, I finally fell asleep.

My eyes popped open as a whispered voice close to my ear sent a stab of fear through my brain. "Shhh, Miss Julia. Miss Julia, you awake?"

"What?" I jerked half awake and tried to sit up but was entangled in the bedcovers. "What . . . who is it?"

"It's me," Lillian whispered. "I think you better get up. Somebody's out in the yard."

"Doing what?" I pulled the covers from under myself, kicked at a blanket, and reached out to turn on a lamp.

"Uh-uh," she whispered, pulling down my arm, "don't turn on

no lights. Here," she said, handing me a robe. "What he's doin' is lookin' in the windows, one after the other."

"Why? He can't see anything with all the lights off." Trembling just a little, I shrugged into the robe and felt for my slippers.

"No'm, I left some on downstairs, so bad people would think somebody was up an' watchin' out for burglars and nekkid men."

"Lillian, for goodness' sake, that could've attracted somebody. What time is it, anyway?"

" 'Bout three. You ready?"

"For what? What're we doing?"

"Runnin' him off. Here," she said, thrusting a pole into my hands. "Hold on to this dustmop an' aim for his face so he can't see. I got the broom an' I'm goin' for where he don't wanta be stuck."

"Wait," I said as she headed for the hall. "Let's call the sheriff."

"No'm, not yet. He hears that siren comin' from way down on Main Street an' he'll be gone 'fore they get here. Then we have to worry 'bout him comin' back."

She had a point, so I put my hand on her shoulder and let her lead me downstairs, where I saw that she'd left a lamp on in the living room and in the library and in the downstairs bathroom, as well as the hood light in the kitchen.

We shuffled from room to room, peeking in, one after the other, our eyes sweeping the windows and seeing nothing. Lillian pushed through the kitchen door from the back hall, me right on her heels and almost tripping on my dustmop. The kitchen was quiet and in order, dimly lit from the light over the stove.

"Nobody here," Lillian whispered. "Maybe he's gone."

"I think he has," I said in a normal tone. "Where'd you see him, anyway?"

"Goin' along the side of the house toward the front. Jus' a-slidin' along like he don't want nobody to see him."

"Are you sure, Lillian? Why were you up looking out the window, anyway?"

"I been checkin' the yard ev'ry time I go to the bathroom, which after all that coffee we had was about ev'ry hour."

"Well," I said, breathing easier now that my heart rate had slowed considerably. "Maybe you saw car lights flash against the house. I don't think anybody's sneaking around. Everything looks fine." Maybe I was trying to reassure myself as well as Lillian because I kept recalling what I'd seen on a certain rain-soaked night.

Lillian frowned, then said, "We didn't check the dinin' room."

Since the dining room opened through double doors into the living room, I'd scanned it from there. But now Lillian pushed through the swinging door from the kitchen, and not wanting to be left alone, I followed, looking over her shoulder.

Nothing was amiss until Lillian screamed, raised her broom, and ran full-bore at the bay window. I screamed, too, for plastered against the window, facing inside overlooking the chair where Helen had sat, was an unclothed figure, spread-eagled and full frontal like the Vitruvian Man.

"Hai, karate!" Lillian bellowed and lunged toward him, jabbing the broom at a spot that would've suffered heavy damage if not for the glass panes.

The man—for it was, without doubt, a man—jumped away from the window and fell backward onto the porch, then tumbled to the ground. While he scrambled to get to his feet, Lillian, still yelling in Japanese, ran to the front door, fumbled with the key, got the door open, and flew across the porch like a shot.

"Lillian, wait!" I yelled, but she was off the porch and rounding the house in hot pursuit, jabbing that bristly broom against the man's backside as he gained purchase and took off across the yard. Being no match for him in a footrace, she stopped halfway across the yard, leaned over to catch her breath, and watched as he disappeared in the shadows of the back hedge.

"He's gone," I said as I caught up with her. Panting, I gasped, "My land, Lillian, you really gave him what-for. Are you all right?"

"Better'n I was," she said. "What does that crazy man mean, comin' 'round here showin' hisself like that with a chile in the house! He better not let me catch him."

"Or me, either," I agreed. "But he's gone now, so let's go in. We've got to report this."

So I called in the sighting to the sheriff's office, enduring a number of questions in the doing.

"Could you identify him?" the dispatcher asked.

"No, I'd never seen anybody like him before."

"What did he look like?" she asked. "Any distinguishing marks, scars, tattoos, things like that?"

"I didn't notice any." Like Miss Vinnie, I hadn't been looking at his face.

"Fat or thin?"

"I'm not sure—about medium, maybe."

"Tall or short?"

"I'll measure the window and call you back."

"Can you describe him?"

"Uh, well, white male, I think. I mean I know he was male, but it was dark behind him and there were no lights on in the dining room. He could've been in between—you know, neither one nor the other. I can't say about his hair color, but he might've had a mustache." I stopped and thought a minute. "But I could've confused it with something else. He didn't have on a stitch."

Finally, having decided that she'd gotten everything I had to give, the dispatcher told me that deputies were already patrolling the streets around my house and I should lock up and stop trying to make a citizen's arrest, although she put it a little nicer than that.

Clicking off the phone with trembling fingers, I joined Lillian at the table. "My goodness, I don't know when I've been so shaken. I might never sleep again."

"Yes'm, it was a sight, all right."

We sat a few minutes in companionable silence, then Lillian said, "I jus' wish I coulda got at him with that broom. I'd learn him to show hisself like that."

"You did a good job of scaring him to death." I managed a smile at the memory of Lillian brandishing her broom. "But I didn't know you knew Japanese."

"Me, *neither*!" she said. "But it jus' come tumblin' out, an' a good thing, too, 'cause I think that scared him worse than my broom."

We laughed at that, easing the tension a little more. But we were still too wound up to go back to bed although there were hours left before dawn. We were sitting at the kitchen table, drinking coffee and reliving the night's activities, when Latisha shuffled in, yawned, and said, "What y'all doin' gettin' up so early?"

"We jus' woke up," Lillian said. "Go on back to bed, honey. It's too early for you."

"Okay," Latisha said, yawning again as she turned away and went back upstairs.

Actually, we were waiting for a report from the deputies, a few of whom were searching the yard with flashlights. Lillian kept getting up and peering out the windows, one after the other. I kept trying to firm up the image of the man plastered against my window, especially what he looked like, because who knew? I might meet him again under more mundane circumstances. I certainly wanted to be able to recognize him and wished I'd focused on his face.

"They not gonna find him in the yard," Lillian announced as she sat back down. "That fool's long gone. I guess they have to look, though."

And soon a deputy rang the doorbell to tell us that they'd found no unclothed men in the yard or in the surrounding blocks.

"But," he said, "there'll be an officer parked in the vicinity, and we'll be doing drive-bys for the rest of the night. He won't be back." The deputy conducted himself in a completely professional manner except for the hint of a twitch at the corner of his mouth. I couldn't blame him. It would've been funny to me, too, if it had happened to someone else.

So we locked the doors again and I followed Lillian up the stairs. We went back to bed, slept late, and got up late to find that Latisha had had Frosted Flakes for breakfast. The remnants were still on the table.

Chapter 27

Latisha herself was curled up on the sofa in the library watching cartoons on television. She was dressed and ready for another day at the Boys and Girls Club, although she was in a sour mood at our lateness.

"I don't know why," she told Lillian, "y'all sit up half the night just talkin', then make somebody else late for what they have to do."

"You're not all that late," Lillian said. "Go on an' get in the car."

Latisha flounced out, mumbling about probably missing the midmorning snack. I was surprised that she wasn't in a better mood since Lillian had told her that Mr. Dobbs had chosen to marry someone else. Knowing that, she shouldn't have been in such a prickly mood. Unless, I thought with a start, Lillian had had second thoughts and was still counting herself as a contestant in the marriage sweepstakes.

It was just one more thing to worry me, for the previous night's visitation was weighing heavily on my mind. I couldn't stop thinking about it. Why my house? Did the man know that Sam was gone? Or had it been Lillian or, Lord help us, Latisha in whom he'd been interested? Before this had happened, I had about talked myself out of attributing what I'd seen that rainy night to the naked man. I had decided that what I'd seen had been something stirred up by the storm.

Now, I wasn't so sure. Maybe what I'd seen then had been merely a glimpse of that which Lillian and I had seen in all his glory the past night. Surely there weren't two men in town who had the urge to put their private parts on public display.

But if there was only one, was the past night his first or second call at my house? The worrisome thing about it was this: If it had been his second visit, what had drawn him back again?

Later that morning I slipped into Lloyd's bedroom at my house. He lived, of course, with his mother and Mr. Pickens in Sam's old house, but occasionally he spent the night with us. I kept his room ready for him, although using it now and then as a guest room and often as an office since he had set up his old computer there for me.

Not being technologically adept, I had nonetheless learned that Google was quicker than a visit to the public library when there was something I wanted to know. And that morning I wanted to know all there was to know about people who engaged in public indecency. First of all, I learned that it's almost always men who divest themselves of clothing and put themselves on display. That was a revelation in and of itself, although I realized that I'd never heard of a naked woman wandering around peering into other people's homes.

I sat back in the chair and stared at the screen. Could that be due to the fact that women could satisfy any deviant urges by wearing perfectly acceptable clothing while baring themselves at the same time? I thought of some of the skimpy dresses I'd seen at the country club. From certain angles, one could view naked flesh from top to bottom and from side to side. I thought also of bikinis and tight jeans and short shorts and the images on television of dancers and exercisers and stripteasers—all of whom wore latex if they wore anything at all, and all of which I turned off if Lloyd was in the room.

I tapped a key and read about public nudity, indecent exposure, and exhibitionism. All the terms amounted to about the same thing—the urge to expose one's privates to unsuspecting strangers in order to surprise, shock, or impress the unwilling observer. That, it seemed, was the entire purpose of the exercise. It was the stranger's shock that gratified the urge to divest oneself.

"Well, bless their pitiful, little hearts," I murmured to myself without a trace of sympathy. If showing off was all they wanted, they didn't know what they were missing.

"Lillian," I said as I entered the kitchen, "do you know what somebody like that man last night really wants?"

"No'm, but I got a good idea."

"I thought I did, too, but that's not it at all. What they really want is to surprise and shock somebody they don't even know. Especially somebody they don't know, like a perfect stranger. The shock they cause is what excites them. Have you ever heard of anything as strange as that?"

"No'm, nor seen anything as strange, either." She hung a washrag on the faucet and turned to me. "I jus' wish I'd got ahold of him. He wouldn't be comin' 'round here no more."

"Hey, Julia," LuAnne Conover said when I answered the phone around noon. "Things are slow here this morning, although we have an open-casket viewing this afternoon, which means I'll be getting off late. Anyway, I thought I'd better check in with you while I could." She stopped, then thought I needed more explanation than that. "We take turns manning the desk when viewings make for long days—people really like to look. Anyway, I'm working through the lunch hour so I can get off close to the regular time, which works out fine because I have a late dinner date. But," she said, assuming her professional voice, "that's not why I called. I just heard that Christy may not be getting married at all. Has Sue said anything to you? I need to cancel my peony order if she's backing out. And not mail our luncheon invitations, either."

"Oh, no, LuAnne, the wedding is definitely on, same date and same time. Christy's beau suggested that they have a destination wedding in New Orleans, but Bob and Sue pointed out how inconvenient for guests that would be, so they dropped that idea. Thank goodness, for I wouldn't have gone."

"Well, I don't know," LuAnne said in a musing tone. "I'd love to have an excuse to go to New Orleans, especially if I had a nice friend to see the sights with."

I knew immediately that the "nice friend" would not have been me but rather a certain Eddie. I made a mental note to ask Sue if LuAnne's invitation had read "and guest" on the RSVP card. Knowing Sue's thoughtfulness, though, I was reasonably sure that it had.

"So," I said, "you already have plans for tonight? I was thinking of asking if you'd have dinner with me—we could go to the club or try that new Italian restaurant on Main Street. Sam won't be back until Sunday night, and the evenings get long without him."

"Oh, that would've been so nice, but Julia"—LuAnne stopped for a little laugh to show that she was teasing—"when a woman has a suitor, you can't wait till the last minute. She'll be busy. But," she went on, "I'll let you know about the restaurant. I've heard that it's very expensive, but that's where we're going."

"I see," I said, adopting the same teasing tone. "I'll just have to be quicker, won't I? How about tomorrow night?"

"Well," LuAnne said, "I don't know. I may have to work if we have a funeral on Sunday. Let's talk tomorrow, okay?"

I didn't push, just agreed that we'd discuss the matter on the following day. But I knew she was leaving the evening open in case her suitor wanted to see her again. I couldn't blame her, for I recalled the eagerness with which I had awaited Sam during our courting days. Except, of course, I had known Sam for years and had had no qualms about his intentions. LuAnne, on the other hand, didn't have a clue as to who or what her suitor was, nor what he was after, either.

As I clicked off the phone, I realized that LuAnne hadn't mentioned the name of her dinner date. I had assumed that it was the same Eddie she'd previously mentioned, because surely she hadn't found another suitable but unattached male in Abbotsville.

I picked up the phone and punched in the number I'd recently used.

"Pickens Investigations," Janelle's soft voice said. "How may I help you?"

"It's Julia Murdoch, Janelle. Is Mr. Pickens in? I need to speak to him, please." Under other circumstances I would've engaged her in conversation, but this call was business related and I didn't have time to fiddle around.

"Pickens here," an abrupt voice said. "What can I do for you, Miss Julia?"

"I'm calling to do something for you. LuAnne Conover and her new friend will be having a late dinner at that new Italian restaurant on Main Street tonight. I suggest that you take your wife to dinner at the same place so you can observe the object of your current investigation."

There was a moment of silence on the line. Then, "How late is late?"

"I don't know. Eight-thirty or so, I suppose. But I'm sure you have your ways of finding out. But let me caution you, Mr. Pickens, I do not want anyone to know what you're up to."

"No one's going to," he said. "Now hang up. I have to make reservations."

I did, realizing as I did that I'd just arranged to have an expensive meal for two added to my bill from Pickens Investigations.

Chapter 28

Lillian walked into the library from the kitchen and leaned against the doorjamb. "What y'all feel like havin' for supper tonight?" she asked.

"Oh, I don't know," I said, thinking that the best reason for having a cook was not having to decide what to serve every day of your life. "Whatever you fix will be fine or whatever Latisha wants." As she turned away, I asked, "Did you get a nap?"

"No'm," she said with a sigh. "Ev'ry time I started driftin' off, a picture of that nekked man sprung up in my mind."

Latisha, walking up behind her, stopped and asked, "What naked man?"

"A picture, Latisha," Lillian said. "Jus' a picture."

Even so, Latisha looked interested, so I changed the subject. "Let's not leave any lights on in the house tonight. Mrs. Allen called to ask if any of us had been sick. She and Penelope got home late last night from Southern Pines and saw our lights on. But leave the yard lights on tonight, Lillian, and maybe you'll sleep better."

"I sure hope she does," Latisha said. "She's been snippy to me all day. I told her she better watch out. She could lose her boyfriend acting like that."

"I'm gonna snip you down to size, little girl," Lillian said. "You better mind what I say."

I stepped in before it went any further. "What do you think of ordering pizza for supper?"

"Yeah!" Latisha said. "I mean, yes, ma'am, let's have pizza."

"I can cook something," Lillian said.

"I know, but let's order pizza. We were up half the night and I, for one, want to go to bed early."

Later, after the three of us had had our fill of pizza, Lillian and I continued to sit at the table. Three slices of the deluxe pepperoni had calmed Latisha down, so she was watching television in the library.

"Lillian," I said, keeping my voice low, "why don't you tell Latisha for sure that you're no longer in danger from Mr. Dobbs? She'd be so much easier to get along with if she knew you're not about to get married."

"I know it," Lillian said, "but if I tell her, she'll tell everybody else and, far as I know, Mr. Dobbs hasn't said anything to Janelle or told anybody else what he intends to do."

"What in the world is he waiting on?"

"Beats me," Lillian said with a shrug, " 'cept he said something about waitin' till the baby come 'cause Janelle be more likely to say yes when she have a new baby an' a new job an' so on, an' learn she can't handle it all by herself."

"That's cold," I said, "but it sounds as if Mr. Dobbs is not quite as confident of his appeal as he seems."

"It sure do, don't it?"

"Well, anyway, it would ease Latisha's concerns and make her easier to live with if you told her something, like maybe that you'd turn him down if he picks you."

"Uh-huh," Lillian said, "I guess it would, 'cept now an' then I don't know if I would or if I wouldn't. You know, if it comes right down to it."

"Lillian!" I cried. "I thought you'd made up your mind."

"I thought I had, too."

She didn't want to talk any more about it after that, so I had to go to bed with the same nagging worry that Latisha had.

"Miss Julia!" Hazel Marie said as soon as I answered the phone the following morning. It was a little after eight o'clock and I had just gotten up from the breakfast table. "Guess who I saw last night."

"Well, I don't know, Hazel Marie. Where were you last night?"

"Oh, J.D. decided almost at the last minute that I needed a night out, so we went out to dinner. He took me to that new Italian restaurant on Main Street, and I have to say that it's as good as I'd heard. Not your usual spaghetti-slash-pizza-parlor at all. They have white tablecloths, candles, and excellent service—wine opened at the table and everything."

I cringed when I heard that for I knew who would be paying for it. "My goodness, what was the occasion?"

"Oh, no occasion. J.D. likes to surprise me with something special now and then. He is just so sweet."

My eyes rolled back at that, but I let it pass. "I'm glad you had a nice evening."

"Oh, I did, but that's not why I called. Guess who else was having dinner there?"

"I don't know. Who?"

"LuAnne and somebody I didn't know, but I think it was the

same man I'd seen her with coming out of the funeral home. She introduced us, but I didn't catch his name."

A stab of fear that my secret arrangement with Mr. Pickens had become known ran through me. "You mean you *met* him? LuAnne saw the two of you?"

"Yes, of course. It's a fairly small place and all the tables were full. We were led right past their table to ours, so of course we stopped and spoke to them. LuAnne looked so nice, and Eddie—yes, that was his name—Eddie stood and shook hands with J.D. He has very nice manners, and LuAnne seemed quite proud to introduce him to us. I may ask them to dinner if I can ever be sure when J.D. will be home."

"That would be very nice. I'm sure LuAnne would appreciate it." I was also sure that Mr. Pickens could really size up Eddie if he came for dinner—find out where he was from, what he did for a living, and what he was doing in Abbotsville. I made a mental note to remind Hazel Marie of her intention if she let the time get away from her, which she had a tendency to do.

Hazel Marie's report on LuAnne and Eddie was interesting, but I was aware that it came from the least critical person I knew. According to Hazel Marie, everyone was nice, pleasant, and mannerly. No one had selfish motives or was engaged in underhanded activities. She took everyone at face value and never let a skeptical thought enter her head. Obviously, since she was dealing with human beings, she was occasionally disappointed in someone. She never let it get her down. She just put that person on her prayer list.

I'd barely clicked off the phone when it rang again. This time it was the head of Pickens Investigations reporting in, and I felt sure I'd get a different assessment from him.

"Running into them in a restaurant was a good move, Miss Julia," he said. "It seemed natural and unplanned, and gave me a few minutes to form a quick opinion. It's not my final opinion, though, just a report of where the investigation stands now."

"Could you tell what he's up to?"

"No, he wasn't wearing a sign."

"Well, I *know* that. But since you deal with so many people who aren't what they seem, I thought you would get a hint if something was askew."

"Askew?" he said. "No, they look as straight as everybody else."

"Then let me ask this: Who paid for their dinner? Him or her?"

"Now, that," Mr. Pickens said, "is the kind of question you should be asking. We were seated across the room and waiters were in the way when they got the bill. But I saw this Eddie hand a card to a waiter. By the way, his name is Cochrane. Eddie Cochrane."

Feeling a burden of worry ease off by learning that LuAnne's dinner date had paid for their meal, I said, "I'm so glad to hear that. Not his name, although that's good to know, but I mean that he has money in his pocket or at least a credit card. Maybe that means his intentions are on the up and up, in spite of the fact that he can't afford to bury his wife."

"*What?*" Mr. Pickens wasn't easily surprised. He was usually two or three steps ahead of me, but not this time. "What do you mean, he can't bury his wife. Is she dead?"

"Of course she's dead, and I assume that she's actually buried. It's just, according to LuAnne, he can't afford a lump sum payment for the interment, so he's making monthly payments to the funeral home. That's how she met him." I stopped, thought about it for a second, then said, "Which means that he's paying to put one woman away while wining and dining another woman, which, in turn, means that he has enough to do both."

"Not necessarily," Mr. Pickens said. "It was Ms. Conover's card because it was Ms. Conover who signed for it."

"I knew it!" I said, overcome with agitation. "I just *knew* it! Mr. Pickens, what're we going to do?"

Chapter 29

After assuring me that he had only just started to penetrate Eddie Cochrane's background and that there was still plenty to uncover, Mr. Pickens told me to hang up and to hang on while he continued to work.

"All right," I said, still distraught over what Mr. Pickens had seen, "but don't forget to tell Hazel Marie when you'll be home so she can invite them to dinner. We can't fiddle around, Mr. Pickens. You need to find out what he's up to before he takes LuAnne to the cleaners. Believe me, she can't afford too many expensive dinners."

"Especially," Mr. Pickens said, "with two bottles of wine."

I'm sure I went white in the face at that. "Oh, no, don't tell me she was *drinking*!"

"Well, *some*body was. I saw a waiter open one bottle at their table and take an empty one away."

"Oh, my goodness," I said with a moan. "Two dinners and two bottles of wine, and she paid for it all. Mr. Pickens, we have to do something. Answering the phone at the Good Shepherd Funeral Home is not a high-end job."

On the other hand, I reminded myself after ending the call, LuAnne was a grown woman and it wasn't my place to tell her what to do, much less what not to do. But surely it was incumbent on me as a longtime friend to issue a warning if Eddie Cochrane was using her.

But Mr. Pickens had issued an order for me to stay out of it, and I was inclined to obey him. If LuAnne even suspected that I distrusted her new friend, she would cut me off completely. How, then, would I be able to instruct Mr. Pickens on how and when to observe and report on their activities?

"Let's have some coffee," I said to Lillian as I walked into the kitchen. "Are you at a stopping place?"

"I can always stop for coffee," she said, adjusting the flame under a pot. " 'Specially on a rainy mornin' like this. The weatherman say it'll stop in a while, but it sure is dreary while it's here."

As we settled at the table, Lillian asked, "Did you get any sleep last night?"

"Surprisingly, yes. How about you?"

"It took me a while to drop off, but I slept good the rest of the night." Lillian stirred two spoonfuls of sugar into her coffee, then went on. "Wonder if that man showed hisself to anybody last night."

"That's exactly what I've been thinking about. Let me show you something." I got up and opened one of our many catchall drawers in the kitchen. Pulling out an old telephone directory, I flipped through it until I found the page I wanted.

"Look at this," I said, laying the open book on the table. "It's a map showing the counties in our free calling area."

"Uh-huh," Lillian said. "Who we callin'?"

"Nobody. Look." Using a pen, I drew a tiny square on the map of Abbot County. "Here's where we are. See, that's Main Street and here's Pitt Street. Hazel Marie lives right about here." I drew another square. "Here's your house, and if I'm halfway right, Miss Vinnie's house is over here."

Lillian leaned closer, studying and quickly grasping the meaning of the map. "Where would that golf course be?"

"It would pretty much take up this whole corner," I said, making a large, curved line in the upper right corner. I put down the pen and uncapped another one with red ink. I drew a tiny red star on the edge of the golf course, put another one where we'd located Miss Vinnie's house, and drew two stars next to my house.

Lillian studied the map. "Why you got two stars next to this house?"

So I told her what I'd seen on that rainy night, although admitting that I was still unsure of what it had been. "It could've been anything—a pillowcase ripped from a clothesline or something a child left outside. It was just a flash of white, although now that I think about it, it seemed to have two legs."

"Law, don't tell me that," Lillian said. "You think he's been here two times?"

"That's what worries me. But look at the map and see where the stars are."

Lillian peered at the map, then looked up at me. "What about whatever James saw at Miss Hazel Marie's house?"

"Oh, I forgot about that." I drew a star in the general area of the Pickens house, then said, "My goodness, that's five sightings within the past couple of weeks."

"And they all right close together," Lillian said. "I mean they all on one side of Main Street—*our* side of Main Street."

"Yes, except for that report of somebody seeing him in Edneyville. That's way over here, almost at the county line."

"Hm-m," Lillian said. "That coulda been somebody hopin' an' not really seein'."

"That's true, so let's concentrate on the sightings around here. There're only five, so he may not have the urge to shock people very often."

"That's more'n enough for me."

"Me, too. But there could be others who've seen him but aren't sure enough to report it. I mean, nobody expects to see a man with no clothes on, so it's easy to talk yourself out of what your own eyes are telling you. Especially if he's dashing from one dark spot to another.

"And here's another thing, Lillian," I went on. "Remember how he just ruined Miss Vinnie's yard? Whacked the heads off all her blooming plants, and she had a yard full. I heard he used a golf club, which ties in with somebody seeing him at the golf course. I remember thinking that it could've been a member of the club or a groundskeeper who worked there. I think, though, that I really thought that it was probably somebody with a guest membership because who would risk arrest after paying those expensive club fees every year?"

Lillian said, "I remember thinkin' it was most likely a teenager 'cause remember how some of them college boys used to go streakin' across a campus? An' streakin' means the same thing as nekked."

"Oh, my gracious, yes," I said with a laugh. "And remember that picture in the paper of a group of naked boys at Wake Forest? A few people swore they could identify the son of a local lawyer. I didn't believe them because all you could see was a bunch of backsides, and one of those is pretty much like all the others."

"Yes'm, but that was diff'rent from what this man's doin'."

"You're right about that," I said. "I don't know what the difference is, but running across a campus in a group just isn't the same as plastering yourself against a window. But let's listen out, Lillian, and see if he's shown himself at other places. It's such a shock, that some people may not believe what they've seen, and he's fast. We found that out the other night."

"He sure is. He took off like a streak of lightnin', which was a good thing for him 'cause I'd've beat the tar outta him if I'd caught him. But if he keeps on doin' it an' we keep puttin' stars on this map, we might figure out who he is or at least where he is."

"Miss Julia!" Hazel Marie said as soon as I picked up the phone and almost before I could say hello. "Are you all right? Lillian's staying with you, isn't she?"

"Yes and yes. What's the matter? What's going on?"

Hazel Marie blew out her breath. "Thank goodness. I was worried about you being there by yourself because he was at it again last night."

"Who? You mean the naked man?"

"You know Ethyl Randolph, don't you? She lives across the street and up one house from us in that little English cottage."

"Yes, I've known her for years. She goes to First Methodist. Why, what happened?"

"Well, you know she lives alone, and late last night she took a trash bag out to the garbage can in her backyard and just as she put the lid back on that man just suddenly appeared in front of her. She said she nearly died of fright right there, and she jumped back so quick that she tripped and sat down hard. She said she thought her end had come, but he just looked at her while she looked at him. Then he whacked the garbage can one lick with some kind of a pole or stick, turned around, and left. The deputies came and everything, but since we sleep upstairs in the back of the house, we didn't know anything about it till this morning. J.D. 's over there now."

I couldn't help but wonder with some skepticism about the instincts and training of a private investigator who could sleep through a neighbor's harrowing experience. But Mr. Pickens was the best, that is to say the only, private investigator we had, so I had to be content with him.

"Well, let me know, Hazel Marie, what he finds out. It just worries me to death that that crazy man seems to come and go at will, and nobody knows who he is."

"I know," she said. "Me, too. But you stay inside, especially when it starts to get dark. That's when he was at Miss Ethyl's and Miss Vinnie's, too. And," Hazel Marie went on, "that's the same time James thinks he saw him in our yard."

As soon as I clicked off the phone, I turned to Lillian. "Get the map and the red pen. He's on the move again."

Leaning over the map on the table, I drew a tiny red star next to where we thought the Randolph house would be.

Straightening up to study the map, Lillian said, "Looks like to me that he's gettin' mighty active. You count all these times together an' he's been showin' hisself just about ev'ry night here lately."

"Yes, and think of this. Just where does he leave his clothes, which is a question I've asked before and nobody has an answer. Does he take them off before he leaves home—wherever that is? Or does he undress when he gets to his target?"

Lillian stared off into the distance. Then she said, "We didn't leave him no time the other night to do anything but run. Let's go look around the back hedge an' see if he left anything."

Chapter 30

"Good idea," I said, although I doubted that a search would turn up anything. The naked man had had plenty of time to come back and pick up anything he'd left. "And look, the sun's coming out. It'll be wet and muddy around the arbor, though, so I'm wearing galoshes." I went into the pantry that served not only as a keeping room for kitchen necessities but as a coat closet and a catchall for everything else. "You want a pair?"

"I guess I better," Lillian said, and we proceeded to step into the rubber boots and slog out to search what Sam laughingly called the back forty.

My yard was not overly large, but it was of a size to host a garden party if I ever felt the urge to have one. Enclosed by a brick wall lined with aging boxwoods, a few crepe myrtles, and several specimen fruit trees, the yard formed a semiformal garden that was easy to keep and pleasant to the eyes. The back wall was centered by a wisteria-covered arbor over a bench. A gate at the far corner behind the boxwoods opened onto the sidewalk that bordered South Oak Street. It was a lovely enclosed garden, if I do say so myself, even though the neighbor behind me had let his privet hedge grow wild and unruly above the brick wall.

Lillian and I tromped around the huge boxwoods in our boots, getting wet from the rainwater dripping from the leaves. Lillian had found a stick that she was using to scrape around the roots.

"Seems like to me," she said, "that he was headed for the gate, 'cause he went catty-cornered 'cross the yard, which shows he's not all that crazy. It's the onliest way he could get out, an' I 'spect it's the way he got in, too."

"I think you're right," I said, brushing against a huge boxwood that sent a shower of water across my back. "He could've undressed under the arbor and left his clothes on the bench. Of course that was before it started raining, so we're not going to find any tracks."

Lillian grunted her agreement, then leaned over with her stick to scrape around a small pile of leaves.

"Miss Julia?" she called. "Come look at this."

I walked toward the gate as she held out the stick. A black cloth matted with mud and leaves was dangling from the end of it. "What is it?"

"A sock," she said. "A man's sock. I found it right beside the gate, where he musta dropped it in his hurry to get out. If we can find the mate to it, we'll know who it belongs to."

"My word, Lillian," I said, "do you know how many unmatched socks there are in Sam's sock drawer? I think the washing machine eats them."

"Yes'm," she said, still intensely studying the muddied sock. "Socks used to have clocks on 'em, but this one's got little curly things instead. Maybe when it dries out we can find out what size it is an' at least know what size of foot used to be in it."

"Maybe, but most men's socks come in a one-size-fits-all because they stretch. I'm not sure the size will help us unless we do like Cinderella's prince and go around trying it on every male foot in town. But," I continued, not wanting to discount the importance of her find, "bring it back to the house, and I'll let the sheriff's office know. They may be able to track it to the owner through odor or something."

I didn't know what I was talking about, but then neither did Lillian. But to my surprise, the sheriff's office was interested enough to send an officer in a patrol car to pick up the sock, so maybe they could do something with it. As it was, the sock was wet and muddy as if it had not only been dropped and rained on but possibly stepped on as well. So it was soon dropped into a plastic bag and on its way to a laboratory.

I had a long telephone conversation with Mildred Allen on Saturday. Since she and her adopted granddaughter, Penelope, had spent part of spring break week visiting Horace, we had all of a day and a half catching up to do. Mildred did most of it, telling me in detail all that they had done while staying at that grand old hotel in Pinehurst.

Breaking into a long account of their shopping expeditions, Mildred suddenly said, "I just love that child. Penelope, I mean. She is so appreciative of the least attention and wide-eyed at anything new. And everything is new to her."

Penelope, barely eight years old, had already had an adventurous life, living mostly from pillar to post, but Mildred had put a stop to that by adopting her. And in return the child was changing Mildred's life, mainly by giving Mildred something besides herself to think of.

"Well, tell me," Mildred said, interrupting her own account of the week, "what's been going on while we were gone? How's Sue getting along with the wedding plans?"

That subject occupied us for several minutes as I told her of the groom's suggestion of having a destination wedding. Mildred would have loved an excuse to go to New Orleans, although she hardly needed an excuse to do whatever she wanted to do.

But speaking of one wedding led to my thinking of another, so I told her of Etta Mae's quandary about getting married. "The thing about it is," I said, "she's been in love with this man for years, but now that she's doing so well on her own, she's having second thoughts. Mainly, I think, because he's running for sheriff in the next election and she thinks he might be using her to get votes. You know, so that he appears to be a settled family man. Voters seem to like that."

"Oh, shoo," Mildred said, "she shouldn't let that stop her. It doesn't matter why a man wants to marry, just that he does. The only thing that matters is what *she* wants."

"Mildred! You know that's not true."

We laughed, but knowing the state of Mildred's marriage to Horace, I wasn't so sure how funny it was. All I knew was that I would not have wanted a marriage like it, yet it had worked for them for close to fifty years and had changed only because Horace was now occupied with crayons and a coloring book and didn't know that he even had a wife.

"How is Horace these days?" I asked.

"Same old, same old," she said with a sigh. "They tell me he's as happy as can be except when it's bathtime. He says he doesn't need to bathe because he hasn't worked hard enough to get sweaty. But, you tell me, Julia, when has he ever? And he doesn't know who I am or remember what he did yesterday, much less years ago. It's like he's living totally in the present. He doesn't remember yesterday and he can't conceive of tomorrow."

Mildred then commented on the fact that such a mental

situation was certainly helpful to anyone with a guilty conscience. "Imagine having everything bad or wrong or cringeworthy that you've ever done or thought being totally erased," she said. "You'd start every day new with no recriminations."

"I think," I said, "that's also called being a Christian."

"Why," Mildred said with a note of wonder in her voice, "I think you may be right. I'd never thought of it that way before."

After hanging up, I realized that I had not reported our run-in with the naked man and almost called her back to warn her about his recent evening visitations.

"Miss Julia?" Lillian said before I could pick up the phone again. "Mr. Sam be home tomorrow, won't he?"

"Yes, and I can't wait."

"Well, I hate to leave you by yourself, but Latisha and me need to go home tonight. I got to get her ready for church tomorrow, iron her dress, plait her hair, and polish her shoes 'cause she's singin' in the choir in the mornin'."

"Oh, of course," I said. "Do whatever you need to do. I'll be all right. Surely that man won't come back to the place where he almost got caught. I'm probably the safest woman in town."

Brave words in the daylight, but I planned as darkness came on to go around the house closing every blind and drawing every curtain upstairs and down. If he came back, he wouldn't be able to see in. Even better, I wouldn't be able to see out. I'd seen all I wanted to see of that man.

Chapter 31

The thing to do, I told myself, was to stay too busy for my imagination to run away with me. To that end, I called LuAnne Conover as I'd promised to do.

"LuAnne? It's Julia. Would you like to go out for dinner tonight? My treat because I'm in need of some company."

"Wel-ll," she said somewhat hesitantly so that I knew she had not heard from Eddie. "I thought I might be busy tonight, but maybe not. Where do you want to go?"

"You decide. I haven't been out in so long that I don't really care. Sam won't be back until late tomorrow, and Lillian and Latisha have to go home, so I'm as free as a bird. Wherever you say will be fine with me."

"Then how about the country club? I really miss that, and there's no reason for the two of us to be home alone."

"My feeling exactly," I said. "I'll pick you up about six-thirty if that suits you."

It did, so I called the clubhouse to make reservations and counted myself lucky that Eddie had apparently made other plans for the evening.

We were led to a table in a quiet corner after speaking to several friends and acquaintances as we threaded our way across the main dining room. LuAnne and I settled ourselves in for an hour of good food and good talk.

"Tell me how you've been, LuAnne," I said after we'd given our orders. "I've had to do all the calling, so I hope that means you've been pleasantly occupied."

"Oh, Julia," she said, leaning toward me, "I surely have. I was beginning to think that there were no gentlemen left anywhere, but then I met Eddie. I must be the luckiest woman alive. Who would believe that I'd meet someone like him in a funeral home of all places?"

"Oh? Well, I'm glad to hear it. Tell me about him. Is he retired? What kind of work did he do?"

I settled in to listen as LuAnne told me all about Eddie Cochrane. It seems that he had held a position in Charlotte's city water department, which I interpreted to mean that he also had a small but regular retirement income. Eddie liked to take long walks, but no runs due to a tricky knee. He used to enjoy an occasional game of tennis, but again the knee had stopped that. He was very neat and particular in his habits, which after Leonard's careless hygiene, LuAnne appreciated.

"I don't know if you've noticed," she said, "but the older a man gets, the less he thinks he needs to bathe. Apparently they think it has something to do with sweating. If they haven't worked up a sweat by cutting the grass or moving furniture, then a Saturday-night bath is plenty. And," LuAnne went on, quoting Leonard with a martyr's sigh, "it saves on the water bill."

"Oh, my goodness," I said, thinking of what Mildred had said about Horace and wanting to laugh, but I could've cried just as easily. What was it with older men and bathing? Thank you, Lord, for Sam, who could stay in the shower until the hot water ran out.

"But Eddie," LuAnne said, a dreamy look passing across her face, "he's as neat and as clean as a pin, and he smells good, too. And he's so thoughtful, just with little things, you know. Making sure that I have everything I need, bringing a flower or two when he picks me up, and calling for no particular reason just to talk to me." LuAnne closed her eyes and sighed. "I couldn't ask for anyone better."

Well, I could.

Of course I couldn't say that, but if I were in the market for an eligible man, I could ask for someone with a little money in his pocket. I wondered how often LuAnne had paid for the wonderful dates they'd had and how long it would take her to realize that she was taking him out rather than the other way around.

But then I thought that maybe their dinner and the two bottles of wine they'd had at the new Italian restaurant on Main Street had been an oddity. Maybe that had been the first and maybe it would be the only time that LuAnne had had to pay the tab. I hoped so, for I wanted my friend to find the man of her dreams, especially since the first man she'd married had turned into a nightmare.

Finally, over dessert LuAnne asked how I was doing. "And how's Sam? I declare, I've been so busy that I've lost track of friends."

"We're doing all right," I said, "same as usual except Sam has been gone all week and I've really missed him. But, before I forget, do we need to do anything more to get ready for Christy's luncheon?"

"No, I think we've covered everything. But it really startled me to hear that the wedding might be held somewhere else. I called Sue, and I'll tell you the truth, Julia, I really think she doesn't like Travis what's-his-name. Oh, of course she'd never say that, but it was in the tone of her voice whenever she mentioned him. You would think that having your daughter marrying a big-time surgeon would have her walking on air. And I understand that he's from an old Virginia family, so Sue ought to be beaming all over the place. But I didn't get that feeling at all. She would never admit it, though."

"I think," I said, "that he just got off on the wrong foot with her, making too many outlandish suggestions and overstepping a little. But Sue will work it out. She's the easiest person in the world to get along with. I think she's just worried that Christy won't stand up for herself."

"Well," LuAnne said, leaning back in her chair with a beatific smile on her face, "when you're in love . . . You know how it is."

No, I didn't. When something seemed too good to be true, I figured that it probably was. LuAnne, however, was in no mood to listen to cautionary advice, no matter how well meant. But it had been time well spent for I had learned a lot about Eddie, although it had been filtered through LuAnne's rose-colored glasses.

After dropping her off at her condo after dinner, I parked the car on the side of the driveway at home, got out, and hurried to the empty house. It was so seldom that our house was empty of everyone that I felt a wave of loneliness as I unlocked the back door. Yet with daylight saving time, the sky was still light and Mildred's house was lit up, as was her yard with the subdued landscape lighting.

I flipped on the kitchen lights, locked the door behind me, and went through the downstairs, turning on lamps and making sure that all the windows were covered with blinds or curtains. If the naked man came for a return visit, he would have to perform without an audience.

I soon got over my unease at being alone and began to enjoy having the house to myself. This, I thought, is the way it would be every day if Lillian decided to marry Chester P. Dobbs. At that thought, I didn't enjoy it quite so much.

After an hour or so of watching a British mystery show on public television, I decided that I was tired enough to sleep without lying awake half the night. I told myself that it didn't matter if someone was even now undressing under the arbor. The naked man could frolic all over the yard if he had a mind to and no one would be watching.

Some while later, although not too much later, right after I'd dropped off into the deepest sleep, I popped straight up in bed. Jerked awake by a loud *BLAM* that still rang in my head, I was even more addled by the scraping and rattling of something peppering down on the roof.

What in the world? I threw off the covers, ran to the side window, and pushed aside the draperies. Standing just on the other side of the hedge and the row of Bradford pear trees that separated our side yards was Mildred in a voluminous gown and a hunting jacket.

"Julia!" she yelled. "Are you all right?"

Struggling to unlock the window, I finally got it up enough to call down to my neighbor. "Mildred? What in the world?"

"You better get down here," she yelled back. "I'm lowering my aim next time."

Good grief, I thought, she's got that shotgun. Nearly stumbling on a bedroom shoe, I grabbed a robe and ran barefoot to the stairs, down them, and out through the kitchen, flipping on lights as I went.

"Don't shoot!" I yelled as I headed for the hedge where Mildred was stalking back and forth with a long gun on her shoulder. "Hold your fire!"

We met at the hedge as I gasped for breath. "What're you *doing*? Are you shooting at my house? Put that gun down!"

"Okay," she said and took the present arms position. "But I didn't shoot at your house, just took the tops off a few pear trees. That naked idiot was running around my house, then he cut across your yard. Did you see him?"

"No," I said, leaning over to catch my breath, "but I wasn't looking. Mildred, you've got to stop taking the law into your own hands. Call the sheriff. Deputies are looking for him already if you haven't run him off for good."

"That's what I meant to do." She ran her hand across the barrel of the gun and said, "This is a twelve-gauge Benelli M3 tactical pump shotgun, loaded with eight—well, seven now—rounds of double-ought buckshot suitable for skeet, clay, target, and home defense. If that won't run him off, I don't know what will."

I started laughing. I couldn't help it. She was so serious yet so ridiculous, standing there in a batiste nightgown under a camouflage jacket, her hair rolled up in pink curlers, caressing a deadly piece of military equipment that she had just recently used so competently.

Catching my breath, I said, "I hope to goodness the safety is on that thing."

"It is now," she said as I heard a click. "Sorry to wake you, but he was prancing around on my back patio, and I'm not going to put up with that. If he thought he was doing me a favor, he was sadly mistaken. I'd like to fill his rear end full of buckshot so he'd have to go to the emergency room and everybody would know who he is."

"Good thinking, Mildred," I said with only a slight edge of sarcasm. "Now, look." I pointed toward her front porch, where Ida Lee and Penelope were standing, clasping each other. "You better go reassure them and then put that gun up. *Way* up."

"I'll put it up, but not that far," she said, hiking up her nightgown as she turned to walk away. "He might come back."

Chapter 32

I went inside and back upstairs, beginning to fume as I thought of what had just happened. The idea of shooting at my house was beyond any neighborly concern Mildred could possibly have had about a naked man. Of course she denied it, saying she'd aimed high, but I knew what I'd heard raining down on my roof.

As I closed the window and pulled the draperies in my bedroom, I saw a sheriff's car drive up to Mildred's front door. A deputy got out, then stepped up onto the porch and out of my sight.

"Well, good," I said aloud, hoping to goodness that he would read the riot act to my neighbor with the itchy finger. Somebody, I thought, had had the good sense to report a gunshot and, I hoped, Mildred would learn the penalty for pulling the trigger on a firearm within the town limits.

She was too quick to take matters into her own hands, and I lived too close for comfort to her.

I woke up Sunday morning with a heart light enough to laugh about Mildred's shootout at the O.K. Corral. Sam and Lloyd would be home by dark, and I could put up with most anything with that to look forward to.

I started dressing for church, then thought, Why? Our new, young pastor was the opposite of Pastor Larry Ledbetter, now retired, who'd tested positive for too many bleeding-heart liberal causes in an effort to stay au courant. The new pastor came very close to preaching a strain of pantheism in which he found God in the creation. That, according to him, is where we should look for Him—in the minutiae of the creation from the very cells that make up everything to the grandeur of sunsets and mountains and space itself.

No, no, no, I wanted to shout. God is no more in the things He has created than an artist is in his canvas. The artist's mark, his style, his choice of subject, may very well reveal the hand that painted the canvas, but the artist himself is outside his creation. He can be pleased with what he's done or he can pick up a brush and change a few things or he can destroy the painting, but he is not *in* it.

That young preacher needed a good talking to, and I wondered if young men and women entered the seminary already convinced of where they stood or if the seminary itself molded them.

Either way, I was of no mind to go sit at the feet of someone who needed a greater dose of Scripture than he was getting. It occurred to me that I should go to Lillian's church to hear Latisha sing in the choir, but their service started early. Not wanting to disturb it by going in late, I stayed home and kept thinking of more good reasons for doing so.

And I'm glad I did for about the time that the offering plates were being passed around in the sanctuary across the street, my phone rang and I was home to answer it.

"Miss Julia? It's Etta Mae Wiggins. How are you?"

"Why, Etta Mae, how nice to hear from you," I said, taking note that she was not in church, either. "How are you?"

"I'm fine, although a little unsure about a few things. I was wondering if I could come talk to you."

Assuring her that I'd be delighted to see her, she agreed to come right over. That left me with more than enough time to worry about what she wanted to talk about.

Was she having trouble meeting her loan payments? Maybe business had fallen off recently or her best employee had resigned. I thought of any number of reasons that she'd want to talk to me but would never have thought of the one that she brought up.

I opened the front door as soon as Etta Mae pulled to the curb and waited as she approached the porch.

"Hey, Miss Julia," she called out, but not quite as cheerily as she usually greeted me. "I hope I didn't keep you from going to church. I didn't even think about it when I called."

"You didn't keep me from anything," I said, holding the door for her. I noticed the jean skirt, T-shirt, and pink tennis shoes she was wearing and knew she'd had no plans for church herself. She looked about eighteen years old from a distance, but the strained look on her face belied that impression close up.

As I welcomed her in, I knew Etta Mae had something of consequence on her mind. She had never been much for chitchat, so it didn't surprise me that she went straight to the nub of her problem as soon as she walked in.

"It's Bobby Lee," she said as I led her to the sofa in the living room. "I don't know what to do with him."

"Well," I said, a little unnerved to be presented with such a problem, "I don't know what to tell you, Etta Mae. Either you marry him or you don't. Nobody else can make that decision. I mean, I assume he still wants to marry you. He's been a little wishy-washy before this, hasn't he?"

"Well, yes, I guess that's what you'd call it. We'd talk about getting married, then something would come up that he had to do first—like go to some kind of FBI training program or something. And I'd get mad and end up marrying somebody else while he was gone."

"But you're not married to anybody else now, are you?"

"No'm. After Mr. Connard died on our wedding night, I've been real careful."

I almost laughed but was able to treat the subject with the appropriate seriousness. "So you're free and Bobby Lee is free. What's holding you back?"

"Oh, I'm going to marry him. I mean, I might as well since I've wanted to for so long. It's what to do with him *after* we're married that's worrying me." She wiggled around on the sofa, cleared her throat, and went on. "See, my single-wide trailer is too small for the two of us. There's hardly enough room for one person, much less two, especially when one of them is so big to start with. Bobby Lee has to turn sideways to get in and out of the shower. I just don't see how both of us can live at the Springer Trailer Park."

"Why, Etta Mae, I wouldn't expect you to. You and Bobby Lee should find a nice house with room for both of you where you can start married life together. I don't see the problem."

"Oh," she said, as the tight look on her face began to soften. "Well, if I'm not living there . . . I mean, if I'm not on the premises, I'm not sure I can manage the park like I've been doing, and, well, I don't want to let you down."

"Etta Mae," I said with a slight eye roll, "do you mean to say that you're worried about moving out of the trailer park?"

"Yes'm, you've let me live there without paying space and

hook-up rent in return for managing the place, so I don't want to just move out and leave you without a manager."

"We'll just find someone else," I said. "Surely you don't think I'd want you to turn down Bobby Lee just so you can stay in your single-wide?"

"Well," she said, "you've already done so much for me, I just didn't want to move out and leave you holding the bag. And Bobby Lee doesn't want to live in a trailer, not even if we changed it for a double-wide. He says it's too much like somebody getting ready to leave. So he wants to look for a house with a foundation and enough room to turn around in, but I wanted to talk to you first."

"Then here's what you should do. Find somebody who can manage the park, preferably somebody settled and trustworthy. Then rent your single-wide to him or her, then get on with getting married. You don't need to worry about me."

"Well, that's a relief," Etta Mae said, "if you're sure. I'll find you somebody good to manage it, don't worry about that." Then, pushing back her hair, she said, "Whew, I guess now all I have to do is tell Bobby Lee where and when to show up to get married."

"Have you thought about it?" I asked as a vagrant thought of offering my house wandered across my mind. "What kind of a wedding are you thinking of?"

"Quick and easy," she said. "Bobby Lee doesn't hold still for very long." She laughed and so did I, but I was just a tad taken aback. "And see, Miss Julia, I've about tried them all at one time or another. My first was a big church wedding right out of high school, and all the cheerleaders were my bridesmaids. Then I had one at the magistrate's office with nobody there but two strangers as witnesses. After that I married Mr. Connard in an almost empty church with Lurline sneering at everything, so I guess the only thing left is to go somewhere special for the wedding."

I swallowed hard, having just escaped an invitation to one destination wedding only now to be presented with another unwanted trip. "That," I said, "might make it difficult for some people to get to—your staff, for instance. They may not be able to travel any distance."

"Yes'm, I know. I'd love to go to Disney World, but Bobby Lee is too busy running for sheriff to be away long enough for me to get my fill of it, so he's promised to take me next year. So right now I'm thinking of maybe just doing it here and going to the Grove Park Inn in Asheville afterward. If," she said, laughing, "we get that far."

I laughed, too, thinking that my understanding of a destination wedding was not quite the same as hers. I liked hers better.

Chapter 33

Etta Mae ended her visit with a quicker step and a lighter heart than when she'd come. But the concern she had expressed that her plans might inconvenience me had touched me. What young woman would consider changing her wedding plans in order to accommodate a part-time employer? Not many.

But if her Bobby Lee was truly committed to marriage this time around, I was presented with another problem: a wedding gift. It would have to be a nice one. Etta Mae had been my good right hand in many excursions when I would have been in the soup but for her. What in the world could I give her that would express my admiration for her and my thanks to her? My old standby, silver, didn't seem quite appropriate for the life she would lead as the wife of a county sheriff, if Bobby Lee won his race. Perhaps a large casserole dish heated by sterno would be something she would use and enjoy when she entertained.

On the other hand, a lovely tea service would be treasured above all other gifts, although possibly never used. But even if a cup of tea was never poured, I knew that the fact of simply owning it, although wrapped in silver cloth and stored away, would give her a sense of social confidence like nothing else.

Maybe she'd eventually have a sideboard on which it could be displayed.

Well, I didn't have to decide right away, and from the way Etta Mae spoke of Bobby Lee's tendency to wander off, I might never have to. Of course, though, I hoped they would marry since that's who she'd wanted for as long as I'd known her.

Just as I headed for the kitchen to find something for lunch, the phone rang again.

"Julia?" Mildred Allen said. "Ida Lee has made some of her good chicken salad and is even now making a plate of sandwiches. Why don't you come over and help me eat them?"

Thinking of the two-day-old package of ham in my refrigerator, I said, "I'd love to."

We sat in white wicker chairs lined with chintz cushions on Mildred's sun porch, a platter of chicken salad sandwiches, crusts removed, and a plate of fruit on a table between us. Mildred was attempting to justify her actions of the night before.

"You should've seen him, Julia," Mildred said. "Naked as a jaybird, however naked that is. He was prancing around right out there on the patio. Of course by the time I'd gone upstairs for my gun, he was already headed toward your house. I had to take the shot or let him figure he could dance on my patio anytime he wanted to. And I did aim high." And to make sure that I took note, she went on. "Just stand back on your way home and look at that row of pear trees. They used to be perfectly aligned, but I took out the tops of a couple of them. That's what you heard on your roof—twigs and things."

"Well, you have to understand that it makes me nervous to have guns going off around me," I said. "And I was sound asleep and completely unprepared to be so rudely awakened. Still, I'm glad you ran him off. I'm getting tired of having him around."

And I proceeded to tell her of the naked man's previous visitations to my house. "It makes me wonder what the attraction is—why he keeps coming back. Of course I don't know how many return visits he's making to the others." Reaching for another sandwich, I said, "Oh, well, Sam will be home tonight, so maybe I've seen the last of him. He doesn't seem to visit women with husbands at home."

"But that doesn't help me," Mildred said, laughing. "Or any of the other women he's been visiting—we're all alone. Maybe he thinks that we need the thrill, but if he thought he was doing me a favor by cavorting in the altogether, he was sadly mistaken. A load of buckshot convinced him of that."

"Who knows," I said, "but he needs to be caught before something drastic happens. Lillian and I have been plotting his appearances on a map, and they're all right around here. And that makes me think that he lives in this area. He disappears so quickly, and the only clue he's left is a black sock by my boxwoods, which may mean that he undressed in my backyard. And because of you and that shotgun, he didn't have time to put his clothes back on—just grabbed them and left. And that means that he was on the street completely nude at least until he found a place to get dressed before going on home, wherever home is, which, taking all that into consideration, can't be far."

Ida Lee slipped in at that point and replenished our tea glasses.

Mildred said, "Is Penelope lying down?"

"Yes, ma'am," Ida Lee said, nodding. "I gave her lunch, and she was ready for a nap after such a busy morning."

As Ida Lee left, Mildred turned to me. "Penelope and Ida Lee went to the AME Zion church this morning. Latisha's choir was singing, and from all reports it was a resounding success."

"Oh, my," I said, "I'm sorry I missed it. I'd thought about going, but then I had a visitor. You remember Etta Mae Wiggins, don't you?" And I went on to tell Mildred of Etta Mae's wedding plans or lack of same. "She didn't exactly say this, but I gathered that she didn't want this wedding to be like any of the others she's had. But she's had so many that she's running out of options." I stopped and thought for a minute. "I'm kind of thinking of offering my house. Remember Binkie and Coleman got married there, and now that I think of it, Etta Mae was a guest and she brought Deputy Bobby Lee Moser with her. That sounds like a good omen to me."

"To me, too," Mildred said. "But don't get too far along on the wedding plans. I don't know her as well as you do, but I've been trying to think of an excuse for having a big do myself. Did you know," she said in wonder, "that Penelope has never been to a party, much less given one?"

"Oh, my goodness," I said. "That poor little thing."

"Yes, and I think it's incumbent on me to remedy that. I mean," she said, stopping for a second, "I know it might be frowned on with Horace in the shape he's in, but life does go on and it might as well go on as happily as we can make it."

"Wouldn't Horace be able to come? I mean for a day or two?"

"Oh, honey, don't ask. He's as healthy as a horse, but he is in another world mentally. He thought Penelope was his baby sister, and he's never had a baby sister. I don't know who he thought I was. One day he said I was the best mother he'd ever had, and the next day he kept asking where my husband was. It's just so sad, but thank goodness for Penelope. She gives me something to get up for every day."

"I'm glad for you, Mildred," I said, and truly I was.

"Well," Mildred went on, "before you get carried away with planning a wedding for Miss Wiggins, give me a chance to think it over. I might like to have a big blowout like I did once before, remember? And to have a wedding along with everything else would be icing on the cake."

"I sure do remember. Wasn't that when Helen Stroud's husband was arrested for fraud and embezzlement right out there in your backyard?"

"Yes, it was, which was sort of the highlight of the day. But think of where she is now. I mean, we know where he is, but the former Mrs. Richard Stroud is now Mrs. Thurlow Jones. It's a good thing we don't know what the future holds, isn't it? If she could've foreseen what was going to happen, she'd probably have left town and never come back."

"Nobody would've been able to foresee that. Even now," I went on with a sigh, "I can hardly believe it. I just hope she's happy, but if not happy, at least that she feels she made a good bargain."

"I doubt we'll ever know with Helen, but I wish her well, too. But listen, Julia, the more I think of it, the better I like the idea of having a great big party and inviting everybody. I haven't done anything social in so long that I hardly remember how." Mildred leaned back with a laugh. "I mean, I've been so taken up with Tonya, then Penelope came along, and now Horace, that I probably owe everybody in town. I didn't even do anything for Christmas, which isn't like me at all."

"But," I reminded her, "you always outdo everybody whenever you do. So if you decide to have a big party, there's one thing I want to ask of you."

"What's that?"

"Please, please don't ask Tina Doland to sing 'Ah, Sweet Mystery of Life' again. I don't think I could stand another of her renditions."

"I thought it was 'People' you didn't like."

"That, too."

Chapter 34

I ended up staying half the afternoon at Mildred's as we whiled away the time, discussing friends and acquaintances of all stripes. Yet under the conversation, anticipation of Sam's arrival was building inside as I pictured him driving home on the interstate. At least I hoped that Lloyd wasn't driving since Sunday-afternoon drivers would be filling the mountain roads. Around three, I left for home, walking carefully down the slight slope of Mildred's lawn toward the boundary of pear trees on the edge of our yards.

Looking up, I saw the jagged tops of a couple of trees where a load of buckshot had shredded leaves and limbs. I shook my head at the sight as a shiver crossed my shoulders. A slight lowering of the gun barrel would have put that load of buckshot through my window and onto my bed. From all reports—mostly from her—Mildred was an excellent shot, having learned at her daddy's knee in the fields of South Carolina and on the veldt of Africa. Still, I was not eager to sleep in her line of fire if I could help it.

"Now tell me about your week," Sam said, pushing back from the table and crossing one leg over the other.

I took our supper dishes to the sink, then came back and sat at the table across from him. Content with having my husband home, I hoped I'd never get over anticipating his homecoming anytime he returned from a trip, even if it had only been to Main Street, Abbotsville.

He and Lloyd had gotten home around five-thirty, stopping first at the Pickenses' house to unload a cooler of fish and drop off Lloyd along with his week's worth of dirty clothes.

Sam had spent the past two hours or so giving me a day-by-day account of the entire week, obviously enjoying again the activities of each day as he recounted what they'd done. I had so regretted Mr. Pickens having to cut short his fishing expedition, but the more Sam talked, the more I realized that it had been a precious time for him and Lloyd.

"That's a fine boy, Julia," Sam said, interrupting one day's account. "A fine young man, I mean. He has a good head on his shoulders, and he's good company. You and Hazel Marie can be proud of him. I already know that Pickens is."

"Oh, well," I said, trying not to smile too broadly. "You know I am. For years I kept watching for some of Wesley Lloyd's unattractive traits to come out, but so far none have. A lot of that is due to you, Sam. You've been part of Lloyd's raising as much as any of us."

Basking in the pleasure of a job well done, as evidenced by Lloyd's maturity, Sam and I smiled at each other.

Then he said, "Well, come on, tell me about your week. Anything going on in town I should know about?"

"Oh, nothing much," I said with a straight face. "Somebody got married. A few others are planning to. Another one is hoping to. Mildred is planning a party. A naked man came to visit. I got shot at, and Lillian speaks Japanese."

"Wha-at?"

I laughed. "She only knows a word or two, but that was enough."

"But who shot at you?" he demanded.

"Oh, that was Mildred, and according to her, she hit exactly what she was aiming at, which was the tops of a few pear trees. You might notice the next time you go out."

"My Lord," Sam said in a prayerful tone. Then, looking up at me, he asked, "I'm afraid to ask, but who was the naked man that came to visit?"

"I wish I knew." And I started telling him of the two visits I'd had by the unknown, undressed man.

"Why didn't you tell me?" Sam demanded. "I'd have come home. Was it the same man both times? Did you call the sheriff? Julia, why didn't you tell me?"

"Hold on," I said, putting my hand on his arm. "The man's not dangerous unless, of course, you have a weak heart. He's just such a surprise, you know. It's not something you'd ordinarily expect to see. And yes, we called the deputies after the second visit because I wasn't sure enough about the first one." I stopped to reconsider. "Still not, truth be told."

"My word," Sam said, rubbing his forehead, "I keep telling myself not to leave you alone, and here's another reason not to."

"Really, Sam, it wasn't as bad as it sounds. And he's not coming back. Lillian and I have already figured out that he only visits women who're alone. So since you're home, we've seen the last of him." None of that seemed to impress him, so I went on. "Of course, I'd really like to catch him. I want to know who it is who can be satisfied with so little."

"For goodness' sake, Julia, how do you know he is? There's no telling what he could do."

"No," I said, "he's quite safe, if you don't count the shock that the sight of him causes. I know, because I googled people like him."

"Well," Sam said, his voice heavy with irony, "that certainly reassures me."

He rose from the table and took a couple of turns around the kitchen. "I don't know what I'm going to do with you. Julia, honey, you worry me to death. There I was, off having the time of my life without a worry in the world, and here you were in danger from an unknown assailant and a half-crazy neighbor with a shotgun. I may never leave town again."

"Oh, it's not that bad," I said, patting his chair. "Come sit down and let me tell you about Helen and Thurlow. I sent you a text that they got married, but I don't have any more details. I sat with him one afternoon when Helen had some things to do, and I saw a different picture than what I'd expected. They may—and I emphasize *may*—really care for each other. Of course it could be that Thurlow simply depends on her, but very briefly I saw and felt something more.

"At least I hope so," I went on. "It makes me sick to my stomach to think of being married to someone as unpalatable as Thurlow Jones. I'd be throwing up all over the place."

"Well," Sam said with a laugh as he resumed his seat, "since Thurlow is apparently already taken, you don't have to worry about that. Now let's hear the rest of it. What else went on while I was gone?"

Relieved to move on to other subjects, I said, "Well, Sue and Bob Hargrove may be having second thoughts about their son-in-law-to-be. It seems that it was his idea that Christy drop out of medical school, and he has lots more ideas which he doesn't mind sharing—all for somebody else to execute. He's been in and out of the Hargrove house for the past week or so, making me think that doctors aren't quite as busy as they once were. Oh," I added with a slight eye roll, "and then there's LuAnne, who has found an unattached man with good manners, so things are looking up for her. I have my doubts about that, but see, Sam, other people have problems, too. It's not just me."

Sam smiled and reached for my hand. "I'll still think twice before leaving you alone again."

"And I hope you always will," I said, smiling back.

Thinking that I had given him enough to worry about, I put off telling him that Lillian was again considering the benefits of marrying Mr. Chester P. Dobbs—if, that is, he offered them to her.

And, feeling fairly sure that Sam would not have approved my decision to hire Mr. Pickens to dig into a friend's love life, I didn't mention that, either. Some things are better left unsaid, and if Eddie Cochrane was all he was cracked up to be, no one would ever have to know what I'd done.

So to engage his mind with other matters, I told Sam about Christy being upset with her mother for putting Travis in the guesthouse rather than in Christy's bedroom.

"Are young people that bold these days?" I asked. "I mean, I know, or at least I suspect, that they don't wait for wedding vows, but are they all so forward about it?"

"It sure seems so," Sam said, nodding. "Do you remember last year when they showed on the news the young man who got down on his knee and asked his girlfriend to marry him in front of hundreds of protesters—and television cameras, of course? It has to be captured on film, you know, else it never happened. I'll admit it was a sweet moment in the midst of rioting and looting and all the rest of it, but then"—he took a breath—"they spoiled it by blatantly announcing that she was pregnant, as if it was the normal progression of events: impregnation, then a public proposal, then a big, fancy wedding with everybody pretending that they haven't been living together for months."

"I do remember that, and I, too, was struck by the total lack of shame or embarrassment that they'd been doing before the wedding what only a wedding is supposed to give them license to do. I don't know, Sam, maybe we've been left behind by a culture run amok." And I wondered again at the rush to marry by Christy and Travis, which was none of my business but would explain a number of things.

"Maybe so," Sam said somberly, "but if so, I'm happy to be left."

Putting my hand on his, I said, "Me, too."

Chapter 35

Monday morning, and Sam was off to the Bluebird café for breakfast with his buddies while I looked over my notes on Christy's bridesmaids' luncheon. Satisfied that everything had been taken care of mainly by LuAnne, I was doubly pleased that we'd arranged to have the luncheon at the inn on the mountain rather than in my dining room. Fearing that Lillian might not have been available was one less thing to weigh on my mind because the fact of the matter was that she seemed to still have some hope that she would be Mr. Dobbs's chosen one.

She let it slip that morning when I asked why she seemed to be moping around. It came pouring out that he had been seen several times over the weekend riding around in the back seat of that old Cadillac with Miss Pearl, Janelle's mother, beside him.

"But what's he doing?" I asked. "Is he courting her now or is he warming her up to ask for Janelle?"

"Law, Miss Julia," Lillian answered, "I don't know, an' I don't know if even he knows. I think that ole man just enjoys havin' everybody want him."

"Yes, well, that would certainly help with one's self-esteem, although I wouldn't think he needed any help. He seems to have plenty of that already."

Lillian turned back to the sink and said, "I just wish I hadn't cooked all them pork chops for him. I didn't know this, but everybody thought my cookin' would win it for me. So now they think he's moved on while I'm grievin' over him."

"Oh, surely not. It's more likely that everybody thinks that you turned him down and he has to take second choice. Or who knows? Maybe third or fourth choice."

That brought a rueful smile to her face. "Not likely," she said. "Mr. Dobbs kinda started lookin' a few years ago as soon as his wife died. Folks started wonderin' who he'd pick to take her place before they got the casket closed. For a while it looked like he wadn't ever gonna remarry, but now that he's decided to, everybody's watchin' every move he makes." She stopped scrubbing a spot in the sink and turned to face me. "I just wish he'd go ahead and make up his mind and quit danglin' a big house an' a big car an' all them white hats in front of us. It just makes me mad as fire the way he's goin' about it."

"Lillian, for goodness' sake," I said. "We've been over this already. What he's dangling in front of you is years of nursing care, feeding and cleaning, and being at his beck and call twenty-four hours a day. You're well out of it if, in fact, you are because I'm convinced that you're the cream of the crop and he's smart enough to know it."

She smiled at that. "Well, all I know is I wish I'd quit thinkin' about it 'cause I know I don't want to be married to him." She gave another swipe across the sink. "I guess I just want him to make up his mind an' get it over with."

"Have you thought about this?" I asked. "That he might've thought that he was God's gift to women, but he's finding out that he isn't. Maybe he hasn't asked anyone because he's afraid everybody'll say no."

"No'm, I don't think so. Everybody who he's had dinner with or rode around with would jump at the chance to be Mrs. Chester P. Dobbs, it don't matter how old an' helpless he gets."

"Everybody except you," I said, "because you see beneath the surface and know what you'd be in for."

"Hm-m, yes'm," she said. "I guess so."

Lillian's continued vacillation over Mr. Dobbs didn't help my state of mind, although I simply could not imagine her actually wanting to marry the man. But who could understand the choices we make when it comes to a life partner? It's a settled fact, as I've said before, that we never fully know the ramifications of our choices until we've already made them.

But the nagging worry over Lillian had to be put aside when Sue Hargrove called and asked if she could drop by for a few minutes that morning.

I was happy to see her when she arrived, although from the tension on her face I knew she had more than a pleasant visit in mind and I thought I knew why.

"Julia," she said as we sat on the sofa in the living room, "I know you're tired of my leaning on you every time you turn around, but I need a clear head and somebody to tell me what to do. Bob can't or won't. He's so hurt that I end up trying to protect him."

"Why, Sue, what is going on? Surely the happy couple hasn't come up with another idea for the wedding?"

"No, it'll be at the church, but I want you to look at this and tell me what you think." Sue handed me an ecru informal with three curlicued initials on the front. "It came in the mail Saturday and I've been trying to interpret it ever since. Read it."

I opened the thick piece of stationery and read:

Dear Mrs. Hargrove,

Thank you for your kind invitation to the nuptials of Christy and Travis. Due to illness in the family, none of us will be able to attend.

Yours sincerely,

It was signed with an unreadable scrawl.

"This is from his mother?" I asked.

Sue nodded as tears sprang to her eyes. "I don't know what to think. It's so cold and formal that it makes me think something is wrong with us."

"Oh, Sue, no. You know that's not true."

"I don't know what to think. Maybe they don't want him to get married, I just don't know."

"Have you met any of his family?"

"No, and it looks like we never will. If Christy would just put the wedding off, Bob and I could invite Travis's family down so we could get to know each other. It's this rush to marry to fit in with Travis's residency plans that's causing the problem."

"I don't know, Sue," I said, reading the note again. "I'm wondering if there's not a rift in the whole family. I have to be honest and say that this note is barely polite."

"That's what Bob said."

"Have you asked Travis about it?"

"No, he had to go back to Durham this morning, but I showed it to Christy. She just said she wasn't surprised because Travis isn't close to his family. She didn't seem bothered by it, but I am."

"Yes, I would be, too. She's marrying not only Travis but his family as well. How many of them did you send invitations to?"

"About ten or so, I think. I did think it was strange that Travis's list was so short. The groom's list is usually about the same as the bride's, but he said he'd been away in school for so long that he'd lost touch. Anyway, this note from his mother is the only response I've had, and I'm thinking that it covers the wedding and the bridesmaids' luncheon as well. So I wanted you and LuAnne to know that Travis's mother and grandmother won't be coming."

Glancing at the note again, I asked, "And Travis hasn't said anything? Given any explanation?"

"Not a word. When they first told us about getting married, I asked Travis for his mother's phone number, thinking to introduce ourselves, but he said that she wasn't well and not to bother." Sue took the note from me and slipped it back into the envelope. "This is not what we wanted for Christy. It seems all wrong, and last night when Christy made a joke about eloping, I, well, it was almost the last straw, and I thought to myself, 'Why don't you?'"

"Completely understandable," I said. "But, Sue, you really should point out to Christy how family problems can become her problems. She should at least know what they are before becoming part of the family."

"I know. I just wish they would put things off for a while. I don't care that everything is reserved and planned. I'd feel so much better if they waited so that Christy would know what she's getting into."

"Just be ready to catch her if it comes to that," I said, aching for my friend's understandable concern.

Chapter 36

As soon as Sue left, I called LuAnne at the funeral home to let her know the change of plans. She was on her break, so I had to wait for her to come to the phone.

"LuAnne?" I said when she finally picked up. "Sorry to call on your break, but I figured you'd want to know about this as soon as possible. We need to decide what to do."

"Why? What's going on?"

"I really don't know, but Sue was just here showing me the reply to the wedding invitation that came from Travis's mother. I'll tell you the truth, LuAnne, I was shocked to read it. Just two sentences, one thanking her for the invitation and the other saying that none of them will be coming."

"*None* of them?"

"Not a one, and Sue and I think that probably covers our luncheon, too. In other words, we may not get a reply at all."

"Well, that's pretty tacky, especially since I've already bought a charm for his mother and grandmother to memorialize the day. I'm not sure the store will take them back."

"It doesn't matter," I said. "But the more I think about it, the more insulted I feel. We ought to wrap up those charms and send them along with a syrupy note saying how much we missed their company. They'd get the message of how we feel about them snubbing a wedding of this magnitude."

"Why, Julia, that would really turn the screws," LuAnne said. "We'd be killing them with kindness. I like it. But I guess the bridesmaids are all Christy's friends and cousins, although I wondered about that when I addressed the invitations. Travis doesn't have any sisters?"

"I don't know," I said, "but apparently Christy knew they wouldn't come and didn't ask them. You'd think that she would've talked to Sue long before this if his family is really on the outs with each other."

"It doesn't surprise me that she didn't," LuAnne said, then came out with a surprisingly perspicacious insight as she was wont to do now and then. "Believe me, Christy knows Travis has a family problem. She just didn't want to tell anybody, especially her parents, because they'd try to talk her out of marrying him. She's closing her eyes to all of it, thinking that it'll work out when they're married. It won't, of course, but she doesn't want to hear it."

"You're probably right," I said and sighed at the problems we create for ourselves. "I'll call the inn's dining room and tell them to prepare for two less. No need to pay for meals that won't be eaten." Preparing to end the call so that LuAnne would still have a few minutes left on her break, I said, "Well, we'll still have a nice time and I'm looking forward to it. Thank you again, LuAnne, for all you've done to get ready for it. You really know how to prepare for a party."

"I do, don't I?" she said with a complacency that surprised me. "It's just recently hit me that I have a knack for giving parties. In fact, I've been thinking about starting a party business. I'm getting tired of being around so many sad and grieving people all the time. I think it's rubbing off on me, but partygoers are happy and they're looking forward to a good time. I'm thinking I need to be around more people like that. So," she went on before I could respond, "don't you want to throw a party sometime soon?"

"No," I said, "but I know someone who does."

"Who?"

"Mildred. She mentioned to me just yesterday that she's thinking of having a big blowout—that's how she put it."

"Oh, my goodness! That would be perfect to start my business with. What would she be, Julia—a customer or a client?" And before I could respond, she answered herself. "A client, that's what she'd be. Or maybe a patron? What do you think?"

"I think," I said, "that you should think this through a little more. Are you going to keep the job you have and plan parties, too? Can you do both? What about when you have to work late or when there's a funeral at the same time a party is scheduled?"

"Oh, shoo, Julia, of course I've thought it through. The beauty part of being a party planner is that the dates are set up so far ahead of time, I'll know when I need to be off. I can arrange my hours here around that."

Yes, I thought, but funerals don't exactly fit in with party dates. Nobody sends out Hold the Date cards in case there's a funeral, but I didn't say anything. As a matter of fact, LuAnne may have come up with an ideal plan for herself. She was good at planning and preparing for whatever was needed. She never forgot anything. She knew who should be invited and who was too mad at somebody to be included. The only problem I could see would be the scarcity of party *givers*. Abbotsville was a fairly social community, but I doubted there were enough parties given to support a business dedicated to giving them.

"And besides," LuAnne went on, "I'll have the best help in the world. You know, if I need help to bring in extra chairs or to pick up things beforehand. Eddie's already promised to help me. So it's the perfect time to strike out on my own if I'm ever going to do it."

"Maybe so, but you know what they say when you start something new: 'Don't give up your day job.'"

"Don't be a party pooper, Julia," LuAnne said in a fairly sharp tone. "You don't know how seriously I've looked into this. Eddie told me that his wife had worked in a doctor's office, but she'd also sold cleaning supplies out of their garage for years and it really made a difference in their income. He helped her, of course, with deliveries and so forth, so he knows about customer lists, ordering, tax filings, and so forth. And he'll help me get started and not charge me a thing until I get established. That's hard to pass up, you know."

"Maybe you can start with one or two parties a month and see how they fit in with the funeral home schedule."

"Eddie thinks I ought to go for broke. He thinks it'll be too much for me to do two jobs at the same time. But with him helping, I think I can."

"LuAnne," I said as plainly as I knew how, "talk to your CPA and your lawyer before you do anything. A lot of people get in trouble because they don't know any better or don't want to know any better. I don't want the IRS coming after you."

"Oh, Julia, for goodness' sake, you worry too much."

"Yes, well, but I'm not in the Atlanta pen, either, am I?"

Finally getting off the phone, I was left with my nerves on edge. For LuAnne to give up a low-paying job with benefits for another low-paying job without benefits made no sense to me. Oh, I understood the attraction of owning a business, but it had to be a business that would support itself as well as its owner. And planning parties in a small town just did not seem to be a moneymaker to me. For instance, I gave two large parties a year—one in the spring when the azaleas bloomed and another early in December to open the Christmas season. These were called receptions or drop-ins or teas, depending on the level of formality I wanted to indicate. They were fairly large affairs that required a good bit of planning, which after years of doing them, I could do in my sleep.

In addition, I often gave small luncheons or dinner parties throughout the year for which I had an in-house planner by the name of Lillian.

In other words, I had no need of a party planner. I would hire LuAnne as an obligation to a friend and not because I needed her assistance. Frankly, though, I simply could not see how such a business could succeed in a small town, and it worried me that LuAnne's Eddie was encouraging her to jump into it. A man who'd held the same civic job for thirty or more years did not emanate much of an entrepreneurial spirit to my way of thinking.

Although, I mused, I may have misunderstood. Maybe Eddie was encouraging LuAnne to keep her job and plan parties on the side as his wife had done with cleaning agents.

That would have put me off right there. I wasn't one who would be eager to replicate a situation to suit someone else, but LuAnne would only see that parties weren't the same as Brillo pads.

I needed to talk to Mr. Pickens. As far as I knew, he'd done nothing to look into Eddie Cochrane's background, or if he had, he had certainly not reported to me. One thing was for sure, though, and that was that Eddie was having a great influence on LuAnne.

Chapter 37

After further consideration, though, I realized that I might be thankful to have access to a professional party planner if Lillian left me. In that case, not only the way I entertained but everything in the daily routine of my life would change. Losing her would be like the earth shaking and heaving and settling into different conformations. And if that happened, I'd be grateful to have LuAnne in charge of my social calendar.

On the other hand, however, I could just retire from all formal interactions that called for polishing silver, lighting candles, and serving cucumber sandwiches.

But I couldn't worry about that now. I needed to find out what Mr. Pickens had learned about Eddie Cochrane. Why, I ask you, was Eddie so eager for LuAnne to start a new business? Why was he so interested in what she did? Party planning didn't sound like a moneymaker to me. Why did it to him?

Hearing Sam come in and eager to learn what he thought of LuAnne's commercial plans, I hurried into the hall to meet him.

"That," I said, smiling a welcome, "was the longest breakfast on record. I'm surprised that the Bluebird didn't run you all off."

Sam laughed. "Oh, we adjourned hours ago. Several of us went over to the high school and watched the big earthmovers work. That's going to be a great campus when they finish." The county commission had finally committed to replacing a building or two of the city high school, something they'd put off doing for years.

"What's the latest news around town?" I asked, referring to the fact that I teased him about getting all the gossip along with the Bluebird's famous breakfasts.

We walked back to the library together. "Well," Sam said, sinking down onto the sofa, "we spent a good bit of time discussing the local night visitor, trying to decide if he's flashing or streaking or what. Jim Watson said he's displaying, like a male bird trying to attract a female."

"Oh, for goodness' sake," I said. "Does anybody think public nudity attracts anybody? Maybe somebody with a net, I guess."

Sam smiled. "Maybe so. The consensus was that he's not dangerous, but that he ought to be stopped before he gives some old lady a heart attack. But nobody had any good ideas of how to stop him since nobody knows who he is."

"I know. I have thought of everybody I know, and I just can't picture any of them making such an idiot of himself." I stopped and thought for a minute. "Actually, the one person who has the gall to do such a thing is the one person it couldn't possibly be."

Sam raised his eyebrows. "Thurlow Jones?"

"Right. He's just crazy enough to disrobe and run around shocking everybody. In fact, I'm surprised he hasn't ever done so. But not now. The poor man can't even turn over by himself, much less get out of bed. And, believe me, what Lillian and I saw was not shackled in casts."

"Milton Avery suggested that we set up watchers and try to catch him, but after I told them about Mildred patrolling the area, that idea got shot down pretty fast. Still, we all agreed that something ought to be done. We just couldn't decide what it should be." Sam laughed. "A fine group of vigilantes we turned out to be."

I smiled at the thought, but it lingered in my mind because something did indeed need to be done.

After a few minutes of discussing the weather, a new thought occurred to me. "Sam, do you realize," I said, "that not one person who's been visited by that man has any idea who he is?"

"What do you mean?"

"I mean that not Miss Vinnie or Ethyl Randolph or Mildred or Lillian or I have been able to describe him. Not one soul has been able to say 'He looked like so-and-so' or 'I thought he was somebody or another.' And I'll tell you the truth, I can't even describe his looks, and I was looking right at him through the windowpanes. I don't know if he's a blond or a brunette. I can't say if he's young or old, although the way he can run argues against being all that old. Lillian mentioned that she thought he wore a mask like the Lone Ranger wears, but I think I would've noticed that and I didn't." I frowned, trying to picture again my close-up view of the naked man. "I don't know why I can't picture what he looks like. The sheriff's dispatcher asked me to describe him and I couldn't do it just minutes after being face-to-face with him."

"Well," Sam said drily, "I'd say you were slightly distracted."

"That," I said with a laugh, "is undoubtedly true. But," I went on, recalling my earlier intention, "I wanted to tell you the latest news from LuAnne. She's apparently thinking of giving up her job, or trying to do two jobs at the same time, and her new boyfriend is encouraging her. I don't suppose you've met him, but have you heard anything about him?"

"I must not've since I didn't know she had a new boyfriend. Who is he?"

"His name is Eddie Cochrane and she met him at the funeral home when he came in to pay the loan he had to take out to bury his wife." And I went on to tell Sam about their dinner and luncheon dates and how LuAnne seemed to be heavily influenced by him. I told him everything I knew about Eddie Cochrane and everything I worried about concerning LuAnne's interest in him—everything, in fact, except what I had set into motion with a phone call to Mr. Pickens.

"Honey," Sam said, "the hardest thing in the world is to stop somebody who's plainly heading for a cliff when they're determined to run toward it. All you can do is point out the danger ahead, but who knows? She might do quite well once her business gets started. What kind of a business is it?"

"Planning parties."

Sam's eyebrows shot up. "Parties? You mean birthday, anniversary, wedding, and so forth parties?"

"I guess so. I'm not sure she's thought that far ahead, although she claims she has. And she could do all of those. She's very good with details. I just don't know if there's a need for such a business here in town, but what worries me is that Eddie seems to be encouraging her, and for all I know, he has no experience in opening a business or running one."

"Would you hire her—or them if he's in it with her?"

"Only if I didn't have Lillian. Otherwise, I'd hire them only because I'd feel obligated to help her out."

"Well," Sam said, picking up the newspaper, "you do have Lillian, so I wouldn't worry about it."

"I'm trying not to."

"Oh, by the way," Sam said, lowering the newspaper, "Bob Hargrove had breakfast with us this morning, and we rode together over to the high school. That son-in-law-to-be is coming back for a few days. Bob says that he'll be glad when they get married and things settle down. He says Sue gets so uptight when Travis is around that he's worried about her. From all that, I'd say that LuAnne should look into adding weddings to her business. She could relieve mothers of the bride from a lot of the details."

"That's not a bad idea except that wedding planning is sort of a distinct entity in itself. But the more LuAnne can offer, the more business she'll have. I keep thinking of Margaret Ridley—remember her? She's passed on now, but when I first moved here she was known for her parties. Every year on the second of January, she sent out Hold the Date cards to just about every woman in town—from top to bottom. She planned three parties for three days in a row for sometime in May when her yard was in full bloom, and each lady was invited for one specific day. And that was the only entertaining she did for the whole year. She said she got her obligations paid back all at one time when her house was clean and ready for company. And the beauty part of it was that she only had to clean and prepare the house once instead of three separate times. And after those three days, she just sat back and waited for everybody she'd invited to pay her back."

"Maybe," Sam said, "giving parties is more involved than I thought."

"Yes" I agreed, "there's certainly an art to it and a lot of strategic planning as well."

Chapter 38

Two days later the town, at least that part of town in which we lived, was in an uproar. Lillian came in late, saying she'd stopped at the grocery store and everybody was talking about it, so she'd waited around to get a consensus. She didn't put it quite like that, just said she wanted to hear what they were planning to do. Since most of the early-morning shoppers were women, the consensus was that the naked man needed to be caught and horsewhipped.

According to Lillian, they had been stirred up by the several sightings of the man during the previous evening, specifically during prime time when there was nothing on but reruns anyway.

Then our telephone started ringing with neighbors and friends asking if we were all right. As soon as I heard that he'd been in the vicinity, I made a few phone calls myself. I checked on Hazel Marie, although it took three tries before I no longer got a busy signal. She was all right even though she only had James between her and no help at all. Mr. Pickens was off again somewhere, making me think I should look into hiring an out-of-town investigator even though the Main Street merchants were forever urging us to buy local.

Then I called Mildred. "Are you all right?" I asked.

Answering with a question, she responded, "Shouldn't I be? What's going on?"

I sighed. "Well, it seems that the naked man was on the move last night. The sheriff got three or four calls, mostly reporting only glimpses or glances of what somebody thought they'd seen. Lillian heard all about it at the grocery store this morning."

"So he wasn't plastered to a window or dancing on a patio?"

"Apparently not, but it's worrisome all the same. It's as if he's working up to something."

"The thing to do," Mildred said, "is to have everybody buy a bottle of NyQuil. When that unclothed idiot learns he doesn't have an audience, he'll stay at home."

I had to laugh at the thought of a town of medicated sleepers. "I'm glad he didn't disturb you. But, Mildred, it might be a good idea to have your gardener stay a few nights in the pool house. Just having a man on the premises seems to be a deterrent."

"Well," Mildred said in her ironic way, "that's sad news to all the widows in town. If you haven't noticed, there're not enough men to go around. I know, because I've looked."

"Oh, Mildred," I said, laughing. "You're too much. Just remember, though, that Sam is home if you need any help or get worried or scared. I think the man is unhinged, which is bad enough, but I doubt that he's dangerous once you get over the shock of seeing him."

In fact, I thought but didn't say, the only danger associated with him was a woman with a shotgun.

After hanging up, I found myself feeling edgy and unable to stop thinking of who the naked man could be. I just could not believe that he was anyone I knew, which was about everyone in town. It seemed unlikely that a man would live a normal life up to a certain age—whatever that happened to be—and suddenly develop an irresistible urge to show off what is normally kept under wraps.

So if that was the case, the naked man had to be somebody who was new in town, which had the benefit of explaining why no one who'd seen him could identify him. I immediately thought of Eddie Cochrane, the only newcomer I knew, but certainly not the only newcomer to Abbotsville. People were always moving in, especially well-heeled retirees who stayed until they moved out in hearses. Since they generally spent the time in between on a golf course, I doubted that any of them had the energy to accost lonely women after dark.

Still, Eddie Cochrane stayed in my mind, making me more depressed the longer I thought of him. It would devastate LuAnne to learn that she'd been taken in by someone in thrall to deviant public conduct. That's what my Google search implied—that cavorting naked in public was compulsive behavior, therefore the poor man couldn't help himself.

I'm not sure I believed that. I mean, maybe he couldn't help undressing—he'd have to take a bath sometime—but he didn't have to go outside and scare people half to death.

I firmly put Eddie Cochrane out of my mind, telling myself that the only thing that recommended him as the naked man was the fact that he'd only recently moved to town. There could be a dozen or more who had also recently moved to town. I didn't know them all, and any one of them could be the offender.

Except, I thought, stopping in my tracks halfway up the stairs, the naked man had confined himself to a particular area of town, indicating some knowledge of who lived where. And in addition, unless she'd just recently had a sighting, LuAnne had not been honored by a visitation and, since she lived alone, you would think that she would be a prime target. Except, I thought again, if it was Eddie, no matter how strong his compulsion, he would not risk being recognized by someone who knew him so well. He would stay away from her.

I didn't like thinking these thoughts. I kept feeling more and more sorry for LuAnne, knowing how bad she would feel if any of them turned out to be true. I decided to track down Mr. Pickens and tell him I'd changed my mind. If the unclothed fool happened to be Eddie, I didn't want to be the one who identified him. I had no business being judge and jury over anybody.

And to that end, I turned around and went back downstairs just as the doorbell rang.

"Hey," Hazel Marie said as I opened the door. "If you're busy, I can come back another time."

"No, of course I'm not busy. It's good to see you. Come in." I held the door open for her while wondering what had prompted a drop-in visit from J. D. Pickens's wife and the friend with whom I had more in common than any other. She had been my first husband's paramour, an arrangement that had produced Lloyd, whose sixteen-year existence had redeemed any number of sins, large and small, as well as several of my own.

"I have to pick up the twins from preschool in a little while," she said, following me into the living room. "But I have a few minutes and I just have to talk to somebody."

"Have a seat," I said, pointing to the sofa. "Now tell me what's going on. It's not Lloyd, is it?" An immediate flash of concern for the boy ran through me.

"No, oh, no, Lloyd's fine. He had a wonderful time with Sam

on their fishing trip. But I declare, Miss Julia, he's growing up so fast I can barely stand it. He's thinking of colleges these days."

"My goodness," I murmured.

"But, listen, I don't know what bothers me the most—what Miss Ethyl told me or J.D.'s reaction to it. I couldn't believe that he could be so insensitive as to laugh when I told him what she'd said. After thinking about it, though, I'm wondering if I was wrong, but at first he just made me so mad."

I understood completely. J. D. Pickens could enrage me by being infuriatingly right as well as being infuriatingly pleased with himself for being right. But I knew better than to run him down to Hazel Marie. She might be angry with him momentarily, but he could do little wrong in her eyes. I veered the conversation onto another track.

"You mentioned Miss Ethyl. You mean Ethyl Randolph, your neighbor?"

"Yes. See, I'd had her on my mind ever since she was scared out of her wits last week when that man showed up in her yard. So I made some cookies yesterday and took them to her, and Miss Julia, she's still not over the trauma she suffered."

"Didn't she fall or something? I hope she didn't break anything."

"No, but she did fall from the surprise or shock or something, because apparently the man just appeared out of the dark, right in front of her. He was close enough to touch, or for him to touch her. Anyway, I visited for a little while because she was still so shaken by the awful experience that she couldn't stop crying. Bless her heart, she just sat there dabbing at her eyes with a monogrammed handkerchief while tears just flowed down her face."

"Didn't it happen last week sometime?"

"Yes, and I thought it was a little strange that she was still so traumatized. I mean, crying and all. But then she started telling me about it, how she'd gone out back to put something in the garbage can, and when she turned around, there he was—as naked, she said, as the day he was born. She said she was so shocked that she stepped back and tripped and then she sat down hard and fell back so that she was looking up at him. And he just stood there, looming over her. She said she just knew he was going to ravish her and then she really started crying." Hazel Marie stopped, squinched up her mouth, and went on. "Miss Julia, you know how I love to read those little romance novels and somebody's always getting ravished in them. But I'd never heard of it really happening until Miss Ethyl thought it was going to."

"You mean . . . ?"

"No, but she thought it was. She said she was so frightened with him standing over her and looking down at her that her whole body just went limp as she grasped clumps of grass in both hands and waited for her fate. She said she knew she couldn't run—she's scheduled for a knee replacement next month—so she was at his mercy. But then that man whacked the garbage can with a stick or a walking cane or something and turned around and left her lying there."

"My word," I said. "How terrifying."

"Yes, but that's when J.D. started laughing. He didn't have a bit of sympathy for her even though the experience was worse for her than for most."

"Why? I mean, if he didn't even touch her . . . ?"

"Well," Hazel Marie said, "I didn't know this, but she's never been married—"

"I thought she was a widow."

"I did, too, but, no, she's a single lady and always has been, so I finally understood why she kept saying, 'I had no idea; I had no idea.' It—*he*—was all so new to her because she's lived such a sheltered life, and I guess the shock of seeing the real thing just kinda unhinged her."

"Hazel Marie," I said, almost strangling with my urge to laugh. "Honey, that's the funniest story I've ever heard. Please don't be mad at me, but the thought of Miss Ethyl going seventy-something years before learning what she was missing is hilarious." And I demonstrated it by giving into a fit of laughter.

"I'm sorry," I said, wiping a few tears from my face. "I know it wasn't funny to her, but . . ." And I was off again.

Hazel Marie's face softened into a smile, then finally she joined me in a full-bodied laugh. "I know," she said finally. "I mean, I didn't at first. I just felt so sorry for her, thinking how afraid she must've been, and I got mad when J.D. saw only the funny side." She wiped her eyes and said, "Typical male reaction, I guess—they're so proud of themselves. I tried to explain it to him, telling him that she was still afraid because she kept reliving the experience over and over in her mind. She said she even dreamed about it.

"But J.D. said, 'Honey, she may still be afraid, but I'll tell you the truth, it sounds like she was more disappointed than anything else.'"

Chapter 39

When Hazel Marie left with plans to bake another batch of cookies to comfort Miss Ethyl, I hurried to the kitchen.

"Lillian," I said, "you'll never believe this, but . . ." And I told her about Miss Ethyl's harrowing experience. "I know I shouldn't laugh, but it seems to me that there's a huge difference between rape and ravishment. Of course up to this point at least, the naked man hasn't been interested in either one. He certainly had his chance with Miss Ethyl and he didn't take it."

"I know about rape," Lillian said, "but not about the other. What's the difference?"

"Well, I'm no expert, but I think willingness or lack of it on the part of the woman is the difference. At least that's the way Hazel Marie's romance books tell it. The ravish*ee* always falls into the arms of the ravish*er* by the end of the book. But it seems that my Google search was right. The naked man is only interested in showing off. Still, I've had about enough of it. The unfulfilled expectation is playing havoc with some sensitive souls in this town."

Picking up the ringing phone, I said, "Hello?"

Hazel Marie asked, "Has Helen called you?"

"No, is she . . . ?"

"Then let's hang up so that she can." And she hung up.

"Well," I said, staring at the phone in my hand, "that's strange." But I clicked it off, too, and waited for the phone to ring again.

When it did, I snatched it up. "Yes?"

Mildred Allen said, "Has Helen called you?"

"No, but . . ."

"Call me back when she does." And she hung up.

I sat down and watched the phone, waiting for it to ring. When it didn't for several minutes, I wondered if I'd misunderstood. Maybe they meant that I was supposed to call Helen. Why? Did she need help with Thurlow? Had he gotten worse? Was he on the way to the hospital?

Tentatively, I tapped in Helen's number and got a busy signal. There was nothing to do but wait and wonder how Hazel Marie and Mildred knew that Helen would call me.

A prayer chain, of *course*! That's what it was. I readily admit that over the years we had become somewhat lax about availing ourselves of the benefits of participating in a prayer chain. To tell the truth I had all but forgotten about either starting a chain or being one of the links. Yet twenty years ago a prayer chain would be started every week or so with prayers being requested on behalf of someone we knew or knew of. It was an excellent way to stay abreast of the current events in town, like when Evelyn Bennett had to go to the emergency room after cutting her hand with a bread knife, or when Mrs. Earl Sanderson had her third great-grandchild, or when Bud Langston walked out on his wife and headed for Harrah's casino over on the Cherokee Indian reservation and for parts unknown afterward.

In other words, the prayer chain had been a quick and easy way to pass along the latest news and to give the participants a reason to stop a few minutes in a busy day to engage in prayer. It also encouraged a sense of community—everybody knew what was happening to everybody else. That was all well and good until you yourself became the subject of a prayer request. I knew from experience that having your own intimate details discussed and passed along was not always a comfortable spot to be in, especially since requests for prayers often fell into the category of gossip. Some links in a prayer chain insisted on knowing all the details, factual or speculative, so they could, as they claimed, pray intelligently. As if the Lord didn't know what was going on.

Of course Helen was the least likely among us to fall back on the comfort of having all of her friends praying for her. She was much too self-sufficient to think of needing that much attention, as well as too self-contained to admit she had a problem in the first place.

But still the phone didn't ring, so I began to wonder if Helen had forgotten me. Or maybe, I thought, she didn't intend to include me. Just before I started having my feelings hurt or becoming indignant at being left out, my phone finally rang.

"Julia? It's Helen, can you talk?"

"Can I talk?" I took a deep breath. "Helen, I've waited thirty minutes for you to call. Of course I can talk."

"Well, I'm organizing a committee to put a stop to that crazy man who's upsetting the entire town. We need a way to let one another know when he's on his way from one house to the other like he was last night. He was here—I saw him from the bedroom window, then Miss Vinnie saw him again at her house, and I've just heard from Joan Curtis. She lives in the Oldham house on Taft Street, and her husband is out of town for a few days, which, she said, is very unusual. So tell me how that man would know she would be alone."

"Oh, my," I said as a shiver ran down my back. "That is scary to think about."

"Yes, and I'm tired of being scared. I've already figured out that he goes after women who live alone, as well as women who're alone temporarily, like you, Julia, when Sam was out of town. And I'm assuming that since Thurlow can't get out of bed, I qualify as a woman living alone because this is the second time he's been in our yard—that I know of. But, and here's the question, how does he know what's going on in our homes—how does he know who's home and who's not?"

"I've wondered that myself," I said. "But don't discount some other possibilities. He may get around more than we know. He could be a mailman or a garbage collector and have ways of figuring out who's alone. He's been at my house two or three times that I know of, but I'm not sitting up watching for him, so he could've been here without my knowing it."

"I know," Helen said, "and that worries me, too. What is he doing around our houses when we don't even know he's on the premises?"

"I wonder, too. Maybe he sits in the bushes and just watches. But it's very strange that he seems to know so much about the people in this area. Except he could be visiting people in other areas of the town on the nights he's not around here."

"No," Helen said. "I posed that very possibility when I talked to the sheriff earlier today. He told me that they've gotten no reports of a naked man from any other area of the entire county—just the few blocks around us." Helen paused, then said, "I'll tell you the truth, Julia, the sheriff did not seem all that interested when I pointed it out to him."

"Keep that in mind in November. I'll get some pamphlets to you so you'll know who to vote for." Having done my duty to Etta Mae, I returned to the purpose of the call. "Anyway, what kind of organizing are you doing?"

"I just think that we all should get together and make some plans. For instance, if somebody sees him, she could call whoever lives nearby, who would then be on the lookout to see which way he goes. We might be able to pin down where he lives or identify the car he drives. So," Helen summed up, "what do you think?"

"I think it's a whole lot better than sitting around wondering if he's outside looking in. But, Helen, be very careful. Mildred has already shot at him, and we don't want to encourage anybody to take up arms."

"My goodness, no. But can you come over about three today? I'll have a large map and we can track him on that. If he wants to be seen, we'll give him what he wants."

After concluding the call, I felt a whole lot better. At least we'd be doing something, which was better than sitting around waiting for something to happen. I went out to the kitchen and got out my makeshift map. It really wasn't detailed enough, so if Helen had an actual map, we'd be able to tell how far apart the targeted houses were as well as trace the man's path on any particular night.

Hearing from all the other victims would also tell us something else—the timing of the man's escapades. Was he out at all hours of the night? It certainly seemed so since he'd been at my house in the early evening in a rainstorm and again at three o'clock in the morning. When did he sleep? And another thing—did he show up in front of some lonely woman on specific nights of the week? Did he venture out on the same night of the following week? He could be a traveling salesman or a shift worker.

We needed to start a dossier in which everything anybody knew about him was listed, compared, and filed. When that was done, chances were that somebody who was meeting at Helen's house today would know exactly who he was.

Chapter 40

But, no, it didn't work out that way. There were about twelve or so ladies who gathered at Helen's or, to be more specific, Thurlow's house, and most of us were too entranced with the decorative changes Helen had made to turn our minds to entrapping a naked man. She allowed each lady as soon as she entered the foyer a few minutes to look around, peek into the several rooms on each side, then began to herd us into the library, where folding chairs and a large map of Abbot County had been set up.

I found an empty chair beside Sue Hargrove and took it, speaking to her as I did. She looked tired and strained, which, of course, I did not mention. I just said, "I didn't know that you'd seen the naked man, Sue. He's really getting around."

"Oh, I haven't seen him." She smiled grimly. "I've been too busy to look out a window, but one of my neighbors has. So I thought I'd better be a part of whatever Helen has in mind."

"Well, I'm glad to see you. How are the wedding plans?"

"Don't ask," Sue said with a twist of her mouth. "Let's talk sometime."

I nodded as Helen rapped on the table to get our attention.

We settled down and waited to hear what we could do to put an end to a community nuisance.

Helen was an experienced organizer of committees, ad hoc and otherwise, and she got us on track right away by stating the problem. "I am absolutely incensed," she said, "that this man is allowed to flout the laws against trespassing, indecency, and endangering the citizenry. It's time to put a stop to his free-ranging activities, and if the sheriff won't do it, we will."

"Amen," Miss Vinnie said, and everybody clapped in agreement.

"The dispatcher had the nerve to snicker when I called," Mary Beth Winston said, "even though I'd been scared out of my wits. I don't care what anybody says, a buck naked man looking in your picture window isn't normal."

I hadn't heard that Mary Beth had had a sighting or that Inez Whitman and Sarah Griffin had as well. But looking carefully at the large map at the front of the room, I could see that their homes were not only marked in red but were well within the vaguely circular boundary that Helen had drawn around the area where the naked man had appeared.

Sarah said, "Well, at least he made me decide to go into assisted living. I'm putting my house on the market next week if anybody's interested."

"It seems to me," Helen said, using a pointer to illustrate what she was saying, "that he lives or stays temporarily either right in the center of this area or right outside the circle. He has to be planning ahead how and where he can go to be safe. I'm inclined to think that he's close enough to be on foot, but everybody should listen out for a parked car on the street suddenly starting up, say around ten or eleven at night."

"Later than that, too, Helen," I said. "He was at my house at three a.m. last week."

"I think," Miss Vinnie said, "that we should ask our neighbors if they have anybody visiting them. I mean, this just recently started up, so he could be somebody from out of town."

"Oh, I hope it is," Sarah said. "I keep looking at every man I see, wondering, 'Is it you? Is it you?'"

"I know what you mean," the lady beside her said. "I'd just hate for him to be a neighbor who has shoveled my walk or brought in my groceries."

"Oh, that would be terrible," somebody else said. "I hope it's a teenager doing something on a dare and not somebody I know."

"It's not a teenager," Mildred said firmly. "He'd pick a different audience if it was."

It took a minute, but a ripple of laughter crossed the room as we thought of the unlikelihood of a teenager being attracted to those of us of a certain age, which was all of us.

Helen rapped on the table to regain our attention. "Ladies, ladies, I'm passing around a sheet of paper. Please put your names and phone numbers on it. Ellie, my helper, will make a copy for each of you, so don't leave without one. I've already reduced the map and made copies of it for you. Now, remember, if you see the naked man or even think you see him, check the map and call your neighbors to watch for him. What we want is the *direction* in which he goes so we can track him. If it's always the same way, we may be able to figure out where he is when he's not out showing off."

I raised my hand. "Helen, we should try to determine the timing, too. We need to know if he's out wandering around on the same days of the week every week, although it seems as if he's not around some weeks at all. I mean, there're a few days when nobody sees him and then he'll be seen several days in a row. We might be able to determine if he's on a schedule or something."

"Yes, good idea," she said. Then she said to the room, "When the paper gets to you, jot down the date or dates of your sightings and I'll collate them."

Ethyl Randolph leaned over to Hazel Marie and whispered, "She'll do what to them?"

Hazel Marie whispered back, "Line them up, I think."

After passing out copies of the paper listing the appearances of the naked man, as well as the days and times that they had occurred, Helen urged us to let it be known if and when we see him again.

"Enter these phone numbers in your cell phones," Helen said, "and keep your phones near you, especially at night. If you see him, call your neighbors who live in the direction he's going in, then call me."

"Even if it's the middle of the night?" Miss Vinnie asked. "Some people have reason to be up then, but not everybody."

"Yes," Helen said. "We want everybody to be on the lookout so we'll know where he goes and especially where he leaves the area. That, I hope, will tell us where he lives and who he is."

"What if we're in a car?" Miss Ethyl asked. "Like we're coming home from a prayer meeting or something? You're not supposed to use a phone while you're driving."

"Well, Ethyl," Helen said a little tiredly, "use your horn. Make some noise and keep on making it. What you want is to get somebody's attention so they'll know to watch for him and see which way he goes. And to let the next person know he's on the way." Sounding as if she hoped not, she asked, "Any more questions? Anybody have anything else to add?"

I stood up and said, "This probably won't amount to anything, but Lillian found a man's sock in my yard the morning after the night it rained so heavily. I turned it in to the sheriff and it's been sent to a criminology lab. I don't know what they can determine from it, so I'm just reporting it."

I sat back down as someone asked what it looked like.

"Oh," I said, standing again. "It was black with little white scribbles on it."

"Oh, my goodness," a voice in the back said. "My dentist has a pair just like that."

A murmur of alarm ran through the room, but Helen quickly took charge. "Belk's had those exact same socks on sale. I bought four pairs for Thurlow, but believe me, he hasn't been running through anybody's yard."

Then she thanked us for coming and dismissed us. So much for learning anything from a stray sock.

As I walked outside, Sue hurried to join me. "Did you walk?" she asked.

"Yes, I needed the exercise."

"Then let me drive you home."

I was only too happy to crawl in beside her, especially since it looked as if we'd get another shower soon. Sue drove the three blocks to my house, then pulled to the curb, put the car in park, and turned off the ignition. She wanted to talk.

"Sorry, Julia, for using your shoulder to cry on, but I sometimes think that I'll lose my mind before this wedding is over."

"I'm so sorry that you're having a hard time," I said, "but don't worry about my shoulder. Cry on it anytime you want. What's going on now?"

"Criticism," Sue said. "I can't do anything without Christy criticizing the way I do it or for doing it at all. It's as if she's been saving it all up for years. Just this morning I told her that the florist needed to know what kind of flowers she wanted in her bouquet, and she told me that I worried too much about unimportant things. Then she said that I've been buried in this dinky little town too long, that I'm not aware of what's going on in the world, and that nobody's interested in Emily Post or Amy Vanderbilt any longer. My problem, she said, is that I'm not *woke*."

"Not *woke*? What does that mean?"

"I don't know, but I'll tell you, Julia, we have spent a fortune on her education—private schools, prep school, semester abroad, private university, medical school, and so on, and she talks like a street person who's never been in a classroom, and half the time I don't know what she's talking about."

Sue wasn't the only one. There were so many new words in the culture and on the market I'd never heard of that it was as if I'd slept a year or so instead of overnight. And everybody except me tossed them around in conversation as if the words could be found in the *Oxford English Dictionary*. Words like *woke, cancel, Zoom, FaceTime*, and so on no longer meant what I'd thought they meant—they were part of a whole new language. I couldn't keep up with them and figured that if I'd lived this long without needing them in my vocabulary, I could just keep on without them.

But I hated to hear how unreasonable Christy was being with her mother and how deeply it was hurting Sue. The pre-wedding weeks should have been a time precious to both of them, yet it wasn't. I may have been prejudiced, but it seemed to me that it was more Christy's fault than Sue's. And I wondered if Christy was as prickly and outspoken with her fiancé as she was with her mother, but I doubted it.

Just one more thing to worry about because it was no way to begin a lifetime together.

Sue seemed to have read my thoughts. She brought me back to the here and now by saying, "I'm really concerned about her, Julia. When she first came home she was so excited and thrilled about Travis and the wedding plans and teasing me about planning an old-fashioned wedding. But lately she's been quiet, almost sullen, and nothing I do pleases her. And it all started when I put my foot down about them sleeping in the same room. But," she said in her own defense, "it's my house, and Christy should've known how I'd feel about that. Anyway, she's unhappy and I don't know what to do about it."

"Maybe it's just wedding jitters," I said. "A lot of brides-to-be have second thoughts as it gets closer."

"Well, if it is," Sue said, "I hope she has third and fourth thoughts about it. Travis is as pleasant and thoughtful as he can be to me and to Bob, but I'm finally seeing that all the complaints and suggestions and criticisms from Christy start with him. He passes them on to her, who unloads them onto us."

"Well, my goodness," I said, "that's downright devious. It's no wonder that Christy isn't her usual cheerful self. She's between a rock and a hard place, and so are you and Bob."

"I know," Sue said miserably. "And I don't know what to do except pray about it, which I'm doing." She stopped, swallowed hard, and added, "Constantly."

Chapter 41

After a few more minutes of platitude-laden comments, which were all I could offer my friend, I thanked Sue for the ride and went into the house. It was obvious to me and to Sue that Christy was headed for an unhappy marriage, but what could be done if Christy herself didn't see it?

But maybe she was beginning to, I thought, and comforted my own concerns by hoping that she was. I mentally added Christy and Sue, then Bob, and to be on the safe side Travis as well, to my prayer list. Then I called Mr. Pickens to tell him what I'd decided to do.

"Janelle?" I said when she answered his phone. "Julia Murdoch here. May I speak to Mr. Pickens, please?"

In his curt, take-charge way, Mr. Pickens immediately took my call. "What's up, Miss Julia?"

"I'm having second thoughts, Mr. Pickens, about interfering in a friend's affairs and—"

"They're not having an affair," he said. "At least not yet. They're still in the getting-to-know-you stage, which is pretty close to coming to an end. I'd say almost any day now."

I was shocked into silence for he was telling me more than I'd asked for. I mean, how did he know? I hadn't hired him to peek into bedroom windows or to listen in on private conversations. What LuAnne did in her spare time should not have been any of my business.

"Mr. Pickens," I finally managed to say, "I want to unhire you. Please send me a bill for what you've already done and don't do any more. I'm ashamed of myself for going this far, and I want to stop it now."

"Uh-huh," he said, completely unfazed at being fired. "You want what I've already found out? You might as well since you'll be paying for it."

"Well, I guess I do, since you put it that way."

"Okay, I'll send a written report with my bill, but the subject has no criminal activities on the books, not even a traffic citation. His taxes have been paid on time. His only outstanding debt is to the Good Shepherd Funeral Home. He's on Social Security and he gets a small check every month from a retirement account from the city of Charlotte. So far he's about the most boring subject I've ever had, but I'm ready to dig into his personal life. That's where we'll find what you're looking for, if it's there to find. So hold on to your hat."

"No, you hold on to yours, Mr. Pickens. I don't want you to go any further. This was not a good idea, and I want it stopped. Please send me a bill, and our business will be concluded."

"Then thank you for your business," he said, completely unperturbed by losing a client. "I'm here if you need me again."

"I think not," I said. Then after a second, I added, "Remember, Mr. Pickens, not a word of this to a soul."

I thought my conscience would settle down and stop bothering me once I'd let Mr. Pickens go. It didn't. It just switched subjects on which to trouble me.

What if, I thought, Eddie Cochrane was the man who was displaying himself to elderly ladies who thought they had put such possibilities long behind them? What if one or more of them had a sudden heart attack brought on by fear or anticipation? What if I could have brought an end to the speculation about the naked man's identity as well as changed the number one topic of conversation at every barbershop, hair salon, and bridge club in town? And most important, what if I could've saved LuAnne from the embarrassment of having been taken in by a wolf in sheep's clothing or, rather, in no clothing at all? And it could've been done simply by keeping Mr. Pickens on my payroll with no one being the wiser.

No, I thought, much better to leave it to Helen and her crew of up-in-arms housewives, retired schoolteachers, and widow ladies. That way no one person, namely me, could be blamed when the great reveal occurred. Because there was one thing I could count on: LuAnne would never in this world forgive me if I had anything to do with not only revealing Eddie Cochrane as the compulsive disrober but in putting him away.

For surely, I assured myself, whoever he was would be put away, either in jail or in a hospital, although there did seem to be a revolving door on both of them. He could be back on the street before we turned around.

And it struck me that even if it was Eddie, not a woman among us would be able to pick him out of a lineup because nobody had

had the presence of mind to look at his face. Not a soul would be able to make a facial identification even if he'd been caught red-handed or bare-bottomed.

The more I thought of Christy and her mother, to say nothing of LuAnne with her hopes for the future and Lillian with her wavering over Mr. Dobbs, the lower my spirits dropped. And I might as well add Etta Mae Wiggins to the list, because who knew what she would do. Weddings—the planned ones as well as the hoped-for ones—were supposed to be happy, joyous occasions, and not a one of these seemed to qualify.

I wandered into the kitchen, sat down at the table, and heaved a sigh. "Well, Lillian," I said, "Helen has us set up to identify the naked man, except if he's new in town we won't know who he is even if we meet him face-to-face. I don't know how it's going to work out, but I guess doing something is better than doing nothing. And on top of that," I went on, "I've been looking forward to a lot of weddings taking place, but they all seem to be falling apart."

Lillian checked on the roast in the oven. Then she looked up and asked, "Who all's gettin' married 'sides Christy?"

"Why, you for one. At least you were considering the possibility. And Etta Mae is about to marry the man she's wanted for years, yet I haven't heard a word from her. She may have changed her mind for all I know. And we all wish that Janelle would have better luck than Mr. Dobbs, although I don't mean to disparage the man even though he's hardly suitable for a teenage bride. And the biggest dud of all was Helen and Thurlow's wedding, which took place in secret so we didn't have a chance to talk about it and be shocked by it. And now Sue Hargrove is having heavy doubts about Christy's choice and Christy may be, too. And here we are in the wedding month of June and the invitations have gone out, yet the Hargrove family all seem to be miserable." I sighed again. "I declare," I said, "there just seems to be a cloud of dread hanging over all of us, and that's not the way weddings should be."

"It's that nekkid man's fault," Lillian said. "He's got everybody all upset and scared and scandalized so they can't think of nothin' else."

"You may be right," I said. "But Helen has some ideas of how to find out more about him. But you know what I just thought of? He keeps coming back to the same places. For instance, he hasn't been to your house, has he? Or to any of your neighbors'?"

"No'm, not that anybody knows of. But I'm still worried that he'll show hisself to Latisha and scare her to death. A sight like that could stunt her growth."

"You're right," I said, "but more and more it looks as if he's confining himself to older women who live alone or who happen to be alone. Which shows how strange he is in the first place. I just hope that Helen will be able to discover who he is. But remember that you and Latisha can move over here any time you get nervous about being alone. Now that Sam is home, I doubt he'll be coming back here. And if he doesn't, it will show that he knows more about us than he should, and that's really scary."

My phone rang then, interrupting my soliloquy on craziness in general.

"Julia?" Mildred Allen said when I answered. "I've made up my mind. I'm going to have a party and I want you to hold the date—the first Saturday in July. Christy's wedding is the third Saturday in June, so two weeks later will be perfect. We'll celebrate Independence Day with barbecue and music and fireworks and anything else I can think of. What do you think of that?"

"I think it's a grand idea. What can I do to help?"

"Not a thing, although I might think of something later on. I'm going to get invitations in the mail right away so people won't plan beach trips and so on. I may even bring Horace home for a few days, but on second thought, I probably won't. Bless his heart, he wouldn't know where he was. Anyway, put it on your calendar because I'm counting on you and Sam being here."

"We'll look forward to it," I said and felt my spirits begin to lift. Maybe, I thought, a party was exactly what I needed.

Chapter 42

The night was quiet with no telephones ringing, which meant, I hoped, that our night visitor had not been on the loose. Maybe he had heard of Helen's plan to entrap him and reveal his identity. If he craved attention, he'd certainly get it from her if she caught him. She'd have his picture in the local paper as well as in the Asheville *Citizen Times*, and who knows? He might even be shown on television, although in that case he'd be adequately covered or blurred out.

When Lillian came in that morning a few minutes late, her arms full of white paper sacks, she said, "Nothin' sounded good to me this mornin', so I went to the bakery. I got some honey buns an' some cinnamon rolls, an' I hope you or Mr. Sam don't have your mouths set for bacon an' eggs 'cause I'm not in the cookin' mood."

"That's fine," I said, "but I hope you're not getting sick. Do you feel all right?"

"I feel better'n I thought I would if you want to know the truth. Mr. Dobbs fin'lly proposed to Janelle last night, an' now that he's done it an' got it out of his system, I'm glad."

"Oh, my goodness," I said, patting my chest. "What did she

say? How did he do it? Does that mean that Miss Pearl is okay with it? Tell me what happened, Lillian."

"Well, the way I heard it was like this, an' I heard it straight from Miss Pearl herself. He talked it over several times with her, an' it took a while to get straightened out 'cause all along she thought he'd been courtin' her. But she was fin'lly all right with it, 'specially when she thought of all the benefits not only to Janelle but to her, too. Like livin' with them an' helpin' with the baby when they move into that big blue house 'cause his son that lives there now with his family is gonna build another one."

"Well, I guess that's better than them all living crowded together, but it sounds like all the plans were made before Janelle was asked what she thought."

"Yes'm, that's about what happened," Lillian said as she stacked rolls and buns on a plate, "but Mr. Dobbs—like I already figured out—he's not used to havin' his plans changed."

"You mean—?"

"I mean he come to see Janelle last night an' brought a great big flower arrangement about the size of a casket spray an', from what I hear, a great big diamond ring, 'cause he was already gettin' nervous about her turnin' him down 'cause he's so old an' rickety. I mean he was already beginnin' to see that every woman over fifty years old in town would jump at the chance to marry him, but not every teenage girl would. 'Specially not every teenage girl as smart as Janelle."

"Sounds like he was trying to dazzle her with flowers and diamonds."

"Oh, yes'm, that's what he was tryin' to do. An' Miss Pearl said that he offered to throw in all the first Mrs. Dobbs's white hats, too, but Janelle said she didn't wear hats. An' she wouldn't take his flowers 'cause she said she didn't have a vase big enough, an' she appreciated him offerin' her a ring, but she was pretty sure that the first Mrs. Dobbs was wearin' that very ring in her casket when Janelle went with her mama to the visitation an' she was pretty sure it wouldn't fit her."

"Surely he wasn't going to move it straight from one hand to the other?"

"Yes'm, that's what he was doin', all right. He prob'bly thought why buy a ring when I already got one? An' most ladies wouldn't care where it come from as long as they got it."

"So," I said, "Janelle turned him down? How did he take it?"

"Well, the way Miss Pearl told it was that Janelle went to bed an' left Mr. Dobbs an' her in the livin' room. An' he stayed a couple of hours, ate supper with Miss Pearl an' everything, so he could say bein' turned down really didn't bother him. He was just offerin' to help Janelle out 'cause he felt sorry for her."

"I guess," I said, "he has to uphold his dignity any way he can. But who knows? It may be the truth. He has more sense than to think Janelle would be in love with him."

"Yes'm, but you got to give him credit for tryin'. If he hadn't tried, he'd never know if Janelle would or if she wouldn't."

I suddenly sat up straight in my chair and said, "I just thought of something, Lillian. If there's one person in this town who knows everybody and who everybody else knows, it's Mr. Dobbs. He gets around all over the place, talking to people, and keeping up with what's going on, and who's going and who's coming. He's like Abbotsville's goodwill ambassador."

"Yes'm, he sure is."

"Well, I'm thinking that he may know more about the naked man than any of us. He may even be able to figure out who it is if he put his mind to it. Why don't you invite him over here for a glass of lemonade one afternoon?"

"No'm," Lillian said, shaking her head, "I don't mind givin' him some lemonade, but if I invite him over, you know what he'll think. An' everybody else will, too."

"No, what?"

"That I'm chasin' after him, 'specially since Janelle turned him down."

"Oh, Lillian, surely not, but if so I can fix that. I will issue the invitation and we'll visit with him in the living room—all proper and aboveboard."

Lillian took her time folding a dishcloth, then she said, "All right, if you think he can help find that crazy man. But I don't want nobody thinkin' I'm tryin' to be next in line after Janelle."

"You know I wouldn't think that since I've always thought you were first in the first place. I'll write a note to Mr. Dobbs if you don't mind handing it to him on your way home. You'll see him, won't you?"

"He's usually settin' out under that big tree next to his pest office. I'll pull over an' let Latisha hand it to him. But I'm not gonna smile at him or hang around to talk to him either there or here at the house 'cause everybody'll be talkin' about me runnin' after him if I do."

"Oh, I don't blame you," I said, properly aghast at the thought. "You'll just be doing a favor for me. But I will ask you to make the lemonade—you know I never get it sweet enough and I'd hate to squinch his mouth up so much he couldn't talk. You wouldn't even have to join us in the living room if you don't want to—"

"I don't," she said. "Miss Julia, you jus' don't know how people talk. An' first thing Mr. Dobbs is gonna do is tell everybody that Miss Julia Murdoch asked his opinion about a town problem 'cause he'll be so proud of that. But even worse, he'll think I'm tryin' to edge into Janelle's place 'cause he'll need something to make him feel good again after she throwed him over."

"My goodness," I said with a smile, "I wasn't aware of all the ramifications of a simple effort to rid the town of a pest, but Mr. Dobbs could be the very one to do it."

I went into the library and drew from its box an engraved informal with its thick matching envelope. Then in my best girls' school script I wrote the following:

Dear Mr. Dobbs,

Would you be so kind as to join me tomorrow afternoon between the hours of three and four for a refreshing glass of lemonade? I would very much like to have the benefit of your advice concerning the current series of disturbing visitations we are undergoing. Your knowledge of the town and its residents could be most helpful. It would be my pleasure to visit with you at your convenience.

Yours very truly,
Julia S. Murdoch

I slipped the note into the envelope, wrote Mr. Dobbs's name on the outside, and, leaving it unsealed, took it into Lillian. "Read it," I said, "and be sure it's all right. I'm not accustomed to sending personal notes to unattached gentlemen, you know."

Lillian opened the note, read it quickly, and said, "I hope you know what you're doin'."

"I do. Of all the people in this town, Mr. Dobbs knows what's going on. The sheriff would be wise to make him an honorary deputy."

Lillian laughed. "He already has." She waved the note around. "As for this, it's pro'bly a good idea, just don't get me in it. I mean, I'll make the lemonade, but I don't want to do no visitin' with him. That man thinks so much of hisself, he'll think I'm runnin' after him, an' that's something I won't ever do." And she turned away, mumbling, "I don't care how many white hats is in that closet."

Chapter 43

The following afternoon I mentally prepared for my visit with Mr. Chester P. Dobbs, hoping that I could set him at ease even while discussing the deviant behavior of an unknown Abbotsville resident or visitor. Mr. Dobbs was known for knowing what went on in town but certainly not known for talking about it. He could easily take offense at my assumption that he not only knew what I wanted to know but that he would divulge it to me. But, I assured myself, if he did take offense, he would do it in the most courteous manner possible.

Lillian was adamant in her determination to have nothing to do with him other than make the lemonade, place the glasses and pitcher on a tray, and leave the tray on the coffee table in the living room.

"Just play like I'm not even here," she said as I rolled my eyes just a tiny bit.

When the doorbell rang at exactly three minutes past three, I hurried to welcome Mr. Dobbs into my home. He, too, had carefully prepared for his visit. Although he wore what he always wore—black summer-weight suit, white shirt, black tie, and a black derby hat, held now in his hand—it was evident that each article of clothing had been freshly cleaned and pressed. His full head of white hair gleamed in the afternoon sun, and the silver handle of his walking stick looked freshly polished.

"Good afternoon, Mr. Dobbs," I said, noting the long Cadillac purring at the curb to keep the interior and the driver cool. "Thank you for coming. Please come in."

When he smiled, I noticed a full set of teeth, but whether his own or not I couldn't tell. He walked slowly, stiffly erect, into the living room and eased creakily into a wing chair beside the fireplace. A slight whiff of bay rum with a medicinal undertone wafted in his wake as he placed his hat on his knee and his cane near to hand.

While chatting easily about a few local matters, asking after his health, and taking note of the weather, I poured the lemonade that Lillian had left, then placed a small table with a coaster on it beside his chair.

Taking the wing chair opposite his, I gradually led up to opening a discussion on the naked man, although I was having trouble deciding how best to do it. Mr. Dobbs, as I've previously indicated, was of the old school, strictly correct in his manners and in his personal conduct. He was likely to be offended by the careless use of such terminology as *naked*, *bare-bottomed*, *ravishment*, or even *deviant*, and certainly not any word with *s-e-x* associated with it. This was going to be more difficult than I'd thought.

Finally, though, I hit upon the best way to open the discussion—like my predecessors of an earlier age, I turned to the French language for my rescue.

"Mr. Dobbs," I said, "I'm sure you have heard of the unknown individual who has been terrorizing certain residents by appearing at night in a state of dishabille. The sheriff has apparently been unable to identify him, much less catch him, so a few of us who have been taken aback by his sudden appearances are banding together to put a stop to them. With your knowledge of the town and its inhabitants, I am wondering if you have any suggestions for us—who he might be or how we might identify him. That is," I stumbled on, "do you have any help you might offer to a group of helpless women who are at their wits' end?"

"Ah, Mrs. Murdoch, ma'am," Mr. Dobbs said, carefully placing his empty glass on the coaster. "Naturally I've heard of your situation and I am most sympathetic. It's shocking that such behavior has been allowed to go on as it has. I, too, have spoken to the sheriff about it, but it doesn't seem to be a priority with him. But," he said diplomatically, "perhaps I'm wrong. I'm not aware of all that goes on in his department."

Seeing an opening to fill, I asked, "Have you met the young man who is running against him this year? Moser is his name, Bobby Lee Moser. He is a former deputy and a recent graduate of an FBI training class."

"Ah, yes," he said with a smile. "I know Mr. Bobby Lee well."

I nodded, satisfied with the note of approval I heard in his voice. "But of course," I said, "we don't want to wait until November to solve our problem. The sooner we get whoever it is off the street, the better."

"I couldn't agree more," Mr. Dobbs said. "If it goes on much longer, it will affect the number of summer tourists we have, which in turn will affect the businesses on Main Street, and that will affect the tax base of the town and the county."

I hadn't thought of such ramifications, but now I saw that the naked man could be more of a widespread problem than merely giving palpitations to a few lonely ladies.

"So," Mr. Dobbs went on, "I appreciate being consulted by your civic-minded group, ma'am, and I'd like to help wherever I can. Since it's hard to conceive of long-term and well-known residents suddenly developing strange habits, it occurs to me that a list of newcomers to our town might be helpful."

"Indeed it would, and I assure you that anything you hear or see that would help bring these shameful episodes to an end would be appreciated. Some of the ladies are so frightened that they're thinking of moving away."

He frowned. "Well, we certainly don't want that. But making a list may be the limit of my help since I myself am always early to bed and have never had occasion to run into the scoundrel you seek. But," he added, raising his eyebrows, "am I correct in thinking that he is on the move only at night?"

"Yes, that's when he's always been seen. But you have already jumped two or three paces ahead of me by assuming right away that he is a newcomer. I think so, too, and a list would be quite helpful."

Mr. Dobbs rubbed his fingers lightly across his mouth, his face taking on a thoughtful cast as he considered the problem. "What, may I ask, will you do if you happen to catch or entrap him?"

"I'm not sure we've thought that far ahead. Call the sheriff, certainly."

"Hm-m," Mr. Dobbs said, "let me cogitate about this for a while. I don't want to put any of you ladies in a perilous situation, so if you all could wait a couple of months, I'm sure his appearances will dry up of their own accord."

"Really? Why? I mean, why would they?"

"Mosquitoes," he said, preparing to rise with the help of his cane. "They get bad in July and August and on into the fall if it's a warm fall. It's one of Dobbs Best Pest Control's busiest times."

"Oh, well," I said, having expected better advice than that.

"I'm not sure we can wait for nature to take its course, Mr. Dobbs. We want to be rid of him now."

"Then I shall give it more thought, and I'll get that newcomer list to you within the next day or two. Would you like their addresses as well?"

"Yes, if you have them. We're already plotting his raids in the neighborhood on a map, trying to determine if he's living among us or if he enters the area from outside. Anything you can do to help will be greatly appreciated."

"Then," he said, leaning on his cane to get to his feet, "I must take my leave. It's been a great pleasure, Mrs. Murdoch. Please give my regards to Mr. Sam and to Miss Lillian as well."

I walked him to the door, thanked him again, and saw him out. Then turning toward the kitchen, I called, "He's gone, Lillian. You can come out now."

Sunday afternoon, Mr. Dobbs sent a list by way of his driver. There were seventeen names and addresses on it, and the only one I had even heard of was that of Edward G. Cochrane, aka Eddie Cochrane. Mr. Dobbs also sent a note saying that the list was limited to the names of men who had moved within the town limits during the past six weeks as he had little knowledge of county residents. Some were listed with their wives, but a few appeared to be men who lived alone.

As soon as the list arrived, I quickly made a copy, then took the original to Helen, knowing that she would not delay in marking the location of each newcomer on her map.

A few minutes after eleven that night, Sam and I were upstairs in the bedroom preparing for bed. We'd spent the hours since supper continuing to discuss the names on the list. Lillian had known none of them, but she was sure that a certain Lester Lafitte was the name of someone who had recently moved from New Orleans to Abbotsville. Given the name, it was probably a good guess.

Sam was a little done in that none of the names were familiar to him. "I used to know everybody in town," he said, "but now I can barely keep up with who lives next door."

"Oh, poo, Sam," I said. "It's the same people who've lived there for forty years." As I slipped off my shoes and untied the belt on my bathrobe before crawling in beside Sam, I asked, "Do you know where 1015 Arrowwood Lane is? That's where LuAnne's new friend lives."

"It's off Lincoln Drive in the North End voting district, not far from here. There're several old houses that've been turned into apartments. Some rooming houses, too, I think."

"That would make sense, I guess, for a widower."

"A recent one, anyway," Sam said, pulling up the sheet. "He'll need time to decide—"

"Shhh," I said sharply, stopping in midcrawl onto the bed.

"What . . . ?"

"*Listen!* You hear that?" I ran to the side window and pushed it up. The undulating wail of a car horn blared in the night air. "It's *him*! Somebody's seen him. Or maybe caught him! Come on, Sam! *Hurry!*"

And out of the room I ran, pulling on my robe as I went, with Sam bounding after me, shouting, "Wait! Wait, Julia. Where're you going?"

"Get your keys!" I yelled, unlocking the kitchen door and heading for his car, the nearest one in the driveway. I threw open the driver's-side door, crawled across the seat and the console, and ended up sideways on my knees in the passenger's place. "Crank it up!" I yelled, frantically pushing the switch to open the window. "Hurry, Sam, somebody's got him hemmed in."

That thought may have given him an extra impetus, for he cranked the car, whirled it around, and flew onto the street. And just as quickly took the corner where Polk met South Oak on screeching tires while I held on for dear life. With the window down, my upper body thrust out of it, I strained to pinpoint the location of the insistent horn, trying to determine the direction we should go in.

"*Right!*" I screamed. "Turn right!" Sam did, as I leaned with the pull of the car and held on to the window frame. And still the horn blared in the night air.

"Right again!" I yelled, then, "Left! Left! Turn left!"

The brakes squealed as Sam slammed on them, then backed up a few feet and turned left, and that's when we saw all the lights.

"Oh, my word," I said, drawing back from the open window. "It's the Pickens house."

Sam screeched to a halt near the house, which was all he could do since two cars were parked haphazardly in the middle of the street. A few people milled about on Hazel Marie's front lawn, while in the driveway some men were concentrated around a familiar Oldsmobile with its hood raised. And still the horn filled the night air with ear-splitting decibels.

"Oh, my goodness," I said, deflating. "They haven't caught him. That's James's old car."

And with that I caught sight of Lloyd among the men leaning under the hood. With a few gestures to James, one of the men seemed to suggest what to do. James reached in and fiddled a little, then the horn abruptly stopped. You can't appreciate the beauty of silence until you've been bombarded for minutes on end by a car horn.

Seeing Hazel Marie in her gown and robe in the side yard, I opened my door. "I won't be but a minute."

Nodding to several neighbors in various stages of dress, I walked over to Hazel Marie. "What happened?"

"We were all asleep or almost asleep," Hazel Marie said, "when that horn started up. It was awful. It woke the twins and James came down and he couldn't stop it, and I didn't know what to do." Hazel Marie wrung her hands. "And, wouldn't you know, J.D.'s not here, and I thought the naked man was breaking in, and James is no help at all unless he's in the kitchen."

"It's all right, Hazel Marie," I said, putting my arm around her shoulders. "It wasn't your fault. And one good thing: Look how many people turned out to help. That should give you some comfort."

Seeing Lloyd turn back toward the house, I stopped him. "Lloyd," I said, "what happened? What turned on that horn?"

He grinned. "No telling. Somebody trying to get into the car or somebody hitting it or it could've been a short in the wiring. James had locked it, then couldn't find his keys, so I guess it about woke up the whole town."

"So it wasn't the man we're all looking for?"

"Could've been, I guess," Lloyd said. "But if it was, he's long gone by now."

After reassuring Hazel Marie, who kept shaking her head and mumbling, "James, James, what next?" I went back to our car. Sam was still sitting behind the wheel, talking through the window with one of the neighbors.

"All set?" he asked as I crawled in and rolled up my window.

"Yes, but what a letdown. I was just sure somebody had caught him."

"One good thing, though," Sam said.

"Then for goodness' sake tell me what it is."

"I was wearing pajamas tonight."

Chapter 44

I got up the next morning with Mr. Dobbs's list on my mind. It was the only thing we had to work with, but what good was a list of seventeen male newcomers to Abbotsville? And no telling how many more we had essentially discounted because they'd set up housekeeping in the county. We had no reason to assume that the naked man was located in town other than the fact that he could disappear so quickly.

I found myself tempted to ask Mr. Pickens to resume his surveillance of the area, if in fact he had done any. Maybe I hadn't given him enough time, and maybe I hadn't given him enough rope. Instead of hiring him to focus on Eddie, I should've aimed him toward our night visitor, whoever he was. Then if he turned out to be LuAnne's Eddie, she couldn't blame me for meddling in her business.

And furthermore, I should've suggested that Mr. Pickens spend some nights sheltering in a few hedges until the wretched man appeared. Then whoever he turned out to be would not be laid at my door.

So, again, what should we do with what we had? I couldn't see assigning seventeen sixty-plus-year-old women to stake out seventeen positions to take note of who came and went, and in what state of dress they did either one.

Maybe Helen would know how to use Mr. Dobbs's list to our best advantage. Barring that, I couldn't see that we'd advanced our mission at all. We had, however, added another set of experienced eyes and ears—those belonging to Mr. Dobbs—which might pay off in the long run.

But there was one thing I could do and perhaps I was the only one who could do it. I could be there to catch LuAnne if the naked man turned out to be her Eddie. For I have to admit that I was still leaning that way, maybe because no one else seemed to fit. Not that he did, other than being new in town and, don't forget, one of those people who invites but has to borrow to pay for anything. That was suspicious to begin with, to say nothing of having a wife who was not fully put away. How could LuAnne think of Eddie as unattached and available while he continued to make monthly payments to get her settled?

This was a time to prove my friendship if I hadn't done it a million times before. She was going to need a shoulder to lean on. In many ways, LuAnne believed what she wanted to believe. She had a way of overlooking anything that didn't fit with what she wanted to see. She would have a dozen excuses for Eddie's inability to pay for an expensive dinner, just as she would excuse anything else that didn't fit with her romantic view of him.

So, even though it was late morning and I knew she was at work, I called her. "Are you busy?" I asked when she answered.

"Oh, Julia? No, not right now, but you never know around here. How are you?"

"I'm fine," I answered. "I was just thinking of you and realizing that we'd not seen each other in a while. How is Eddie?"

"Won-der-ful," she breathed with a rapturous sigh, and my

heart sank. How far had their relationship gone? I declare, just let a few days pass by and no telling what could go on.

I cleared my throat. "Well, I was just wondering if you and Eddie could join Sam and me for dinner tonight—maybe at the club?" I hadn't cleared that with Sam, but he was always amenable to the plans I made and it had occurred to me that it would be good to get Sam's assessment of Eddie Cochrane.

"Oh, I'm afraid we can't tonight," LuAnne said. "Eddie's leaving really early in the morning for Charlotte for a couple of days. He has a few loose ends to tie up on his wife's estate, and I want him to have a full night's sleep before getting on the road. Maybe another time?"

"Of course. But it's been a while since we've even seen each other. Why don't you and I go to dinner and catch up? Sam will be just as happy putting his feet up and reading without my interrupting him."

"I'd love to do that," LuAnne said, "but I need to clean out the car and get it gassed up, so it's ready for him."

"He doesn't have a car?"

"Oh, he has one, but it's old and not very comfortable. Actually it's been a while since he's taken a road trip, so I'm a little worried about him." She giggled a little. "And my car, of course."

We quickly adjusted our plans, deciding to meet for lunch, but it was all I could do not to scream, "He's driving *your* car? Where is *his*? What *else* are you doing for him?"

We met at the club, knowing it would be quiet and conducive to an intimate talk. We met in the lobby and I'll have to say that

LuAnne looked better than I'd ever seen her. As a matter of fact, she was glowing, her eyes sparkled, and I think her teeth had been whitened. Either the woman was in love or she'd just gotten a raise.

"You look wonderful, LuAnne," I said, giving credit where credit was due. "What have you done to yourself?"

"I'm happy, Julia," she said. "It makes all the difference in the world."

And indeed it did. Normally, LuAnne had a strained, concentrated look on her face as if she needed to do something and she was running out of time to get it done. Now she looked softer and unhurried. I mentally sighed for I was reasonably sure that she hadn't gotten a raise.

After giving our orders, I listened to LuAnne's chatter about the funeral home and Eddie. I reminded myself that I was there to prepare her for disappointment and to remind her that there were plenty more fish in the sea.

Not that I knew that for sure, but it stood to reason that there were better catches than Eddie Cochrane. Could she not see that? She had paid for at least one dinner—but what a dinner it had been, complete with two bottles of wine—and now he was driving her car. What else had she given him?

Mentally squaring my shoulders, I interrupted the flow of exclamations about Eddie's abilities, accomplishments, manners, thoughtfulness, and on and on. Nobody, I thought, was that wonderful.

"LuAnne," I said, breaking in, "don't you think you'd do well to date around a little? I know that Eddie seems perfect, but nobody is, and it wouldn't hurt to do a little comparison shopping."

"No," she said firmly, "because when you find exactly what you want, why should you keep looking? Oh, Julia, if you'd just get to know him, you'd understand why I feel this way. I don't need to do any more shopping. He's one of a kind."

More than she knew, I thought, for if Eddie was who I thought he was, he'd be the only man in town who enjoyed prancing around in the nude. At the same time, I marked on a mental calendar the two nights that Eddie would be in Charlotte. If the naked man showed up during that time, I'd know he wasn't LuAnne's Eddie. Unless, of course, Eddie was smart enough to let it be known that he would be in Charlotte, while crouching instead in the nearest boxwood hedge.

"Well, LuAnne," I said, picking up my fork as our salads were placed before us, "I just hope you won't do something you'll regret. There's no hurry, you know. What's that old saying, Marry in haste, repent in leisure?"

"Oh, Julia," LuAnne said, "you always see the down side of everything."

"No, I don't," I said, immediately on the defensive. "I just don't want to see you jump into something too quickly. All I'm suggesting is that you slow down and not do something you'll regret."

"Well, I'll just tell you this: If he asks me, I'll jump. I've already told you that I was made to be a wife. This living alone and eating alone and sleeping alone is for a different kind of person. I want to be married."

"LuAnne," I said, throwing caution to the wind, "no, you don't. If that was true, you'd still be married to Leonard and you're not. You couldn't wait to get out of that marriage."

"That's not true," LuAnne said, "and you know it. I would've stayed if he hadn't flaunted that girlfriend of his. If Leonard had had the decency to keep her hidden away and not made a public display, I could've put up with it."

Well, I thought, speaking of public displays, how would she

deal with a man who was compelled to make a public display of himself in all his natural glory? But I couldn't say that because I didn't know. I only suspected.

"Well," I said, backing off, "I just want the best for you, and only you can know what that is. So let's talk about something else. Is there anything we need to do for Christy's luncheon? It'll be here before you know it."

"I know, and I've already arranged to have Thursday and Friday off. The peonies will come in on Thursday, and I'll make sure they're arranged and in place by Thursday night. I can check on the table settings at the same time. You and I should be there by eleven on Friday, just in case there's some last-minute problem."

"LuAnne, you are wonderful. You've done everything and I've done nothing. No wonder everybody loves to work with you."

She smiled, pleased at the compliment. "Oh, not really, but I'm really looking forward to Christy's wedding. It's a real love story—she's giving up everything for love."

I let it pass, but I thought, Yes, she is, more's the pity.

Chapter 45

After a few days of consideration, I felt I'd done all I could do to tap the brakes on LuAnne's headlong rush to be a wife again. It still seemed to me that instead of becoming a wife she was in danger of becoming a divorcée twice over. They say that it becomes easier after the first one, which is probably true with anything. But divorce is what happens when you marry someone you don't really know and don't like when you find out about them. I felt that I knew Eddie Cochrane better than LuAnne did. At least I knew enough to suspect more, whereas she didn't want to know anything.

The problem with that was this: Sooner or later you would learn it all—the good, the bad, and the indifferent—and one day you would wake up knowing exactly what you had married. It can be an eye-opener. I know, because I've been through it, and so had LuAnne with Leonard, her philandering first husband, which should've taught her a few things but apparently hadn't.

I tapped my fingers on the table beside the sofa, thinking, thinking. Since I hadn't made a dent in LuAnne's determination to anoint Eddie to sainthood, what if I went at it from another angle? What if I made sure that Eddie knew the extent of LuAnne's financial situation? With her willingness to finance expensive dinners and loan him her car with a full gas tank, as well as having start-up money for a new business, he may have formed an unrealistic view of her financial situation. And LuAnne was not above leading people to believe that she was better off than she actually was. She carried it off quite well and I admired her for it.

But Eddie wouldn't, especially if part of his attraction to her was based on an assumption of wealth.

But no, I told myself, I could not interfere to the extent of letting Eddie know that LuAnne had not signed a prenuptial agreement with her first husband because there had been nothing, pre- or postnuptial, to agree to.

Nonetheless, something had to be done, and the best outcome would be to identify the naked man. I had thought that Eddie's trip to Charlotte would eliminate him if the naked man made a visit while he was gone, but all had been quiet. Did that mean that Eddie was the naked man and couldn't make a night visit in Abbotsville because he had business in Charlotte? It certainly didn't rule him out, but it didn't definitely rule him in, either.

So I still didn't know one way or the other. If it turned out to be Eddie, as I suspected, the problem would be solved. LuAnne would drop him like a hot potato and she would be the first to condemn him.

I heard the distant rumblings of thunder heralding an afternoon shower, which put an end to my vague thought of taking a walk. It reminded me of what it had been like before air-conditioning units were as common as furnaces. The first thing that had to be done was to go around the house, pulling down windows to prevent rain from blowing in. It also reminded me of how air-conditioning had reformed the South by making it possible for people to work in huge plants, live in multistoried buildings, and simply to exist in the high humidity and sultry temperatures of a long afternoon in the Deep South.

Just as I'd decided to go to the kitchen and talk with Lillian, the telephone rang.

"*Miss Julia!*" Etta Mae Wiggins sang out as soon as I answered. "I can't believe it! It's just wonderful, and Bobby Lee is walking on air! We're both so excited. I just had to thank you, because I know you had a lot to do with it. So thank you, thank you. And now"—she paused to take a breath—"I have to decide what to wear. I don't guess white would do, would it?"

"Slow down, Etta Mae. What're you talking about?"

"Why, the wedding, of course. Mrs. Allen just called and, Miss Julia, she *asked* me, as if I might not want to do it. And of course I do. It's just perfect, especially for Bobby Lee. I mean, how in the world would he ever come up with a more perfect way to reach so many voters? I don't know how you thought of it or how you got Mrs. Allen involved, but I am ever so grateful. But I don't know what to wear."

"Etta Mae, listen to me. I do not know what you're talking about. What is Mrs. Allen doing?"

There was a second of silence. "You mean you really don't know?"

"No, I really don't."

"Well, I hope I'm not telling something out of school, because I can't imagine that Mrs. Allen would do something like this and not invite you. Oh, gosh," Etta Mae said, her voice dropping in disbelief, "do you think she would? I guess I've really stepped in it, haven't I?"

"Just tell me."

"Well, she called a little while ago and said she's having a big party—indoors and out—and inviting everybody she knows, which would include you, wouldn't it? And she said she'd heard that I was getting married but hadn't decided where or when, and she thought her party would be the perfect time and place and she'll fix up an altar inside or out, whatever I want. And then, and then, she said we could double up and have a campaign rally at the same time if Bobby Lee wanted to hand out pamphlets and so on. She said there'd be a couple of hundred people there, and Bobby Lee's never had much more than forty anywhere he's been, but that's better than the man he's running against, and besides, it's still a long time till November."

"Well, my goodness," I said, amazed at what Mildred had come up with from the brief conversation we'd had when she'd mentioned having a party. "Don't worry about talking out of school, Etta Mae. I have been invited to her party if we're talking about the one on the first Saturday of July. I just didn't know about her plans for a wedding and a campaign rally along with it. But it all sounds wonderful and it's very typical of what Mildred likes to do. She'll probably thank you and Bobby Lee for giving her the perfect reasons to have a party."

"Oh, she has. I mean, she did. But I still can't get over it."

"One thing, though, Etta Mae," I said in all seriousness, "if you agree to this, you and Bobby Lee have to follow through. She'll invite everybody in town, and she'll spend a mint of money on food and flowers and entertainment. It'll be done right, and people will be talking about it for years to come. So if you agree to it, he can't be running off to the FBI and there can't be an extra marriage thrown in by you."

Etta Mae started laughing so hard that she could barely get the words out. "I've already told Bobby Lee the same thing, but don't worry, he wants the sheriff's job so bad that he won't take a chance on anything else."

"Well, I would think he'd want you more than that."

"Yes'm, but you know," Etta Mae said, the laughter fading away, "I think he really does. Miss Julia, I don't know why everybody is so good to me, but I am so grateful. I just hope it doesn't all fall apart."

"You deserve to have a wonderful wedding, Etta Mae, and I'm delighted that Mildred is in a party mood. You just let her do whatever she wants to do for you, and you and Bobby Lee enjoy every minute of it."

"I'm going to try," she said. "I mean, I will. It's just hard to believe, but I still don't know what to wear."

"Let's wait and see what Mildred has planned. You know, inside or out, that sort of thing. For instance, you wouldn't want a dress with a cathedral train if she puts the altar outside."

"I don't think I'd want one anyway, since I'm not sure what a cathedral train is."

"A very long one, requiring several children in England to carry it. But I'll tell you what. Why don't you ask Hazel Marie to help you decide what to wear? The two of you can go shopping once you know the type of dress you want."

"Oh, I'd love that," Etta Mae said. "Would you go with us?"

"I'd love to."

Chapter 46

"Mildred?" I said when I called her as soon as Etta Mae hung up. "How did you come up with such a wonderful idea?"

"Which one of my wonderful ideas are you talking about?"

"Etta Mae just called, and she is thrilled out of her mind. You're doing a very good deed, Mildred, so what can I do to help?"

"Not a thing. I already have a pile of lists and notes of things to do because it's only a few weeks away and I usually plan this sort of thing months ahead of time. But the first thing we're doing is lining up the barbecue folks to be sure they can be here. They'll start the night before, you know, so prepare for my yard lights to be on."

I laughed. "I'm already used to your yard lights being on. I expect there'll be all kinds of goings and comings that entire night, too."

"Oh, yes. The best idea I've had was to combine a wedding and a campaign rally with a plain old party. Etta Mae assures me that her Bobby Lee will want to invite all the deputies and the EMTs, which gives me a chance to do something for them, too. You know how helpful they were when Horace was such a problem. I'm very excited about it. So you and Sam be prepared to come for the entire afternoon and on into that Saturday night. And that reminds me to double-check on the musicians, too. I have a couple of bands lined up—one's a great bluegrass band and who knows what the other one is, but there won't be any downtime while they take breaks." She stopped, drew a deep breath, then went on. "Just think, Julia, we'll have Christy's wedding this weekend, then my big blowout soon afterward. We'll need the rest of the summer to recuperate."

"And that reminds me that I should check on Sue," I said, realizing how near Christy's big day was. "Have you heard from her?"

"No, but I will," Mildred said. "I have Ida Lee calling on my other line with invitations to the party. It's too late to issue written invitations, and this way we'll know exactly who's coming and who's not. And so far, nobody's not."

"I don't doubt that," I said. "Everybody loves your parties."

"Yes, and this one's going to be a doozy."

Over the next day or so I learned more about how Mildred was turning a big party into a doozy. She'd consulted with Helen about Thurlow's needs, and even though at first he'd said he was in no shape to attend a party, Mildred went right ahead preparing for him. She arranged for a hospital bed to be set up on the pool house patio, as well as a wheelchair and three EMTs to get Thurlow in and out, or up and down, whichever he wanted.

Mildred invited the town as well as the county commissioners, on the assumption that they might need to do a little politicking along with Deputy Moser. She didn't overlook the churches, either, as there were a number of preachers and their families on her list. And of course there were our friends—the Pickens family, who was asked to bring along Ronnie, Thurlow's Great Dane, to visit with him, as well as the Hargroves; LuAnne, who was thrilled to be able to show off her Eddie; Miss Vinnie; Miss Ethyl; and several others who'd been traumatized by a glimpse of male nakedness.

When I told Mildred of having Mr. Dobbs over for lemonade, she immediately said, "And I didn't even think of him! He'll get an invitation tonight, and so will Lillian and Latisha, and that Janelle girl. Might as well ask her mother, too. Who else, Julia? Help me think so I won't leave anybody out. Oh," she said suddenly, "I know what I can do. I'll have a wooden dance floor set up near the pool, because I've got a quartet coming that sings all the good ole sixties songs. Did you ever do the shag, Julia?"

"Not very well."

"Me, either, but I loved that dance. Wait a second, I've got to make a note to myself to invite Christy and Travis. They'll probably be in Baltimore, but I'd love my party to be the first invitation they get as a married couple."

"Have you spoken to Sue lately?" I asked.

"We talked on Monday, I think it was. She sounded tired, but getting your only child married is enough to tire you out."

"I know, but I'm also wondering if it's not more than that. She and Christy don't seem to be getting along very well."

"Well," Mildred said, "that's a shame. I'm already looking forward to Penelope's wedding, but of course there'll be debutante dances and so forth before that."

"Christy did them all," I said, recalling the flurry of parties for the Hargroves' daughter some few years before. "And I remember how much Sue enjoyed the season. And Christy, too. The two of them got along so well, and Christy came out at the Rhododendron Ball in Asheville and the Governor's Ball in Raleigh. Even Bob had a good time, and he's not much of a party person. But Sam says Bob doesn't have much to say these days."

"Well," Mildred said, "there's just been the three of them for so long, I guess they're having to adjust to adding a son. Maybe that's all it is. And that reminds me. I must put the new doctor that Bob brought in on my list. It'll be a good way to introduce him and his wife to the town."

"I'm not sure he has a wife, but be sure to let him know that your parties are not typical of what goes on around here. You set too high a standard for the rest of us, Mildred."

"I do," she said with her usual complacency, "don't I?"

When I walked into the kitchen that afternoon, Lillian whispered, "Mr. Sam taking a nap in the library, so don't go waking him up."

"Is he feeling all right?"

"He said he feels fine. He just gettin' ready for all the weddin's and parties comin' up real soon."

"Oh, for goodness' sake," I said, laughing. "Well, I need to call Sue Hargrove, so I'll go upstairs and not disturb his beauty sleep."

I had planned to discuss Sue's seeming unhappiness with Sam because it had occurred to me that she might not be well. It simply was not like her to let small disagreements, even with her daughter, bring her so low. Perhaps, I thought, Bob had said something to Sam that would explain what was wrong between mother and daughter—other than their daughter dropping out of medical school without warning, announcing an imminent wedding as well as plans for moving away, and expecting complete acceptance of a stranger as a son-in-law. It was all a little much to expect from doting parents, and it troubled me that Christy—that delightful, bubbly young woman—couldn't or wouldn't understand her mother's lack of enthusiasm.

"Sue?" I asked when she answered her phone. "It's Julia. How are you? Am I interrupting anything?"

"Oh, Julia, it's good to hear from you. No, I'm in the bedroom with the excuse of taking a nap. But I can't sleep. I just needed some time to myself. Bob can go to the office, but I have to come up with an excuse."

"Oh, Sue, I'm so sorry you're still having problems, but surely when the wedding is over things will settle down. It's just a very hard time for a lot of brides—so much is expected of them."

"Yes, I think we've been out almost every night. Christy has so many friends who want to do something for her. But just another week and it'll be over." And Sue began to cry.

"Oh, Sue, is it that bad? What is going on?"

"I'm sorry," she said, sniffling. "No, I'm just tired. And Christy is all upset. We went to Asheville to pick up some gifts and she was expecting Travis to be here when we got back. Instead there was a message that he'll be delayed and won't be here till Monday. That gives them almost a full week before the wedding, more than enough time for whatever they need to do, yet Christy was thrown into a tailspin. How in the world is she going to stand being married to a doctor who has to change plans all the time, I don't know. You'd think being a doctor's daughter would've prepared her for being a doctor's wife. Yet somehow or another, the change of plans has become my fault."

"That's ridiculous, Sue," I said, taking umbrage for my friend's sake. "And I hope you told her so."

"It's hard to tell her anything these days."

"Sue," I said with a change of tone, "are you sure that Christy even *wants* to get married? This is all so unlike her that I can't help but feel there's something going on underneath."

"I've told her a dozen times that she can back out anytime she wants to. There's nothing worse than getting caught up in events so much that you feel you can't get out, and I don't want that to be happening to her. But she's quiet, almost sullen, and always mad with me when Travis is away and when he's here. And she blames it all on the fact that I don't like him. And, Julia, that's not true. I like him all right. I just think he's a bad influence on her because she's never been like this until he came along."

"Only one more week, Sue, and it'll be over. Maybe a little distance between you and Christy will help smooth things over. Are they planning to come back for Mildred's party?"

"It'll depend on Travis's on-call schedule, I guess. All I know is that he'll be here most of the week before the wedding because there're several couples parties for them."

"Then let's enjoy what we know. LuAnne and I are really looking forward to the bridesmaids' luncheon on Friday. And listen, as soon as the wedding is over, I want to talk to you about LuAnne. That'll give you something to think about instead of worrying about Christy."

"What's going on with LuAnne?"

"I'm afraid she's thinking of getting married now that she's found the perfect man."

"Oh, for goodness' sake," Sue said. "I've about had my fill of perfect men."

Chapter 47

As it turned out, I didn't go shopping for a wedding dress with Etta Mae and Hazel Marie. They decided to go on Monday morning, and to hear them tell it later Etta Mae tried on dresses all over Asheville and down across Greenville as well. I would've been worn out, but apparently they found the perfect one. But perfection is in the eye of the beholder, and the one they chose was a mix of what we used to call an afternoon dress because it was ankle length and a hippie style because, well, you'd have to see it. When they showed it to me, I was just as glad that I hadn't been along when they made their choice. It was perfectly appropriate, and made of natural linen—not white but almost—and plenty of it in the skirt but very little above the waist.

Etta Mae had called me that Sunday afternoon before and paid me the highest of compliments. She asked me to be her matron of honor, but after giving it consideration, I suggested that Hazel Marie would be more suitable. Not such a contrast of age differences, you know, and after arguing about it for a few minutes, she saw the wisdom of having a younger woman at her side.

"Etta Mae," I said during that same conversation, "have you

thought of who will marry you? Who will do the actual ceremony, I mean?"

"Oh, gosh, no," she said. "I've been so excited about the whole thing that I haven't thought of that."

"What about the preacher of your church?"

"I hate to say this, Miss Julia, but I don't have a church. I've usually worked on Sunday mornings and I guess I've just gotten out of the habit of going. Oh, my goodness, what if nobody wants to do it because I'm so slack?"

"What about Bobby Lee? Does he have a church home?"

She sighed. "No'm, he's worse than I am."

"Well, there's something you can do to start your marriage off right. You both can get back in church. Remind Bobby Lee that voters like churchgoing candidates."

"I'll do that," she said. "I'll start us off right because this marriage is going to work."

"Good. And I'll talk to Mildred. She's inviting a number of preachers, so we'll find somebody who will do the honors. If not, I'll talk to our preacher, but I hope we can find somebody a little more understanding than he is. Although he'd jump at the chance to marry two men or two women, he seems to draw the line at non-churchgoers."

"That's kinda strange."

"You don't know the half of it."

So things were set in motion to get Etta Mae married, so much so that Christy's big, formal wedding began to fade into the background for me. Everybody was agog at the thought of Mildred's party, which would include not only barbecue and fixings but a wedding, some politicking, and a large dash of bluegrass music and buck dancing.

I offered to help wherever Mildred needed it, but otherwise I stayed out of the way. I couldn't help but think that excitement over Mildred's party had lessened the anticipation of Christy's wedding, but Sue didn't mention any disappointment, so I didn't, either. I think she just wanted it to be over.

About midmorning on the Tuesday of Christy's wedding week, I answered the doorbell and found Mr. Pickens waiting to be let in.

"Why, Mr. Pickens," I said, "how nice to see you. Do come in."

"Just thought I'd drop by instead of trusting the mail," he said, making me wonder if the U.S. mail was having more trouble than I'd heard.

We went into the living room, where he opened a briefcase and removed a few papers.

"I have your bill here," he said, handing it to me. "And," he went on, pulling out a few more sheets, "my written report on Eddie Cochrane."

"Shhh," I said, glancing toward the hall. "Nobody knows about that but you and me, and I don't want anybody knowing it, especially since it's over and done with."

"Oh, sorry," he said. "Forgot that you might not be alone."

"Lillian's here, and I trust her with everything. Except this, because I'm a little ashamed for setting it in motion. But, Mr. Pickens, since we've gone this far with it, can you tell me if you picked up anything about this person that worries you? I mean, even though I've told you to stop, I'm not sure that I really want you to."

"No, I can't say I found anything that really worries me, but I've barely scratched the surface. He seems a little dandified, precise, and what I'd call prissy, but that's a type like any other. Doesn't have to mean anything."

"All right, then let's leave that alone and turn to something else. You've heard, of course, about the idiot who's running around with no clothes on, and it surprises me that you haven't made him your number one priority. Especially since he's been seen around your house and your neighbor's."

"Just had my hands full lately," he said, which was a poor excuse in my opinion. "Been in and out of town a good bit."

"Well, if you need official employment before proceeding, I will engage you to track down that man, unmask him, so to speak, put some clothes on him, and take him to jail. I want to know who he is, and I want rid of him. Somebody's going to get hurt if he's not soon stopped."

I told him then about Helen's attempt to organize a committee to track the man's method of operation, which, of course, he already knew about from Hazel Marie.

"Yeah," he said with a slight patronizing smile, "your plans didn't work so well with James's car going off like that."

"They worked fine," I shot back. "People gathered around just as they were supposed to, and if that man had been there he would've been caught. Or at least seen up close so that he might've been recognized."

"I hear that you and Lillian got a good look and almost caught him."

"We did, although it was Lillian who really went after him. But what do you say, Mr. Pickens? Will you take the job? There're a lot of women who would be ever so thankful to you for ridding us of this pestilence. They, I mean we, are losing a lot of sleep."

"Okay, I accept the case."

"Good. Now, the way I see it is that you should spend a few

nights outside, but not walking around and patrolling. That would put him off right away. You need to hide somewhere where he's been known to visit and wait for him to show up. There's Miss Ethyl's house, for instance, and certainly mine, which he's visited only when Sam's been away. He's been seen at Mildred Allen's house at least twice, and I do think that he's been around your house, too. You just need to plan on spending a few nights outside, Mr. Pickens. That's the only way you'll catch him."

"I hear you," he said, fastening his briefcase and standing. "I'll start on it right away. But the rest of you need to leave it to me. Don't encourage anybody to go after him. If he shows up anywhere, everybody needs to stay inside and out of the way. I'll give you my cell number, which you can distribute, so if anybody sees him, tell them to call me. I'll be roving around for the next few nights."

"Yes, okay. But what if the naked man hears your phone ring? Won't it scare him off to hear a Nellie Stevens holly bush get a phone call?"

The hint of a smile flickered at the corners of his mouth. "I'll put it on vibrate."

"Oh, of course. Yes, that'll work. But just a minute, Mr. Pickens," I said, rising, "I'll give you a check for the business done and we'll start fresh with this new assignment."

Chapter 48

Sam pushed aside his dessert plate that evening, then said, "You want to go to Raleigh with me tomorrow?"

"Why are you going to Raleigh?"

"The governor's called a meeting of the executive committee I'm on—some legal situation has come up. I'll go down tomorrow afternoon, have meetings all day Wednesday, and be home probably midday Thursday. Maybe Friday. I'll tell you what. Plan on Saturday morning for sure."

"You're not going to get hung up down there, are you? Remember that Christy's wedding is that afternoon. Bob might need a little hand-holding to get him through it."

"I'll be back long before then. But why don't you come with me?"

"What in the world would I do in Raleigh while you're in a committee meeting?"

"You can go shopping or just lie around in a hotel room."

"Well, thank you, anyway, but I have too much to do here. LuAnne and I have to go over everything for the bridesmaids' luncheon on Friday, and I need to discuss with Helen the best use of Mr. Pickens now that he's working for us, and I'd like to take Sue to lunch this week, maybe tomorrow, to give her a break. In fact, I'll call her tonight and see if she's free. And I'd like to do something for Etta Mae for her wedding, but that might have to wait till next week. So again, thank you, anyway, but I'd better stay here."

"I don't much like leaving you alone. Would Lillian and Latisha come stay with you?"

"Oh, I don't think that'll be necessary. Now that we have Mr. Pickens guarding the ramparts, there shouldn't be a problem. In fact, it wouldn't surprise me if we've seen the last of the naked man. I don't think he'll want to take a chance of getting caught." I stopped, drumming my fingers on the table and thinking.

"Do you realize what I've just done?" I asked as a few things began to come together in my mind. "I'm assuming that he will know that we've hired Mr. Pickens, which in turn means that I'm also assuming he's somebody we know and who knows us and what we're doing."

"Interesting," Sam said. "But it does seem so. You have any candidates?"

"Well, I did, until I began to feel so ashamed of myself that I'm trying to come up with somebody else. Suspicion is a pernicious thing, you know. Have just one little question about somebody and it can quickly put a questionable light on everything else about him."

"Who?" Sam asked.

"Who what?"

"Who did you suspect?"

"Oh, well, don't tell anybody, but LuAnne's new boyfriend, Eddie Cochrane. I mean, whoever is running around naked only started doing it since she started seeing him. So the timing is right, and he has never displayed himself to her, yet she's a single woman, which is the kind he seems to prefer. He may be afraid she'd recognize him, although so far nobody has had the presence of mind to look at his face."

Sam smiled at that and, after hearing Lillian start down the stairs, I decided to change the subject.

"I told you, didn't I, that Janelle turned down Mr. Dobbs's marriage proposal? And Lillian says that it has run through the community like a shock wave. Just about everybody thinks that Janelle cooked her goose by not grabbing him when she could. Everybody, that is, except her own mother, who seems to have a few attractions of her own because it seems that Mr. Dobbs has now shifted his interest in her direction."

"My word," Sam said, his eyebrows jumping up in surprise, "who would've thought that a ninety-year-old man could create such interest?"

"I think he's only eighty-nine."

"Well, if he's able to turn from daughter to mother, he's a better man than I am."

"There's not a man anywhere to compare with you, Sam. But I'm just glad that his attention is focused far from Lillian, because I'm not sure that she could resist him if he came after her. Oh," I went on, "she says she could, but being at the top of the social pyramid would be awfully hard to turn down. So I just wish he'd go ahead and marry somebody so all the interested ladies could calm down."

Sam smiled. "He's really kept things stirred up, hasn't he?"

"Yes, and I think he thoroughly enjoyed doing it. Until, that is, the one he chose turned him down. So thank goodness for Mr. Pickens deciding he needs some office help, because having a job made it easier for Janelle to say no. And speaking of Mr. Pickens,"

I went on, "I am really counting on him to put a stop to all the nakedness we're being subjected to."

"*All* the nakedness? It's only one, isn't it?"

"You know what I mean. Anyway," I said, "with Mr. Pickens on guard duty while you're gone, I won't be afraid. In fact, I'm hoping that the naked man does show up so he can be caught, identified, and incarcerated. And if it's LuAnne's new honey, well, that's just too bad.

"In fact," I went on, warming to my subject, "I'm wondering if I shouldn't tell Mr. Pickens to stake out her Eddie and follow him the next few nights. That would be different from what he's planning to do, which is to hide near one of the houses where the naked man has already appeared and hope he's picked the right one, although most of the targeted houses are fairly close together. What do you think, Sam?"

"I think that you've hired a professional, so you should leave the implementation to him. What I want you to do is pull all the curtains, lock all the doors, and stay inside before it gets dark every night that I'm gone."

"Miss Julia," Lillian said, late the next afternoon as she came out of the pantry with her huge pocketbook. "Latisha and me can come back an' stay with you while Mr. Sam's gone."

"I know, and I thank you for it, but with Mr. Pickens on duty I feel perfectly safe. In fact, if you were to come back, that might be the very thing that would keep the naked man away. I don't think he'd want to tangle with you again. But here's the thing, Lillian, which I wouldn't tell Sam, but I *want* that miscreant to show up so that Mr. Pickens can catch him. And to that end, I've told everybody I know, and some I don't, that Sam is out of town and I'm alone. If that doesn't draw him out, I don't know what will, given his propensity for older women."

"Of course," I said, half to myself, "I've told Mr. Pickens to stake out Arrowwood Lane so he can follow a certain suspect if he makes a move tonight. Which means that if he's not the naked man, the rest of us—the ones he's previously visited—will be on our own. I hope I've not outsmarted myself."

"Well," Lillian said, "I hope you know what you're doin' 'cause sometimes you don't. But call us if you change your mind."

"Thanks, Lillian, you know I will if I get scared enough. But, I declare, as much as Mr. Pickens aggravates me, I feel perfectly safe knowing he's around."

Nonetheless, as soon as Lillian left, I went around the house closing off any view of the yard on all sides, except for one window in the library that overlooked the back garden. A deep, comfortable chair provided an ideal lookout for any goings or comings across our backyard. I placed my cell phone, my car keys, and a magazine on the table beside the chair. I intended to be the bait to draw a performance from the naked man. I would be ideally situated to get an eyeful if he decided to give me the shock of my life.

And if everything worked according to plan, Mr. Pickens would be close on his heels. I hated to think of being the one to call LuAnne and tell her that Eddie was being booked for public indecency, but with all the unusual marriages, either consummated or contemplated, among us, hers would be stopped in its tracks.

So, leaving the front of the house in darkness, I sat lit up like the star of a show as I waited for the real show to begin. Three hours later I was still sitting and no one, clad or unclad, had appeared. Where was he? Had he gotten his compulsive behavior out of his system?

Maybe he wasn't as tuned in to our comings and goings as I had thought. So as I crawled into bed, I thought, I think I can fix that.

Chapter 49

I spent the following morning making phone calls to just about everybody I knew—friendly calls checking on their well-being, discussing the upcoming weddings, and asking about children and grandchildren, yet making sure that I mentioned Sam's absence for the next couple of days. After that I made a trip to the drugstore, replenishing my vitamin supply and talking with my friendly pharmacist in the presence of several other customers, making sure to mention Sam's fishing trip.

On my way home, I stopped at the Gulf station and filled the gas tank, then went inside and bought a copy of *The New York Times* to see how far off the wall their writers had gotten. Waiting in line to pay for the paper, I chatted with a landscaper I knew, mentioning as I did that Sam was out of town for a few days.

Not, I assure you, that I thought that any of those I'd spoken to had any connection to the naked man. I just knew how news could spread even from your most trusted friend to her husband to his coworker to his wife to her bridge club to their various Sunday school classes and on and on. Once a perfect stranger stopped me on the sidewalk to ask if Lloyd had passed his driver's test a couple of weeks before.

Satisfied that I had done all I could to spread the news of my temporarily single state, I went home, had tuna fish salad for lunch, and took a nap in preparation for a busy night.

After supper and after Lillian had left, I went around the house preparing it for the vigil I intended to keep that evening. I turned off all the lights except for those in the library, locked all the doors, and closed all the curtains and blinds except for the one on the window overlooking the backyard. Then I turned on only those outside lights mounted under the eaves on the corners of the house. They weren't bright enough to illuminate the entire yard; rather they cast a dim romantic glow from the house to the bordering hedges—just enough, it seemed to me, to tempt the unknown man to display himself for the select audience that would be ready and waiting for him.

And, I firmly told myself, if I were to be treated to a backyard solo performance, I was going to force myself to ignore the central feature and concentrate on the man's face. I was going to know who he was—or wasn't—before the night was over.

So I waited. And waited, and flipped through a magazine without reading any articles, and kept waiting. Traffic slowed on Polk Street in front of my house around ten o'clock when I heard the clock in the courthouse tower begin to strike. After that, the house seemed to settle as the night outside the arc of light in my yard grew thicker. A little after midnight, a group of teenagers, laughing as they headed home, walked by on South Oak, the street that ran along the side of the house. I knew my expected visitor would not come as long as they were within earshot, so I took that opportunity to visit the bathroom and get a slice of Lillian's chocolate cake.

And still I sat and waited, wondering if the naked man had suddenly lost the compulsions that drove him. Maybe he only had them when the moon was full. Maybe the urge came and went according to some chart in the *Farmers' Almanac*. What if he had been miraculously cured and we would go to our graves never having learned who he was?

Yet I was convinced that if I gave up and went to bed, he would come as surely as I was sitting there. I wondered where Mr. Pickens was. Was he following Eddie Cochrane? Was he even now watching Eddie with LuAnne? I hoped he wasn't seeing something he shouldn't see. How long would he watch before revealing himself and taking Eddie to jail?

I'd finished the slice of cake but hesitated to leave my post to take the plate to the kitchen. It would be awful if the naked man came when no one was there to see him. That, if I understood it correctly, would defeat the whole purpose of public divestment. He could flit across the yard, glance at my empty chair, and keep on flitting until he came upon a lonely woman taking out her trash at an ungodly hour.

I think I nodded off for a few minutes but suddenly jerked fully awake. A horn sounded, far off and briefly. I sat up, straining to hear it again, but to no avail. Had it been the angry honk of a frustrated driver or had it been the beginning of a signal of things to come? I didn't know, but I was fully awake and ready for whatever happened next.

Nothing did, and the longer I waited, the more agitated I became. It was as if the whole town, maybe the whole state, was waiting for something to happen. I stood up, then sat back down. Then I heard another horn go off in the distance but from another direction. What was going on and what was I supposed to do? Who was I supposed to call? My hands were shaking as I grabbed the smartphone on the table and started tapping. Helen's phone was busy, and so was Hazel Marie's, and so was Mildred's. Then I realized that I was keeping my phone busy as well. I stopped trying to call out in case somebody was trying to call in, but I had to know if the man was on the move and from which direction he was coming. I tapped Mr. Pickens's number, then just as quickly untapped him. He might still be hidden in a boxwood bush and something like the *1812 Overture* would give him away if he'd forgotten to put it on vibrate. I couldn't risk it, so I tried Mildred again.

"Are you awake?" I asked, relieved to get an answer.

"Yes, are you?"

"Uh, yes, I've been waiting for something to happen. Did you hear a car horn a few minutes ago? Way off in the distance? And then another one?"

"No, but I saw somebody or something creep behind my pool house a few minutes ago. Could've been him, or maybe a bear. They're active now. I was just trying to decide whether to call the sheriff or Mr. Pickens or whomever."

"Are you upstairs? Which way are you looking?"

"I'm downstairs looking out the kitchen window toward the garage and the pool beyond that. Where—"

"*Mildred!*" I hissed, my face pressed against the window. "I see him!" Or I thought I did. "He's coming through our hedge. Get your car! We can't let him get away!"

I snatched up my pocketbook and car keys and ran for the kitchen door. Calling people on the phone took too long. We couldn't let him get away this time. I ran for the car, jumped in, locked the door, cranked the engine, and heard a horrendous splintering crash from Mildred's direction. Her yard was lit up like Broadway, so I had no trouble seeing the black Town Car barrel down her curved driveway, leaving the garage door behind, hanging by one hinge.

Sam kept telling me that I shouldn't back out onto Polk Street, but it was too much trouble to turn around in the drive. I wished

I had, though, because just as I whirled backward into the street, Mildred's car turned out of her drive and the front of her car met the back of mine on Polk. I heard the crunch of metal and a tinkle of glass, but it was all very lightly done with the collision barely felt in either front seat. I lowered my window and waved for Mildred to follow, then stepped on the gas and spun around the corner onto South Oak. And just as quickly, I pulled to the curb, parked, cut the lights, and got out.

Mildred slid to a stop beside me and lowered her passenger-side window. "Sorry for running into you," she said, "but what do we do now?"

"Park in front of me and turn off your lights. If he's in my backyard, he may hit the sidewalk any minute. Light him up with your brights and follow him. And blow your horn so everybody'll know where we are."

Mildred slid her car to the curb as I regained the driver's seat in mine. We sat in the dark for what seemed an hour but was probably only a few minutes. Where was he? He could've doubled back and recrossed Mildred's yard by then. Or he may have been so tempted by the light in my window that he was waiting to put on a show for whoever appeared. It depended, I surmised, on the strength of his compulsion to act out.

Mildred screamed "There he is!" as a long-legged figure dressed only in an unbuttoned shirt and running shoes slid out of the gate at the foot of my garden and melted into the shadows of the overgrown privet hedge of my neighbor.

Hurriedly turning on the ignition with shaking hands, I put the car in gear. I flipped on the bright lights just as Mildred's lights went up. It was like daylight with American- and German-made headlights lighting up the entire block even beyond the next streetlight. There wasn't a dark hiding place anywhere.

I pressed down on my horn to keep up a constant din and Mildred did the same as house lights began to come on all along the street. The naked man—half naked now, to be precise—seemed confused, and who wouldn't be? He couldn't get through the privet hedge, so he took a few steps in our direction, saw the futility of that, and turned to run from us, his unbuttoned shirt flapping in the breeze as he put on a burst of speed.

Mildred eased her car along right behind him and I eased along behind her, both of us pressing those deep, resonant horns for all we were worth. Any minute now I expected the running man to dash into somebody's yard and go to ground in the interior of a block where cars couldn't follow. But neither he nor I had allowed for the pride of place exhibited by local homeowners. Every yard had a fence—picket or rail—or a wall—brick or stone—separating freshly mown grass from the sidewalk. He would have to break his stride to scramble across a boundary and find a hiding place.

So he kept running, keeping his face turned away from us as he headed for the end of the block, where he would have a choice of directions.

Chapter 50

Where was Mr. Pickens? Where was any kind of help? Any second now the man could pull himself together and dash between two houses and cross a few fenced yards where cars could not follow and find a place to hide until we gave up looking for him.

However, I thought with a surge of hope, he'd left the rest of his clothes somewhere. He'd have to emerge from any hiding place before daylight or his bare legs and short shirt would draw unwanted attention even if he buttoned the shirt.

By this time, car horns were going off all over town—I could hear them each time I rested my hand from blowing mine. My cell phone on the seat beside me kept going off as calls came in, but I was too busy driving and watching to answer any of them.

Then it hit me—Bluetooth! My word, I was done in by my ignorance, but I quickly pressed several buttons on the steering wheel, yelling "Hello! Hello!" at each press.

"Where are you?" Mr. Pickens's voice boomed out of the dashboard.

"Uh, on South Oak, headed south. We have him in sight. Where are—? Wait, wait, he's turned onto Taft, headed west. I think it's west. Hurry, Mr. Pickens, he'll get away any minute."

"I'm coming!" he yelled. "But break it off, break it off. You can't catch him by yourself!"

"Well, I know that, Mr. Pickens, but don't worry. Mildred Allen is here, too."

"Oh, Lord," he said.

I hung up. Then, wishing I'd listened more carefully to Lloyd's instructions when I bought the fancy phone, I was finally able to ask for Mildred and get through to her. It would've been almost as easy to have gotten out of the car and run up to hers.

"Stay the course, Mildred!" I yelled. "Don't let him out of your sight. Mr. Pickens is on the way." Not waiting for her response, I threw the phone on the seat and concentrated on trying to predict what the man would do next. He'd had a nice, long run in more ways than one since he'd been able to outwit everybody who had tried to stop him. But we were closing in on him, which meant that we were close to putting an end to his inappropriate behavior, and I didn't want to lose him now.

It seemed to me that he was beginning to flag from the run, although the entourage of three or four dogs loping at his heels was having a high old time. I figured that at any minute the man would abandon the sidewalk for a cross-country run through backyards.

Then he did. He suddenly swerved from the sidewalk and cut in front of Mildred's car in a long diagonal dash across the street, the dogs leaping and yipping around him.

"Mildred!" I said when she answered her phone. "Keep following him! I'll turn at the next block and try to head him off. Don't lose him!"

I sped up, passed Mildred as she crept along, and drove the length of the block to the next intersection. Then I slowed to a crawl, peering along the dark sidewalk for a glimpse of the running man. I kept expecting a sudden eruption of a partial nude from the shadows of trees overhanging the sidewalk.

Thinking that at any minute the man would swerve between two houses and disappear among the garages, gardens, trash cans, fences, and swing sets, I clutched the steering wheel and prayed for the arrival of Mr. Pickens.

Disconnected thoughts ran through my mind as I hunched over the wheel, watching for any movement. Was the man Eddie Cochrane? I wasn't sure. He might've been a little taller than Eddie, who wasn't a big man. Each time the man had glanced to the side to check on our progress, he had shielded his face with his arm, so I'd never gotten a direct look at him. His hair might've been darker than Eddie's, but our bright lights could've distorted the color. Still, if put to the test, I couldn't swear one way or the other who the man was.

But then he seemed to gain a second wind and began to eat up the pavement with powerful strides, while I began to have even more doubts. This was a stranger, and a stranger who most certainly did not have a tricky knee, as Eddie was said to have.

Then I lost him. One minute he'd been pounding the sidewalk, the next minute he was gone. Slowing considerably, I dimmed my lights and inched along, figuring that the naked man was hemmed in by Mildred on the north side of the block and by me on the south. Let him, I thought, hunker down in between. We'd send Mr. Pickens on foot to hunt him down.

"Mr. Pickens?" I said, still unsure of how Bluetooth worked. "Where are you?"

"Passing my house, heading south. Where are you?"

"Keep coming. I'm on Eaton Lane between South Oak and Adams. Mildred is one block to the north, and the man is somewhere in between. Hiding, I guess."

"All right. I'm here. Stay where you are and let me know if you see him." Mr. Pickens issued his orders as I pictured him leaving his car and beginning a search of the block. Then he demanded, "Are you armed?"

"Why, no," I said, wondering if I should be. "But I'd be careful around Mildred. She could be."

"Oh, Lord," he groaned. Then: "I'm out," he said. "On foot. Go home and take Mildred with you."

Before I could answer, there was a roar of motors interspersed with the screeching of brakes as streams of headlights from several cars poured down South Oak on one side and Adams on the other. If I hadn't already known that the town had had its fill of shocked and outraged ladies who were deeply disturbed by the man's lack of decency, I would've realized it then. Cars began to fill the street, parking haphazardly as drivers jumped out and converged on the block. I pulled closer to the curb, decided that I didn't need to join the foot race, and stayed in the car and out of the way.

Chasing down miscreants was, after all, Mr. Pickens's bailiwick and I was just as happy to leave it to him. I did wish for company, however, and thought of Mildred only a block away, probably perspiring in the humid June night as I was, but unwilling to leave until the man was caught.

I powered down all the windows, let the engine idle for the air-conditioning, cut the headlights, and listened intently to the calls, yells, and whistles of the hunters. I thought I recognized Mr. Pickens's voice once, then decided that he was too professional to give himself away to the hunted. I pictured him gliding silently to the man's hiding place and suddenly pouncing on him in the dark.

It occurred to me that as hot as the night was and as sweaty as the man would be after his five- or six-block run, Mr. Pickens would have to be very careful. The naked man would be as slick physically as he had been metaphorically during these several weeks of showcasing his charms.

I smiled at the unlikely thought of him, slippery with perspiration, sliding out of Mr. Pickens's handcuffs and gaining his freedom.

But then it happened so fast that I couldn't take it in. The passenger-door lock popped up, the interior lights came on and then went off as the door opened and closed, but not before he slid in beside me.

"Drive," the almost naked man ordered, panting, as he scooted down beneath the window and the odor of male sweat filled the car. "Or else."

I did as I was told, putting the car in gear and threading my way through the abandoned cars, all the while thinking, You're not Eddie. "Where to?" I asked. "I only have a quarter tank of gas."

He was silent for a while, then he said, "Let me think." He bunched up his shirttail as a covering for his lap and, shoulders slumped, used both hands to hold it there. He looked like a beaten child, and I sensed that whatever had been driving him was no longer in control. I discounted his puny "or else" threat and began to wonder just what to do with him.

"Well," I said, inching along as slowly as I could get away with, "first of all, think of putting on some clothes. There's an ordinance against public indecency. Where did you leave yours?"

He wiped his face with one hand and said, "I'm not sure. I'm all turned around." He sniffed and turned to look out the window.

"Do you know where you live?"

"I'm staying with somebody." He was having trouble doing two things at one time—holding that skimpy shirt in place and wiping the sweat from his eyes.

I was still slowly maneuvering among the cars, including now a couple of sheriff's cars, wondering how best to divest myself of my passenger.

"Well, who? I'll take you to get some clothes."

I wasn't sure he was going to answer. Actually, I wasn't sure that he was able to answer, and I remembered my Google search that said his naked displays were *un*controllable. I also recalled that I hadn't much believed that at the time and still didn't. Yet the man was pitiable, with half the town ready to tar and feather him, and I was moved to compassion as I thought of him being marched to jail as everybody rejoiced in his fall.

He cleared his throat and whispered, "Do you know the Hargroves?"

I was struck dumb, but only for a moment. "Travis?" I asked with a tremor in my voice. "Are you Travis?"

He nodded. "Don't tell them. Please don't tell them. I'll leave. I'll get some help. I thought I was cured. I haven't done anything like this since high school. Just, please, please, just let me leave."

Cautiously reaching an empty street while considering at the same time one option after another in my mind, I kept glancing at him, trying to judge his state of mind. What would he do if I stopped the car, jumped out, and screamed my head off? People would come running—I could see a few on the sidewalk—and Travis would be overwhelmed by justifiably outraged Abbotsvillians. Arrest, arraignment, trial, all to be covered in detail on the front pages of newspapers around the state, along with the names and pictures of each of the Hargroves. Christy would never recover from being the girl who almost married the man with a secret passion—an object lesson for every mother concerned about her daughter.

And what of Travis himself? I owed him no loyalty or protection. He deserved whatever the townspeople wanted to hand out, even a horsewhipping, as someone had suggested. I had no patience with the defense that it was compulsive behavior so he couldn't help himself and should be patted on the head and forgiven. We can all help ourselves if we want to badly enough or the punishment is severe enough.

I glanced again at him, noticed how his hands were shaking, how he shrank from being seen, how young he seemed, and came to a decision without benefit of judge, jury, or panel discussion.

Taking a left turn onto the empty street, I sped up to leave the hunting field behind. "You can sit up now," I said. "I've made up my mind as to what to do with you, but tell me something first. Is Christy expecting?"

He stared at me. "Expecting? You mean . . . ?" He shook his head and managed a weak smile. "With her mother around? No way."

That released a dozen possibilities that ran through my mind until the one I'd already decided on remained. "You have a car?"

"Rental and already turned in. We're using Christy's."

I had to do a little rethinking. "You're staying in their guesthouse?"

He nodded, sniffed wetly, and hung his head.

"Here's what we'll do," I said, turning south and heading for the Hargroves' house several blocks away. "I'll park on the street, but at the back. You slip into the guesthouse, get dressed, throw your things in a bag, and come right back out. Don't contact anybody, not Christy, not *any*body. I'll get you out of town and you can make any explanations from Durham or from Baltimore, I don't care which." I pulled the car to the curb behind the Hargrove house, turned off both motor and lights. "I want you back in this car in fifteen minutes. Now go."

He was out of the car in a New York minute, giving me in his haste a twinkle of his rear end as he left. I timed him, worried that I'd facilitated an escape and wondering what my penalty would be if anybody found out.

He was back in fourteen minutes, throwing a duffel bag in the back seat and crawling, fully clothed though unwashed, into the front seat beside me.

"Thank you," he said. "Thank you more than I can say. And I do promise to get some help. But please, please don't tell the Hargroves. I don't want Christy to know. I want her to think I'm anything but what I am. I left her a note saying I couldn't go through with the wedding. She'll hate me, but that's better than knowing the truth."

He looked around as I headed the car out of town at a fairly fast clip. "Where're we going?"

"Asheville. There'll be a bus to somewhere tonight."

Chapter 51

It was almost six a.m. by the time I got home, but I'd seen Travis off on an early bus after waiting more than two hours for it. Still wondering if I was doing the right thing, I hadn't wanted to leave him on his own. One of those strange urges might take hold again.

We sat in the waiting room for the last hour as he kept assuring me that he could get on the bus on his own. I knew he could. I just didn't know that he would. So I was taking no chances. I wanted him out of town and out of any thought of seeing the Hargroves.

It wasn't long before he began telling me of the burden he'd carried for so long. It was a burden he thought he'd unloaded in a psychiatrist's office but it had roped him in again just when he thought marriage would cure him forever. But now, for all he knew, he would have to bear it to his grave. He ran his hand through his hair and said, "It's such a terrible thing to have to live with. My folks can't understand it—they're ashamed of me, but I can't help it. All the experts agree on that."

I soon had enough of it. "Stop feeling sorry for yourself, Travis," I told him as we sat on the hard seats in the waiting room. "Everybody has problems. Yours are just more noticeable than most."

Then a little later, I began to think that he needed more direction than I'd given him. "What're you going to do if Christy comes to Baltimore?" I asked. "She might just show up, wanting to know what happened to make you walk out on the eve of your wedding."

He gave an audible sigh with a strong whiff of "poor me" and the pungent smell of sweat in it. "I'll move, give up my residency. I don't deserve it or her. I know it would be better if we never saw each other again." He hung his head, slumped his shoulders, and went on. "I've been thinking maybe of going to the mission field, anyway. It's been on my mind a lot lately; maybe it would redeem me. You know, working in Africa or somewhere."

I gave him a sideways glance. "I wouldn't get carried away, Travis."

When his bus was announced, we stood and I gave him a direct glare and a few last-minute instructions. "Remember this: Do not come back to Abbotsville ever again. You've done yourself in there, but my lips are sealed unless you contact Christy. If you do, the sheriff will be contacting you. I want you to cut her off cleanly and for good. Don't answer her calls, her letters, or her emails. Better to hurt her now than for the rest of her life." And then, because I have good manners, I added, "Take care of yourself, Travis, and see a doctor."

I stood outside the station until the bus with him on it had left, heading eastbound for the interstate. Then I drove back to Abbotsville where all was quiet. The hunters of the naked man had given up the chase and gone to bed. I didn't intend to be far behind them.

When Lillian came in, I told her about the night's adventures chasing the naked man but added a reference to an intestinal bug that had cut short my chase and sent me home before the others. That went over so well that I used it with Helen and Mildred and Mr. Pickens, all of whom wanted to know what had happened to me. But mostly they wanted to know what had happened to *him*. It was hard to accept that the naked man had escaped again, especially since we'd had him boxed in. I moaned along with them.

"We had him surrounded," Helen said. "I don't know how he managed to get out of that block without somebody seeing him."

"Just wait," Mildred said. "If he shows up again in my yard, he'll wish he hadn't."

And Mr. Pickens was ready to search inside every house on the targeted block and would have if the sheriff hadn't said they needed probable cause. But of them all, it was Mr. Pickens who kept looking at me as if I might know something, which of course I did, but I wasn't going to tell anybody but Sam, who could then tell Bob and Sue if he wanted to.

So why did I do it? Why did I aid and abet Travis in evading what he clearly had coming to him? I'm not sure, but it was something along the lines of not wanting good, decent people like the Hargroves to have an unhinged naked man attached to their names for the rest of their lives.

I could just hear it. Thirty years from now somebody will say, "Do you remember Dr. Bob Hargrove? He delivered my babies." And her friend will respond, "Oh, yes. Didn't he go around half naked most of the time?"

And Christy would fare no better. No telling what the story would be about her—probably something like being the beautiful girl who'd been jilted by a psychiatric patient she'd met in medical school.

And Sue's heart would ache for them both, knowing how the truth would be twisted and the ones she loved be defined by one episode in their lives.

So I deemed it better that no one know that Christy's intended was the naked man, because what did that say about her judgment, to say nothing of her medical acumen? Better that he be a cad who got cold feet before a wedding than that everybody know what he actually was. I'd done what I could to make sure that nobody ever did.

Sue called late that morning. "Julia?" she said when I answered the phone. "Christy and I are calling everybody to say that the wedding is off."

"Off?" I said, sounding as surprised as I could. "Why? What happened?"

"We're not really sure. Travis was gone when we got up this morning, but he'd left a note saying he couldn't go through with it." Sue sighed, then went on. "I will only tell you, Julia, but it's like a burden has been lifted. I am so relieved, although, of course, Christy bounces from stunned disbelief to crying outrage. She's better now and is helping get the word out to her bridesmaids. But I am so sorry about the luncheon when you and LuAnne have gone to so much trouble. Bob and I will pay for everything."

"Of course you will not," I said. "Don't worry about the luncheon. But what do you think happened to Travis?"

"We just don't know," Sue said. "He's just disappeared. Christy was devastated at first, overcome by shame at being left at the altar, so to speak. But I think she's beginning to handle it now. I'm wondering if all this time when she's been so upset with me that maybe she was having second thoughts about everything just as he obviously was."

"I expect that's exactly the way it was," I said as warmly as I could. "Thank goodness it happened a few days before the wedding instead of a few days afterward."

It wasn't long before most of the town had stopped wondering about the Hargrove wedding—actually, most of the town hadn't been invited anyway. But just about everybody would be welcome at the Allen house that coming Saturday, so they were looking forward, not back, to something that hadn't yet taken place.

I kept waiting for someone to find a pile of men's clothes, minus a shirt, folded and waiting for the owner, but no one did. Maybe someone in need had found them and had put them to good use.

For a few days the talk of the town centered on how close we had come to catching the naked man. Plans were made for the next time he showed up, but no one remarked on the fact that the week came and went with no sightings. That was because there had often been as much as a week or ten days between the man's previous appearances and only, as I now knew, when Travis was in town. No one, to my knowledge, made the connection between his visits and the naked man's displays, nor did anyone comment on the cancellation of Christy's wedding and the continued absence of the naked man.

In fact, it was well after the first frost that the town realized that he was apparently gone for good, or at least until the weather warmed up again.

Mildred could barely spare a thought for him the following week. She was in full party mode with workmen coming and going, musicians checking their sound systems, barbecue chefs preparing the pit, electricians stringing lights on tree branches, extra help in the kitchen, and Ida Lee overseeing everything. I figured, after offering, that my best help consisted of staying out of the way.

But Mildred was in her glory. She loved anything big and showy, and that's exactly what she was getting, even to putting up her Atlanta lawyers and their wives for the weekend in one of the local inns. Even better for her, she had Penelope, for whom she could model Lady Bountiful, having whispered to me that she was teaching her granddaughter how to spend money to its best effect.

Friday afternoon, a large truck parked in her drive. Men jumped out and began to unload folding chairs, then set them up in a small glade of trees in the back corner of Mildred's huge lot. A florist's truck soon followed and pulled out an arch covered with greenery and white (of all things!) roses.

Mildred called me to come over and give my approval. We walked through the kitchen where we spoke to a half dozen ladies who were preparing for the next day. When we got outside, I said, "That's the first time I've seen Janelle in a while. She looks well, but I'm a little surprised that she's not coming as a guest."

And Mildred replied, "I invited her as a guest, but she said if it was all the same to me, she'd rather make the money. Don't worry about her, Julia, that young woman has her head on straight."

We walked together to the glade, which had been made into a perfect outdoor chapel with baskets of roses and baby's breath marking the aisles of folding chairs. It was a shame, I thought, that all the peonies that LuAnne had ordered for the bridesmaids' luncheon hadn't lasted to do double duty. And with that thought, I recalled LuAnne's reaction to the wedding cancellation. I had thought that she would be angry after the time and effort she'd put into make the luncheon a memorable time for Christy.

Instead, she had smiled sadly and said, "Oh, that's too bad. But if he wasn't sure, he was right to get out of it even at the last minute."

I'd stared at her in surprise and she'd said, "What? You thought I'd be mad? I'm not, although I've spent a good deal of money for nothing. But I am sad for Christy and just hope that she'll find somebody as good and kind as Eddie."

Oh, my, I'd thought. I was going to have to keep hearing how wonderful Eddie was, but at least, I told myself, I now knew what he wasn't.

Tentatively and very carefully, I asked, "Are you and Eddie . . . ?" And let her fill in the blank.

"Not," she said with a little of her old fire, "until he finishes with his wife. His first wife, I mean. I'm not sharing anything with another woman, and certainly not a funeral bill."

Friday evening after supper, with the banging of hammers echoing around the neighborhood, as men put the finishing touches on a dance pavilion next to Mildred's pool, Lillian and I lingered at the table.

"What do you hear from Mr. Dobbs, Lillian?" I asked. "I've been so taken up with everything else that I've lost track of the marriage sweepstakes."

Lillian sighed. "I'll tell you the truth, Miss Julia, I'm beginnin' to think that man don't wanta get married at all. I think he thinks he *ought* to, but he don't much *want* to."

"What about Miss Pearl?" I asked. "I thought she'd have the inside lane after Janelle turned him down."

"No'm, I don't think so. He tole somebody he'd about decided he didn't wanta have to break in a new wife. Too much trouble for too little return, he said."

"Well," I said with a full head of indignation, "if that's not the most arrogant thing I've ever heard, I don't know what is. You are well out of it, Lillian, and I hope you stay out."

She tapped her fingers on the table, taking her time to answer. "He's got something else on his mind now. I don't know if this is true, but it's what I heard he's thinkin' of doin'."

"What?"

"He said he never knew how valuable the first Mrs. Dobbs's hats are until so many ladies took a interest in them. I heard that he said he could eat supper off of one a week for jus' about a year an' get that big closet cleared out at the same time."

"Oh, for goodness' sake," I said, "surely not."

"Yes'm, I think that's what he's doin'. An' I'm puttin' my name on his calendar before all the good ones get picked over."

Saturday, about midafternoon, Sam and I walked over to Mildred's spacious lawn. Groups of people were already milling around, some finding chairs and others looking over the food on the table. A band warmed up on the edge of the wooden dance floor so recently constructed. Latisha ran over and greeted us, as did Lloyd, and soon Lillian, who was one of the few women there wearing a hat. But what a hat it was. It looked like a swan about to take flight, but she wore it with such flair that I assumed her pork chops had come out on top again. If that was the case, I hoped she'd be satisfied with just the one.

The crowd ebbed and flowed around Sam and me as we greeted friends and partial strangers alike. In one of the ebbings I saw Mr. Dobbs raise his hat to Ida Lee, who nodded to him without slowing down. After that, Mr. Dobbs seemed to have eyes only for her, turning all the way around to watch her enter the house. Somehow, I didn't think Ida Lee would be interested in a pork chop cook-off. Or be tempted by a hat, either.

Mildred, in a flowing caftan, sailed out to meet us, grabbed my arm, and said, "Come meet our preacher."

We walked over to a group of suit-clad, serious-looking men apparently discussing something theological in nature. Mildred welcomed them, then expertly cut out a man who looked about old enough for high school.

"This is Pastor Danny Davis, Julia," she said. "He's the new preacher at the Living Waters Baptist Church out on Hightower Road. He'll be doing the wedding honors for us."

"Well, now," Pastor Danny said as his face bloomed with a blush that also reddened his ears. "I've been praying about that, and, you know, I like to meet with the happy couple several times, consult with them, you know, before uniting them for life. Just to be sure they're ready for such a big step. So—"

"Don't worry about that," Mildred said, her hand clasping his arm as she walked him toward the glade. "You won't find anybody any readier than these two, believe me."

Mildred made an announcement over the sound system, and people began to converge in the makeshift chapel, where some found chairs and others standing room. Somebody started the music, and Hazel Marie in a stunning pink (Etta Mae's favorite color) dress proceeded down the aisle to the makeshift altar.

Preacher Danny had apparently decided that if he had to do it, he'd do it right. So he motioned to Deputy Bobby Lee Moser, looking ill at ease as he waited for his bride, to join him at the altar. Deputy Moser was a handsome man, tall but broad where it counts, and with an air of confidence that reminded me of Mr. Pickens. He wore a light gray suit with a slight sheen and a string tie. He also wore boots, as did, I later saw, his bride. When the wedding party was assembled at the altar, the music changed to Mendelssohn's "Wedding March," whose soaring notes brought us all to our feet. The congregants turned to the back, where Etta Mae emerged from Mildred's potting shed in all her glory.

She was lovely, her face glowing as she walked to join the man she had loved and kept missing for so long. Something seized up in my chest as I recalled the neediness I'd seen in Etta Mae when I'd first gotten to know her. Deeply wanting to be liked, even loved, she nonetheless put up a belligerent front, afraid enough of rejection to want to be the first to reject. Yet she had come through for me time after time, each time growing in self-confidence and grace. I counted her a dear friend, almost a daughter if I'd been so fortunate to have had one. I dabbed at my eyes as daintily as I could, moved by a crescendo of love for Etta Mae and her Bobby Lee, for Sam, Lloyd, Lillian, Mildred, and everybody I'd ever known. Except maybe Travis.

We threw a little birdseed as the newlyweds left the glade, then joined them for dinner. They cut the cake, posed for pictures, for Mildred had forgotten nothing, then inaugurated the dance floor. It took a while for the new couple to leave since so many people wanted to congratulate them or watch them dance together or, as I later learned, talk to Bobby Lee about his plans for the sheriff's department if, or rather when, he won the election.

Etta Mae ran over to hug me right before they left, thanking me with tears in her eyes for everything I'd ever done for her. "I'd love to sit and talk with you," she said, laughing and crying at the same time. "But Bobby Lee keeps thinking of that bed waiting for us at the Grove Park Inn."

Finally, as the band played "On the Road Again," they did leave, and that seemed to signal the start of some real partying. The bands played louder and faster, people danced on the floor and on the grass, there was more laughter and more groups of men discussing heavy subjects until their wives pulled them to the dance floor.

As the evening grew darker and the lights grew brighter, there was a small flurry of activity on Mildred's patio as a wheelchair was pushed out of the house and positioned for a clear view of the party by the occupant.

"Why, that's Thurlow," I said to Sam. "How good of Helen to bring him. Let's go speak to them."

Thurlow had obviously had his full leg-length casts replaced by shorter ones, although they were covered by a summer-weight blanket. He wore a white shirt with an elegant tie. His hair had been washed and trimmed, but his face still bore the lines of suffering he'd endured. Standing nearby were Mike, Thurlow's nurse, and two competent-looking men who I later learned were off-duty emergency medical technicians, hired for the evening by Helen to ensure Thurlow's well-being.

So many people had gathered around the wheelchair that Sam and I had to wait our turn. I walked over to Helen and said, "I'm so glad to see Thurlow out and around. But tell me, Helen, what is that fur ball he has in his lap?"

She sipped from the glass that someone had handed to her and said, "It's a Maltese and his name is Billie." She smiled. "Don't ask, but after Ronnie you can probably guess."

Ronnie was the Great Dane, named for Thurlow's favorite

president, that had once had the run of Thurlow's house but had been the first to go when Helen moved in. He was now ensconced in the Pickens household, serving as a vigilant caretaker of small children. As far as I had known, Thurlow was still embittered by Ronnie's banishment.

"Helen," I said, greatly impressed with her care of Thurlow, "you couldn't have done a better thing for Thurlow. It was brilliant of you to replace Ronnie with a smaller dog."

"Well," she said with a laugh, "Billie is a lot easier to clean up after."

Sam and I found chairs where, after eating our fill of barbecue and overcoming our emotions about the wedding, we could watch the dancers.

Sam leaned over while I was talking with Miss Vinnie and said, "You don't want to miss this."

I certainly didn't, for there was Christy Hargrove dancing with a young man whom I didn't know. And could they ever dance! She was a marvel, laughing and whirling in the arms of her partner, who gave new meaning to the term *dirty dancing*. The dance floor had emptied to give them room, and I thought that at any minute he was going to pick her up and hold her over his head as Johnny had done with Baby.

"Who *is* that?" I asked Sam, my breath taken away by their spinning, whirling, and twisting movements.

"He's the new doctor that Bob brought into his practice," Sam said, grinning.

"Well, have you ever?" But I watched the well-matched couple with a smile on my face. After this, no one would ever accuse

Christy of pining over a lost love or feel sorry for her for having been left at the altar.

It was well after midnight by the time we crawled into bed that night. What an evening, even an entire day, it had been, but I was ready to end it with several hours of sleep.

"You know," I said, sliding under the covers and backing up close to Sam, "with all that's gone on here lately with so many weddings planned but not followed through on—I'm thinking of Christy's of course, but also of Mr. Dobbs's, and LuAnne's possible one, and maybe one for Janelle, and Etta Mae's and Helen's, which were the only ones that came to fruition—I've had reason to give consideration to what makes a good marriage."

"I hope," Sam said, yawning, "you're not thinking of making any changes."

"No," I said, laughing. "If anything, it just confirms how fortunate I am. But think about it, Sam. When the summer started, there were at least four, maybe five, weddings in the offing. Christy and Travis were the only traditional couple, and look how that turned out. And I worried myself to death over Lillian marrying Mr. Dobbs while he was considering taking a teenage bride, then there were LuAnne and Eddie and you can't know how that worried me to death. I was just convinced that it was Eddie who was showing himself all over town, and I don't know why unless it was because LuAnne had made such a poor choice with her first husband." I stopped and considered what I'd just said. "But then so had I with my first, and look how I lucked out with the second one." Sam's arm tightened around me. "And you know what? I think

Helen may have, too. Isn't it interesting how sometimes opposites attract? There's nobody more opposite than Helen and Thurlow.

"And always," I went on, "in the background of my thinking, there were Etta Mae and her Bobby Lee, and who knew if he'd ever settle down. I'd about decided that she was going to be an old maid, if a thrice-married woman can ever be an old maid."

"Interesting question," Sam said.

"Yes, but there were so many shifts and changes and varying reasons for some to marry and some not to marry that it seemed like musical chairs. And all the while I kept thinking that love stories aren't what they used to be. And believe me, I've read enough of them to know how they used to be."

"How? 'And they lived happily ever after'?"

"Exactly. The ceremony supposedly wipes out all the problems when you and I know that's when troubles are likely to begin. Especially if the ceremony unites two people who don't know what they're doing or who they're doing it with. It makes you wonder why some people ever get married. I mean, just look around at all the misfits and incompatible couples. Just think how miserable Christy would be right now if she'd married Travis. And Lillian and Mr. Dobbs? My word, it makes me shudder to even think of that."

"Uh-huh, true enough," Sam murmured as his breathing deepened.

I smiled and settled in to await sleep.

After a few minutes, my eyes popped open. "Sam? Put on your to-do list to watch out for an ambitious, hardworking, nice young man for Janelle. She needs a husband."

"Um, okay," Sam said.

"You know," I said, "the state of marriage today may worry us, what with all the divorces, living togethers, multiple marriages, and general disregard for its sanctity, but it's still the best chance we have to live happily ever after." I waited a few seconds. "You just have to take your time and be sure you know what you're doing. Don't you think? But, then again, can you ever really know for sure?" I waited a few more seconds for an answer. "Sam? Are you asleep?"

"Uh, not yet."

"Well, be thinking about Helen and Thurlow. We should have them over for dinner sometime and you'll see how close they are. You know, that's the most remarkable and most unlikely coupling of any I've ever seen. What an inspired gift that little dog was! Don't you think? But listen, you won't believe what I heard from Miss Vinnie." I waited for a response. "Sam?" And kept waiting.

"Well," I said, patting his arm, "I'll tell you the rest tomorrow."

ALSO AVAILABLE

MISS JULIA SPEAKS HER MIND

MISS JULIA TAKES OVER

MISS JULIA THROWS A WEDDING

MISS JULIA HITS THE ROAD

MISS JULIA MEETS HER MATCH

MISS JULIA'S SCHOOL OF BEAUTY

MISS JULIA STANDS HER GROUND

MISS JULIA STRIKES BACK

MISS JULIA PAINTS THE TOWN

MISS JULIA DELIVERS THE GOODS

MISS JULIA RENEWS HER VOWS

MISS JULIA ROCKS THE CRADLE

MISS JULIA TO THE RESCUE

MISS JULIA STIRS UP TROUBLE

MISS JULIA'S MARVELOUS MAKEOVER

ETTA MAE'S WORST BAD-LUCK DAY

MISS JULIA LAYS DOWN THE LAW

MISS JULIA INHERITS A MESS

MISS JULIA WEATHERS A STORM

MISS JULIA RAISES THE ROOF

MISS JULIA TAKES THE WHEEL

MISS JULIA KNOWS A THING OR TWO

MISS JULIA HAPPILY EVER AFTER

PENGUIN BOOKS

Ready to find your next great read? Let us help. Visit prh.com/nextread